LESSONS FROM A ONE-NIGHT STAND

PIPER RAYNE

Cover Design: By Hang Le

Line Editor: Joy Editing

Line Editor: Gray Ink Editing

Proofreader: Shawna Gavas, Behind The Writer

ABOUT LESSONS FROM A ONE-NIGHT STAND

If you're a guy like me, and you find yourself having banged your sexy new boss—the school principal—in the back of your Jeep one drunken night, here's a few takeaways based on my experience...

Lesson One: Always get her FULL name.

Lesson Two: Consider asking what she does for a living.

Lesson Three: Find out why she's moved to town. Get details. Details are crucial.

Lesson Four: Don't alter her bio in front of an auditorium of high school students unless you know she has a sense of humor for that sort of thing.

Lesson Five: If you ignore Lesson Four, apologize instead of flirt when you're sent to the principal's office.

Lesson Six: NEVER sleep with her again.

Lesson Seven: Pay attention to this one—it's the most important of them all. Don't fall for your one-night stand.

Class dismissed.

Lessons from a *One-Night Stand*

The Baileys

Austin Bailey - 30 years old
(*Biology Teacher/Baseball Coach*)
Savannah Bailey - 28 years old
(*Runs Bailey Timber Corp*)
Brooklyn Bailey - 25 years old
(*Hotel Maid*)
Rome Bailey - 23 years old
(*Chef*)
Denver Bailey - 23 years old
(*Bush Pilot*)
Juno Bailey - 22 years old
(*Matchmaker*)
Kingston Bailey - 19 years old
(*Smokejumper*)
Phoenix Bailey - 17 years old
(*Student*)
Sedona Bailey - 17 years old
(*Student*)

ONE

Austin

The handsome guy on stage with his jaw hanging wide open, shock and awe in his eyes?

That'd be me. Austin Bailey. Eldest brother of the Bailey clan, guardian to my younger siblings, biology teacher extraordinaire, baseball coach, good neighbor, and all-round pretty great guy.

Before we dive into the fact that karma just raised its middle finger at me, you should hear how my day began.

Today started like every other day. I woke up, got ready, prepared breakfast for my ungrateful twin sisters, Phoenix and Sedona, then we all hopped into my Jeep to head to school.

Of course, Phoenix didn't eat the pancakes. Her exact words, if I remember correctly were, "They taste like cardboard. Can't you just follow the recipe?"

Sedona ate the pancakes, but as soon as we pulled into the parking lot of Lake Starlight High School, where they're seniors, her appreciation for me ended. "Park in the back, I don't want to be seen stepping out of this monstrosity."

I've learned that there's no pleasing a teenager, especially a female one—no offense, ladies, but her comment still irks me. How is my Jeep embarrassing? It has a snorkel so when I off-road, I don't have to spend my money on a new engine and can instead afford to buy her whatever new outfit she wants. She should be grateful, thanking me. But she's seventeen. Pleasing her is impossible.

I purposely park in the first row and honk my horn to announce our arrival, because pissing off Sedona is one of my top five favorite things to do. *I'll miss that come next year.*

Phoenix's stomach rumbles as she exits the car. Sedona has already raced off to the nearest entrance as if that creepy *IT* clown is following her.

I stroll toward the door, reloading my emails on my phone, hoping I received the response I've been waiting for and that it contains good news. Elijah, my star pitcher, cuts me off.

"Coach, I need some advice." He runs his fingers through his long hair.

"How to cut your hair? Come see me. I've got clippers in my office."

It's like a contest these days for the kids to see who can grow their hair and look the most unkempt. I don't get the appeal, and Elijah is the worst of them all.

"No, Coach, Becca broke up with me." There's a hitch in his voice. His eyes scour the courtyard, where most of the kids hang out until the first bell rings.

I stuff my phone into the pocket of my jacket. "Why?"

"Well..." He runs his fingers through his hair again.

For the love of God. Next season if I'm still here, I'm

making a new rule—if your hair covers your eyes, I'm your barber.

Of course, then JP's mom will call to complain. She *always* calls. I think if we changed the flavor of the performance drink we give them from strawberry to lime, she'd call. You know the type. She probably still wipes his ass to make sure he did it right. And though I understand that the Andrews family has had its share of heartbreak, she was like that before *and* after.

I push JP's mom out of my head because just the thought of dealing with her will give me a headache. "What'd you do?"

I open the door to the hallway. With it being Monday morning, my fellow teachers nod, gripping their coffee mugs like life vests.

A group of three girls lingering around one locker follow Elijah as we head down the hall. I'm not blind. He's kind of a big deal around here, and I can guess what path his teenage hormones led him down. They're tricky fuckers to manage.

"You know Sara Pylar?" Elijah asks in a tentative voice.

See? Too bad I can't bet on my players' screw-ups. I wouldn't be working here, that's for sure. I'd be a rich man.

I open up the door to my classroom, and Elijah heads in first.

Do I know Sara Pylar? Of course, I do. She's usually the one in the short skirt with her finger twirling a strand of her hair. The worse her grades are, the more bubble gum she chews while she asks to move to the front row so she can see the smart board better. Sara would eat up and spit out a kid like Elijah if he ever tried to tangle with her.

"Yeah, I know Sara."

He sits in the chair next to my desk. "There was this dare…"

"Nothing good comes from those." I cross my arms.

"JP was razzing me about how I've only ever kissed Becca and that when I go to college, we'll break up and how the girls at college are on another level." His eyes widen, silently asking me.

I went to college. I played in college, and at one time, I thought maybe I'd hit the majors. Then family responsibilities brought me back to Lake Starlight. Now I teach and try to advise kids like Elijah not to make the mistakes I did. Then again, youth is your free pass to do stupid shit.

"Girls in college are the girls you went to high school with but a little older." I sit in my chair, grabbing a pen.

"He said I'd regret not having experience."

My gaze lands on the clock. Elijah has about five minutes before first class bell. I hold up my hand to stop him from rambling. "Listen."

Elijah is good enough to be drafted first round, and this town can't wait to see him succeed. He'll have plenty of temptation come his way over the years, and he needs to decide now how he's going to handle it.

"Did you kiss Sara?" I ask.

"No, but…"

"I'm gonna guess here and tell me if I'm wrong." He closes his mouth, so I continue. "You let your friends get to you. JP, whose mom probably follows him on his dates you do realize, tells you that you don't have enough experience and should kiss another girl."

He's nodding and smirking because everyone knows JP's mom will probably put up spy cameras in his dorm room next year.

"You thought, 'Hey, what if Becca does break my heart

and fall for someone next fall? Where does that leave me?' So, you went into a bedroom or somewhere private with a very willing Sara. Then Becca somehow walked in on you right before you finished debating in your head if you were going to kiss her?"

You see me trying to make it seem like he would never cheat on Becca? Probably bullshit. He's seventeen. He would've kissed Sara and blown his relationship with Becca into smithereens and only realized what a mistake that was down the road.

"Exactly. Coach."

"Now you have to grovel." I check the clock one more time. Three minutes until first bell.

"I did. I went to her house. I texted her."

I stand to let Elijah know he's leaving before my class arrives. "Sorry," I smack him on the back. "You need to pull out the big guns."

His shoulders slump.

"Just think of what makes Becca happy, why she fell in love with you, and you'll figure it out."

"How do you know, Coach?"

I open the door and wait for him to walk through. "Because I was you at one time. And another piece of advice?"

He waits for me on the other side of the door.

"Don't go listening to your friends. They usually give shit advice, and honestly, you usually get a lot more experience with a girlfriend than by flipping around with multiple girls. Teenage boys have shit for brains. Don't listen to them."

I really don't want to know how far he's gotten with Becca. Especially with Phoenix and Sedona being the same age as Elijah.

He looks at me sheepishly. "Well, we have—"

"That's a conversation I don't want to hear and no one else should either. Don't be a dick and kiss and tell." The bell rings. "Go to class."

He turns around. "You mean assembly."

"Assembly?"

We walk out into the hallway where everyone is filing toward the auditorium.

"Yeah, remember Principal Miller had the baby?"

Shit. Now I'm running my fingers through my hair. All the teenage angst had me forgetting that we have to meet the new principal of Lake Starlight High School this morning. The last principal I'll ever be under because next year I'm heading to the college level—I hope.

"Yeah. Go. You don't want to be late."

"Thanks, Coach... for everything." He jogs down the hall, catching up to his friends.

I turn to go through the back entrance since I'll have to sit in a chair in front of all the students so that we can appear as a united front for the new principal. A symbol that says we have their back.

I run smack-dab into Fay Murphy, the office assistant. "Hey, Fay."

"I'm so happy I found you." She seems a tad flustered, and her face has that beet-red overlay she used to get when Principal Miller reprimanded her for not refilling her stapler.

Working without that dictator will be a nice change. Let me tell you, pregnant women do *not* like it when they have to give up coffee—something we all paid the price for.

"What's up?" I keep walking because we're going to be late if we don't hurry.

"We need you to introduce Principal Radcliffe." She

peers behind me then pushes up on her tiptoes to whisper in my ear, "Malcolm, I mean Vice Principal Ealey, called in this morning. I think he was still..."

Fay doesn't have to finish the sentence. Malcolm Ealey went through a public divorce last year and has been spending a lot of his time at the Lucky Tavern, drowning in a helluva lot more than his sorrows. That's why, even though he should have become our temporary principal, the school board decided to hire someone new.

"Why me?"

She hands me a piece of paper. "The kids look up to you, and everyone thinks that the kids will welcome Principal Radcliffe if you introduce her."

Her. Another woman. Hopefully this one is well-caffeinated and not pregnant. We'll all stand a better chance that way.

I accept the piece of paper, looking over what I need to say. "Fine."

I'm not scared of public speaking. I've got two teenage girls at home. You don't know a hostile environment until you're trying to break up a fight between those two.

"You're the best, Austin." Fay squeezes my forearm then walks down the hall.

My footsteps slow as I read over the new principal's bio. What the hell is a Yale graduate doing in Alaska at Lake Starlight High School? After skimming over her education, I fold up the paper. I can wing it from there. Besides the kids couldn't care less about what's printed on that sheet.

Heading into the auditorium, I search out the face of our new principal, but I know everyone here.

"Her meeting with the superintendent is running a tad late, so if you could stall, I'll tap you on the shoulder when it's safe to announce her," Fay informs me.

"I'm not a zoo keeper."

Fay laughs.

I will not miss this part of my job next year.

Before I realize it, I'm in front of the podium, clearing my throat and introducing myself, as if everyone here doesn't already know who I am. Sedona rolls her eyes and looks away. I have no fucking clue why she's so embarrassed of me. I mean, look at me. Six foot two, two-ten, short, neat haircut. I work out four times a week, hike, bike, ski. My muscles aren't from just the gym...

Okay, before I keep sounding like a male-seeking-female want ad, let's get on with how my day went into the shitter in a matter of twenty minutes.

I tell a few jokes, and the kids loosen up a bit. Maybe I should rethink the whole college baseball coach thing and go for stand-up comedy. I'm pretty good at this.

Fay taps my shoulder, and thank God, because I'm running out of material.

I pull the paper out of my back pocket and clear my throat one more time. "All right, everyone. We all know that Principal Miller has left us to enjoy her new baby, so we're welcoming a new principal into our school. Our new principal for the remainder of the year is Dr. Radcliffe. She graduated from Yale with her doctorate in education. She comes here from the lower forty-eight, so make sure you give a big Alaskan welcome!"

About half the kids in the auditorium clap while the rest of them stare at the stage with an expression that only a bunch of unimpressed and uninterested teenagers can manage.

Time to grab their interest and get them to buy in. "Principal Radcliffe's hobbies include streaking during foot-ball games, ferret racing, and taking surveys for money."

The kids roar with laughter, finally looking as if they're interested and want to be here. Fay steps up and nudges me.

"Sorry," I mumble. "We'll bring Dr. Radcliffe out to explain her hobbies in more depth." I turn from the podium at the sound of heels clicking across the stage.

This is the part where my mouth drops open and my testicles jerk up, seeking protection.

See the auburn-haired woman walking right toward me? The one who looks as pissed off as Sedona did when I honked my horn in the parking lot this morning?

Yeah, that's my new boss.

The new principal of Lake Starlight High School.

I don't believe in kissing and telling, but I'll tell you—this is the first and only principal I've ever given an orgasm to in the backseat of my Jeep.

TWO

Holly

"I'm going to kill him," is the first thought that hits my stunned brain. "Slowly."

Since I'm a complete professional, I refuse to let the fact that I slept with the man standing at the mic, staring at me with wide eyes, derail me. So, I smile, one that probably does, but hopefully—fingers crossed—does not show how uncomfortable I am.

My heels click along the stage, the sound overshadowed by the students' laughter, which was spurred on by this ass of a man holding the microphone.

I hadn't regretted the one-night stand that left me panting for more—until now. If anything, I'd wondered if our paths would cross again and hoped for a repeat performance. Now, it's no longer an option. Too bad... he really was a good lay, and I'm happy to report that I did *not* have my beer goggles on the night we were together.

Taking the microphone from his hand, I pretend to be

unfazed by his antics. I've dealt with boys like him before. They're usually under the drinking age though.

"I'm sorry, I..." His face is about as pale as a sack of flour.

"Thank you. Coach Bailey, right?" It'll do him good to think I don't remember him.

He licks his lips. "Yeah."

I pretend that it doesn't spur memories of his magnificently talented tongue...

Whoa, I zoned there for a moment.

Cut me some slack, it had been a while since I was properly taken care of.

I clear my throat into the microphone, ending the whispers and murmurs from the student body now that Coach Bailey has sat down behind me. He can stare at my ass all he wants. He'll never have it in his palms again.

"Good morning, everyone." I turn back to "Coach Bailey." "Thank you for the wonderful introduction and the additions to my bio. I promise to let you do the streaking next time." I give him my best fake smile.

Fay the office assistant's face is fire-engine red as she sneaks a look at Austin, obviously uncomfortable.

Facing the students once again, I'm surprised to still have their attention. "I'm Principal Radcliffe, and what Coach Bailey didn't tell you is that I'm from Florida, born and raised. I can't believe you guys still have snow on the ground. It's been years since I've seen it. I was a professor at Florida State before taking this job."

"Why come here?" a kid near the back row screams.

Everyone laughs.

"Guess I've watched too many Alaska shows on the Discovery Channel."

I earn my own laughs without the help of Coach Bailey.

I have my own reasons but they're not for the student body to know. Thankfully, this job presented itself and people aren't exactly clamoring to work in Alaska so getting this job was easier than I would have thought.

"I want each of you to know that I have an open-door policy. Although I'm only here for the remainder of the school year, since Principal Miller will be returning next year, I hope to get familiar with each of you. For you seniors, I'm making it my commitment to meet with each of you to talk about your future and what path you see yourself headed down. I know most of you will have probably chosen your school or maybe you're weighing your options. But I think I can help you understand what the expectations will be once you reach post-secondary education and help you with what for some, is a difficult transition."

Groans and more mumbling sound from the students.

"I mean, maybe one of you wants to take surveys for money. If that's the case, I would be the go-to person for advice." I turn to face the man whose good looks still make my heart beat uncontrollably. "Right, Coach Bailey?"

The auditorium fills with laughter.

He smiles, leaning back in his chair, one leg resting on his knee. Bastard thinks he's the king of this school. He's about to be struck from his pedestal.

"Well, I'm sure you all want to get on with your day. Please remember, my door is open, always. Have a nice day."

Fay rushes up to the microphone, taking over to instruct the students to head to first period in a single-file line. She snaps at one kid roughhousing with his friend. I totally underestimated her, I'm happy to see.

A few of the teachers approach, introducing themselves before heading off to their classrooms, but Coach Bailey lingers, obviously waiting for me.

The auditorium clears out, and as the custodian—Kip, I think—stacks the chairs, Coach Bailey finally approaches me.

"Holly," he says my name as though he knows me.

Okay, so he kind of does. But knowing I have a racing stripe under my panties is not the same thing as *knowing* me.

"Hello. Austin, right?"

He smirks, biting the inside of his cheek. "Yeah."

"Nice to see you again. Thank you for that humorous introduction. Really got the kids' attention."

He stuffs his hands in his pockets and rocks back on his heels. "Yeah, sorry, I just thought it could use some spicing up."

"So, you won't mind if I send you my resume? You know, since I need to look for another job after Principal Miller returns? Maybe you can spice that up too."

He laughs, his smirk growing. "All right, I deserved that. Truce?"

"Do most women give in so quickly, Austin?" I cross my arms, my blazer pulling on my shoulders.

His gaze floats down my body, concentrating on my breasts for a few moments, then he meets my gaze again. "Most times. You did on Saturday."

I'm clenching my jaw so hard my teeth might turn to dust, but I ignore his reference to Saturday night. "That's a pity then, because all is not forgiven here. Now if you'll excuse me, I need to head to my office and get some work done." I spin on my heel and head off the stage.

"Holly! Hold up." He jogs to catch up to me and lightly grasps my elbow.

"Yes?" I flick my gaze to where he holds my arm, and he drops his hand.

"I just... I don't want to start out on the wrong foot. I do apologize for ambushing your bio. I really am sorry."

Now he knows he can't railroad me. It was a hard lesson for me to learn in life, not to please people by constantly accepting apologies that hold no weight.

"Thank you. I appreciate it. I'm sure I'll see you around the halls."

I walk down the row of chairs until I'm safely in the hallway, at which point I suck in a breath.

Am I really going to have to work with him day after day until the end of the school year?

I bet you're happy you're not me right now. I would be.

I'M NOT IN MY OFFICE FOR FIVE MINUTES BEFORE MY cell phone rings on my desk. My mom's name flashes on the screen.

Damn it. I need this right now like I need a yeast infection.

"Hey, Mom," I answer, sitting down in my desk chair. Ouch. My teeth dig into my bottom lip as I inhale quickly from the stabbing pain centered on my tailbone. I guess Alaskan high schools don't have the budgets for comfortable office chairs that colleges do.

"Good afternoon, or I guess morning for you." She laughs. "I was checking in to see how you're settling in."

"Well, remember I started my new job today?"

"Oh, that's right. You should've called this morning to remind me."

You know that phrase the apple doesn't fall far from the tree? Yeah, that doesn't apply to my mother and me. She's laid-back and believes everything takes care of itself. And I... do not.

"I had a lot to do," I say.

"You always do."

"What's that supposed to mean?" I tap my pen on my desk in agitation.

I swear that a mother's ability to say only three words and still get under her daughter's skin is a special talent bestowed by the heavens.

"Nothing, sweetie. How's the weather in Oregon? Cold?"

Now you know—I lied to my mother.

I know, I know, but I do have my reasons.

I cross my fingers. "Yeah. Good thing we went shopping for that winter coat you told me to buy."

"Told you. You should listen to me more often. I did raise you."

I ignore her taunt. "How are you doing?"

"I'm good. I'm heading into the restaurant for the lunch service. I miss you."

The hardest part of coming here was leaving my mom. That, and lying about it. But she doesn't always understand why I have to do the things I do, and I don't want to hurt her.

"I miss you too. How about we Skype during *The Bachelor* tomorrow night?" I ask, dropping my pen on my desk.

"Perfect. You make a pizza and I'll make one. It'll be just like we're together."

A knock sounds on my office door and I glance over to see Fay standing there.

"It's a date then. Have a great day, Mom."

"You too, sweetie, love you."

"Love you."

I hang up, guilt eating away at my stomach. What she doesn't know is best in this case. In a few months, I'll be back in Florida and she'll never be the wiser.

I wave Fay in.

"I'm sorry, Principal Radcliffe, but—"

"Please call me Holly."

"Principal Miller said that shows a lack of respect for authority."

God bless this sweet woman's heart. "I insist. Call me Holly."

"Okay... I hate to interrupt, but Coach Bailey has asked to be penciled into your schedule. You have an opening during fourth period, and he has a break as well. I wanted to make sure that was okay."

I never want her to feel afraid of me, so I smile sweetly. "Of course, please pencil him in."

I say that while thinking that he needs to stay the hell away from me with his sexy smile and tall, strong build. I could grab Fay by the lapels of her silk jacket donned with shoulder pads and scream in her face, "Do you have any idea how magical his fingers are? I'll cave, Fay. How much is one woman supposed to resist?" But I'm a professional, so I'm not going to do that.

"Great. I'll stick him in then."

Visions of when Austin stuck it in *me* come to mind, and I feel my face heat.

She smiles and shuts the door when she leaves my

office. If I wasn't in a fish bowl in the middle of the front office, I'd let my forehead fall onto my desk.

So far today, I've been humiliated in front of my new school, stood face-to-face with a guy I let finger-fuck me on Saturday night—in his Jeep, no less—and lied to my mother... again.

This move is working out exceptionally well. What more could a girl ask for?

THREE

Austin

“Coach!”

Elijah joins me as I walk to the front office to make sure everything really is water under the bridge with Holly. I want a job coaching at the college level next year, and I know any potential employer will be calling her for a reference. As of right now, I think she’s cast me as the school clown who takes nothing seriously. She has good reason to feel that way, what with the student population probably taking bets on whether she’ll streak during the next football game.

“Not now, Elijah, we can talk at practice.”

“JP asked Becca out!”

A few heads turn our way.

“So beat the shit out of him.” It’s out of my mouth before I can stop myself.

Elijah stops for a second but quickly catches up to me. “Seriously?”

“No. Don’t do that.”

Although I would've. It's clear JP set up Elijah. What a dickwad of a friend. But I'm their mentor and already in deep shit with the principal. This morning, she was nothing like the smiling, satisfied woman in the back of my Jeep on Saturday night.

"I'm so mad at him. I want to punch him in that big bird nose of his."

I tug on Elijah's shirt until we're out of the clogged artery of the main hallway. "Beat him at his own game. You know Becca. You know what she likes and what she doesn't. Not to mention you have one advantage that JP doesn't—Becca loves you." I point at his chest.

Becca walks by a few seconds later, staring at Elijah until he looks at her. Then she scowls, acting as if she hates him.

"Go." I nudge him, and he bumps into Becca, her book almost spilling to the floor, but Elijah catches it and mumbles something.

Becca takes the book out of his hands, murmurs something to herself, and turns the other way, whipping him in the head with her long ponytail.

So maybe she needs some time.

I feel super shitty for leaving Elijah in the hall, looking like a lost puppy, but I have more pressing matters to deal with and that's making sure that Principal Radcliffe and I really are on good terms.

The hallway is clearing out as I walk into the school office. Fay's smiling face is a nice surprise. She's a happy woman generally speaking, but when Principal Miller was here, she often looked on the verge of tears. Principal Miller just wasn't a people person. God help her child. Oh, stop judging me, you don't even know her.

"Hey, Fay," I say as I approach the desk.

"Hi, Austin. Not yet, honey. She's on the phone."

I lean against the counter and snatch a butterscotch candy from the bowl. Fay always has the best treats.

"What's new?" I ask, picking up a pen that's sitting there and tapping it end to end on the counter.

"Gary is working on the float for the Bailey Timber Founder's Day Parade." Her smile reaches from ear to ear, and I know she's remembering some of the Founder's Day moments she shared with my parents.

"That's great. Savannah is coming by tonight to talk logistics. Anything you think we can improve on from last year?" I suck on my candy.

"Knowing Savannah, it's all in place. I think it's great that after what happened with your parents, you guys managed to keep it all intact." Tears well in her eyes. Every year we have this same conversation.

"Yeah."

"You and Savannah have sacrificed so much." Her hand covers mine. "Your parents would be proud." She squeezes my hand.

I place my other hand on top of hers. "That means a lot. Thanks, Fay."

"Did I ever tell you about the time your mother and I went on a double date?"

I could finish the story for her, but she likes to tell it, so I settle in for another rendition of Fay and Beth's wild teenage double date. It's when my mom met my dad.

"Coach Bailey." Holly stands in her open office door. Her jacket is off, leaving her in a sleeveless, cream-colored satin blouse that shows off her muscular arms. I knew she was strong, the way she suspended herself over me, using my roll bar like a pull-up bar while she was riding me.

What? I'm a guy. If I notice something physical about

her, it's going to lead to thoughts of sex and since I know what that's like with her—phenomenal, if I were to pick one word—of course it's going to lead to thoughts of *actual* sex with her. It doesn't make me a pig.

"Another time, Fay." I tap the pen on the counter and leave it there.

She smiles at me like she did when I was fifteen. "Definitely."

I walk into Holly's office, shutting the door because no one needs to overhear the discussion we're about to have.

"Have a seat," she says, sitting down behind her desk, looking all prim and proper with her back straight.

Everything on her desk is neat as a pin. I get the feeling she probably has a vision in her mind of little cut-out lines where each item should be placed.

"Thanks." I sit down on the other side of her desk, feeling as though I showed up to a wedding in a sweat suit. Her pantsuit costs a lot of money, I'd bet, and here I am slumming it in jeans and a button-down. But more than that, it's the energy she's giving off. It's cool and professional and not at all like the woman I met at Lucky's on Saturday night.

The sun pops out from behind a cloud and shines through her window, across her blouse, and I get a perfect vision of her bra. Lacy, like the one I took off her that night. One of those ones without a clasp. Not as easily accessible, but sexy as hell.

Shit. Must refrain from thinking of Holly naked. I change positions—jeans aren't exactly the easiest to hide a hard-on in.

"What can I do for you, Austin?" She clasps her hands on her desk and leans forward.

I'm pretty sure she has no idea that her arms push her

tits together when she does that, but I'm a good boy and resist the urge to keep glancing at her cleavage.

I'm in over my head right now.

I clear my throat. "I wanted to apologize."

"You already did that." Her face is as void of emotion as an A-list actress who's had too much Botox.

"Yeah, I know, but I can't help but think you thought I was full of shit. I think you've pegged me wrong."

"Why do you say that?" She tilts her head ever so slightly.

"I think that you have the impression that I don't take this job seriously, and that can't be further from the truth. I've been here for almost nine years. I've developed the baseball team to the point where some of these boys might get drafted to some big-name schools. I care about the students—"

She holds her hand up for me to stop. That same hand that was holding my dick on Saturday night. Let's just say I don't forget these details. "I know about Elijah Crupe and his potential offers. Whatever your worries are about me, don't worry. I'm a mature adult. You misstepped."

"I had a little fun. If I'd known you were the same woman from Saturday night, I'd have included all the other great qualities I know you possess."

Her eyes flare open and her cheeks flush, but she doesn't look impressed.

You're here to apologize, not flirt with her, idiot.

"Thank you, but I think it's safe to say we're done with the extracurricular activities now." She leans back in her chair.

"You should've stuck with Scrabble, and what was your other hobby? Refinishing furniture? Is that like antiquing?"

She stares at me blankly.

I've offended her. I'm hanging around Phoenix and Sedona too much.

"Let me take a stab at your hobbies, if I may?" She doesn't wait for my permission. "You're probably an outdoorsy kind of guy. One who's out all day doing dangerous or risky things with the excuse of having 'guy time.' You come home late at night, fall onto the couch, and watch some sporting event?"

I smirk. She's good.

"Figures. Guys like you are all the same. So, mock my hobbies if you will, but they are mine, and I'm not going to let you make me feel as if I'm some boring person."

"That's not what I meant."

"If you're done insulting me for the day, please let me get back to work."

"Holly." I stand, my fingers on the edge of her desk. God, I'm such a fuck-up right now. I'm never not in control or one step ahead of someone when we're verbally sparring.

She looks up at me, and if her gorgeous green eyes could give me the middle finger, they would.

Time to cut to the chase.

"Listen, I'm applying for some college-level coaching jobs and they're gonna call here for references and I—"

"There you go thinking I'm going to sabotage your career because you embarrassed me after we slept together. I've looked into your classes and your coaching. All of your players are holding their GPAs where they need to, and your seniors are progressing nicely toward graduation. I'll only speak on those items should someone call, but please don't put me down as a character reference." She raises her eyebrows, dismissing me.

"Thanks, I really appreciate it."

"Goodbye, Austin."

I open the door and walk out of her office, still feeling like shit.

Why is that?

"Everything okay?" Fay asks as I mindlessly walk out of the half door near her desk.

I force a smile. "Perfect."

I wink, which brightens her smile. No need for Fay to worry about the Baileys any more than she already does.

FINALLY, MY SHIT MONDAY ENDS AND I GET TO SPEND the rest of my afternoon on the baseball diamond—freezing my ass off, but I'm outside and teaching the best game there is.

My buddy Jack strolls up and stands beside me. "Rumors are spreading."

I laugh at his parka, hat, and gloves. "You grew up here, right?"

"Funny, asshole. I just got back from Cancun, give me a fucking break. I have to reacclimatize."

"How is wedded bliss?" I ask, watching as the boys warm up by tossing the ball to one another.

"Nah, we're not talking about me. You need to start talking." He rubs his gloved hands together.

"Take off those ridiculous gloves and help with the drills."

"Fine. I tried the nice way." Jack takes off his gloves, grabs his baseball mitt, and steps over to where the boys are. "Tell me, boys, did Coach Bailey embarrass himself this morning?"

The group of boys laugh.

"You should have seen his face," Elijah says.

"He's gonna be dragged around by a collar," JP adds. "She is one hot piece of ass though."

"Lap!" I point.

JP drops his mitt and runs to the light pole and back.

Jack glances over his shoulder, silently asking me if they're telling the truth. I shrug. He laughs and turns around.

"I heard he was practically drooling all over the stage," Jack eggs them on.

Seriously, how fast does word spread in this town? Jack doesn't even work at the school. He helps me out with the team because he shares the same love of the game as I do.

"He stared at her ass the entire time she was speaking," JP says.

The little bastard is back from his lap and I'd make him go again if he was lying. He's not. But damn, I didn't think I was that obvious.

"Then I heard he went and saw her during fourth period," another player says.

"Really? This is all so intriguing. I think I need to visit the principal's office." Jack throws the ball to JP to start the drill, then he steps back over to me and lowers his voice. "So?"

I glance around to make sure no one is coming up from behind. "So, she's my Saturday one-night stand."

Jack bends over in a fit of laughter. "You're shittin' me?"

"Nope." I shake my head.

"Classic. Can't wait to meet the lucky lady."

"Fuck you."

He clasps me on the shoulder. "Is it bad I kinda hope you fall madly in love with her?"

I quirk an eyebrow.

"Then maybe you'll stick around." He shrugs. Other

than crying like a baby when Francie walked down the aisle two weeks ago, he's a typical "show no emotion" Alaskan guy, so I'm surprised he's bringing this up.

"Play your cards right and maybe they'll let you be head coach next year. Maybe they'll even pay you." I laugh.

He smiles. "I'd rather have you here than be the head coach of a bunch of misbehaved high school guys who can't control their hormones."

"It's not like I won't be back."

Jack doesn't say anything, just steps back up to the field. "JP stop egging Elijah. Go run two laps!"

I get what Jack's saying. I'll miss him too. I'll miss everything in Lake Starlight, but my life has been on hold for practically a decade. It's time to live for myself now, and I can't miss the opportunity.

FOUR

Holly

I t's morning, before classes have started, and I walk into the teachers' lounge to find most of the teachers. I guess I was wrong to assume they'd be preparing their lessons in their classrooms rather than in here, gabbing about the students. Half are talking about how Elijah Crupe and JP somebody roughed each other up down at the Lard Have Mercy diner over some girl named Becca. I make a mental note to look up everyone. Elijah I know—Miranda Miller gave him his own special write-up about how colleges are looking at him for a baseball scholarship.

I'm sure Coach Bailey would have a flying fit if Elijah was reprimanded at school for anything. Elijah's record is squeaky clean, but that could be Miranda and Coach Bailey's doing. Scoring a job at the college level would be easier if some hot recruit picked up one of his students.

"Hi, Principal Radcliffe." A woman with chin-length, dark brown hair approaches me, her hand out. "We didn't meet yesterday. I was just returning from my honeymoon. I'm the librarian, Francessca Porter."

Now her golden skin at the beginning of an Alaskan spring makes sense.

"Nice to meet you, Francessca. Please call me Holly. Yes, I stopped in at the library and the substitute told me about your recent wedding. Congratulations."

"Thank you so much. Everyone calls me Francie though, so please feel free." Her friendly smile sets me a bit at ease in this still-new environment.

"Okay, thanks." I mix creamer into my coffee and throw away the straw.

Francie lingers, hemming and hawing, reluctant to tell me something, I think. "Um... there's something else."

I sip my coffee and raise my eyebrows for her to continue.

"My husband, Jack Porter, he's... um... the owner of Hammer Time Hardware and he... is..."

We're going to be here all day and I can't imagine what it is she's so nervous about. I touch her arm. "What is it, Francie?"

Her shoulders sag. "He's Austin Bailey's best friend. I just wanted you to know because I didn't want you to think I'm lying or withholding information. I heard about the whole assembly thing and then the fact he was in your office and you shut the blinds and—"

She's talking a mile a minute, but I catch the part about the blinds and my forehead crinkles. "Hold on, what? I never shut the blinds."

My throat goes dry at the idea that rumors about me are spreading around the school. What is Coach Bailey saying?

"Well, this town's not that small, but you wouldn't know it from the *Lake Starlight Buzz Wheel*. I shouldn't have said anything, it's just you're the new principal and—"

"You have no worries if you're friends with Austin Bailey." I smile, hoping to set her at ease. I really have no idea why she would think that would be an issue for me.

She places her hand over her heart and sighs as if I offended her. "Oh, *I'm* not really. We're friends through marriage, if that's a thing. I mean Austin is just... my *husband's* best friend."

Principal Miller sure did a number on this school. They all walk around as though I'm going to be giving out ruler spankings.

"Stop. It's fine. What is this *Lake Starlight Buzz Wheel* thing you mentioned?"

Her face reddens, and even though it was just the two of us talking, the room grows silent. Great. I smile through the awkwardness.

"It's a gossip site?" She says it like she's guessing the correct answer. She might as well have put in the words "What is" as though she were a contestant on *Jeopardy*.

"Gossip site?"

A chair squeals across the linoleum floor. "It covers all the news in Lake Starlight," Fay says.

"Gossip," someone else clarifies.

"Yeah, and the daily news is erased every day, so you have to be sure to read it before midnight, otherwise you'll have no idea what it said or who it was about." Fay acts as though it's getting confidential files from the US government.

I don't need to know who's sleeping with whom or not paying their taxes. Other people's business is not my own. "That's a little tasteless."

"It is, but no one knows who writes it, so we can't stop

them," Francie says. Her smirk tells me she's been a lifelong reader of the blog.

Everyone in the teachers' lounge is staring at me, and it dawns on me why Francie brought it up in the first place. A thin layer of sweat breaks out on my hairline.

"Am I to assume I was in this blog last night?" I ask.

Silence blankets the small room like fresh snow.

Fay's eyes stray away from mine, as they always seem to when I ask her a question she doesn't want to answer.

Francie bites her lip and nods.

"Well, I can assure you that whatever they said, it was wrong," I announce so the entire room hears it.

No one argues. It was probably something related to Austin's stupid stunt in the auditorium yesterday.

"I mean, Fay can attest that the blinds were open when Coach Bailey came to my office yesterday."

No one responds. Not even Fay.

"I mean, it's ridiculous that I'm even in the blog. I'm not that interesting."

"Well, you were the Jeep mystery girl, so of course you were in the blog," a teacher behind me says.

"What?" Coffee sputters out of my mouth onto my light pink blouse.

"Oh, let me help." Fay runs over to the faucet and comes back armed with a wet paper towel.

"Thanks." I try to take it from her, but her eyes are a millimeter away from my tit as she tries to stick a hand up my blouse to work out the stain. I swat her hand away with my free one. "Really, I can get it."

"I've got a Tide stick in my desk." She tosses the paper towel into the garbage can and is about to run out the door except it opens before she reaches it.

Austin stands there wearing jeans and another button-

down, this one striped with a sweater over it. He looks so...
delectable. Damn him.

"Francie!" His voice booms through the room, inter-
rupting the conversation we were having. His arms swoop
Francie up in a hug bear hug. "How was Cancun? Did you
swim with the dolphins like we did on our senior trip?"

Francie's eyes catch mine. Not his friend, my ass.

"Yeah, thanks, Austin." She pats his shoulders to put
her down.

"Tell me about it!"

Francie looks at me and back to him.

"Oh, morning, Holly." He gives me a nod. "Coffee stain
already? Sign of a bad day to come, huh?"

I wish I had that Tide stick, so I could jab it in his eye.

"Oh, I almost forgot," Fay says, flustered as she runs
toward the door.

"No, Fay, it's fine." I chase after her.

Murmurs commence as I wind through the tables of
teachers, and I catch the words "fogged-up windows,"
"Jeep," and "handprint." I stop beside a table of three
teachers and look down at them—one man, two women, all
in their fifties. The man looks away, but the women hold my
gaze.

"Okay, everyone." I place my hands on my hips.
"Someone is going to tell me what you've heard."

Austin walks toward me. "Holly, let's go to your office."

I hold up my hand. "Nope. Someone tell me."

My patience is at an all-time low, and if they thought
Miranda Miller was bad, wait until they see my temper. It
doesn't show itself often, but let's just say it channels Joe
Pesci in *Goodfellas*.

"Sweetie." Fay's hand lands on my forearm. She purses
her lips, unsure, and I nod at her to continue. "There were

pictures of some mystery girl in Austin's Jeep on Saturday night. Austin, you know... it was big news because... well, he doesn't get a lot of—"

"Fay," Austin snips.

"I pegged it for Sedona and Jamison," another faculty member calls.

Who the hell are Sedona and Jamison?

"So, after seeing Austin turn white as a ghost at the assembly, and then someone overheard you two talking afterward..." Fay continues.

My gaze shoots to Custodian Kip, who was the only one left in the auditorium. He stares down at his coffee. Chicken shit.

"Buzz Wheel put two and two together, and everyone figures it was you in his Jeep on Saturday night," Fay finishes in a whisper accompanied by a wince.

"Oh, my God." I cover my mouth with my hand and run through the halls until I enter the bathroom, where I lose my entire breakfast.

Teenage girls' "ugh" and "gross" ring out as my knees press into the bathroom floor. Not my proudest moment, but if I'm picking, neither is having the entire town know about my one-night stand.

"Hi, girls, can you give us some privacy?" I recognize Francie's voice.

"Sure. Miss... or Mrs. Porter now." They say missus as if she's the queen. Oh, to be a teenager when marriage seemed so magical.

The sound of running water stops, and I hear the girls shuffle out.

A knock hits the stall door. "Holly? It's Francie. I'm sorry, I should've given you a heads-up."

I stand, flush the toilet, and try to collect myself. "It's

okay. It's just so..." Tears threaten. I'm new to this town and I'm already being rumored about.

"Want some gum?" She holds a piece under the stall door. "I have mints too."

I accept the gum. "Gum's great, thanks."

"Do you want to talk?"

"No, thank you. I think I need to just go on with my day."

"Well, you know where to find me if you do." She pauses before she continues. "Um... Austin really wants to come in and talk to you."

"Please tell him no, I'll talk to him later."

Francie lets a small chuckle loose. "Oh, you really don't know Austin, he's—"

"Not going to accept no. Thanks, Francie." His deep rumble echoes through the empty bathroom.

"I meant what I said, Holly, whenever you want," she says before her heels click on the tile as she leaves the bathroom.

Austin wastes no time in climbing on the toilet seat in the stall next to me and peering over the divider. "Thanks for flushing the toilet."

"Thanks for making me Saturday night news." I close the lid of the toilet, sit on it, and bring my legs up to my chest.

"I'm just as much of a victim in this as you."

I look at him with narrowed eyes. "The guy is never the victim when it comes to these things and we both know it. There's a double standard—I'm the slut and you're the king."

He chuckles. "Believe me, I'm not seen as a one-night-stand king around here, and no one sees you as the slut.

Promise. Not to mention it's all hearsay. There's not one shred of evidence it was actually you."

"People don't need evidence. I'm just starting here and now people are going to see me as the woman who slept with a man she didn't know and later found out he was her employee." I bring my forehead to my knees.

"Can you unlock the door and come out so we can have a proper conversation?"

"No."

"Come on. You definitely need a hug, and if you remember, my arms are pretty good at the hugging thing."

My brain betrays me, and I smile.

"That's all I need, a picture of me hugging you in the girls' bathroom at school. Might as well etch my name and number on the door under 'For a good time call.'"

"Let's not go too far. You are older than these girls and that could be seen as trying to lure—"

"Austin!"

He chuckles again. "Come on, don't make me crawl under the door and unlock it."

I stare at him. He shrugs, and I can tell that if I don't do as he asks, he's going to do it for me. I stand and unlock the door.

"Good." He jumps down and is in front of me in a second. His arms open, waving me into his body.

My brain betrays me again and I step into him. His arms wrap around my body, holding me tight.

"See, doesn't this make all that worry go away?"

"No," I mumble, but it kind of does. I feel safe and protected in his arms.

"It's today's news, and tomorrow it will be someone else. Don't sweat this, okay? The Buzz Wheel isn't something to be crying over." He leans back, his thumb wiping the tears off my cheek.

His smile warms me, and for the first time since I arrived in Lake Starlight, I feel as though I have an ally. Which I could really use, given why I came here in the first place.

"Thanks," I say into his hard chest.

He squeezes me. "Any time. I know we got off on the wrong foot—after we got off"—I chuckle into his chest—"but I want you to know, I'm here for you if you need me."

"I appreciate that."

We pull apart, and I use a paper towel to dab at my makeup. We leave the bathroom after the first period bell has rung, so all the students are in their classrooms.

"You better go," I say when we reach the hall.

"Francie's in my class until I get there."

I stand there, taking in his chiseled jaw and stubble that's darker than the tips of his hair—something I don't think is from a salon, but comes to him naturally—his lean, muscled body, and his brown eyes, and I realize that this man may not be what I pegged him for after the auditorium incident. I think he really might be one of the good guys.

"You good?" he asks in a way that makes me think I may have been staring at him longer than I thought I was.

"Yeah. Thanks."

He squeezes my hand before releasing it. "You're welcome."

He winks at me with a grin, and this time my stomach flip and flops as if I'm a student here and not the principal. I'm unsure whether I'm happy about my discovery or not. Because knowing Austin isn't the jerk I thought he was is only going to make it that much harder to stay away from him.

FIVE

Austin

"*Austin!*" my sister Savannah screams when she walks in the front door of the house.

Jesus, does she ever not sound like she's in a panic?

No, not really, but that's Savannah for you. She's younger than me by two years, and when my parents passed nine years ago, we took the reins and equally divided the family duties between us to try to get our seven brothers and sisters into adulthood in one piece. I took the bulk of the domestic duties, and she took over learning the family lumber business. She lived with us for a few years at first, but she's had her own place for a while now.

I don't know if it was the weight of that kind of responsibility at such a young age that turned her into the type-A, always serious and doesn't seem to know how to have fun anymore woman she is today, or whether she would've been that way anyway. But suffice it to say that on most days, Savannah is wound tight.

"In the kitchen," I say in my regular voice because she's only *one* room away.

I hear her make a pit stop in the family room, where Sedona and her boyfriend, Jamison, are watching TV.

"I don't think the two of you should be sitting so close," Savannah says then walks into the kitchen. "Did you see those two? They have a blanket over their laps. Come on, Austin, you remember being a teenager, right?"

I point a knife in her direction. "You stick to your responsibilities and I'll stick to mine. Jamison is harmless. They aren't in her room. They're in plain sight where I can surprise them and pop into the room whenever I want." I turn my attention back to cutting up the chicken.

"I'm starving." She picks up a piece of broccoli, pops it into her mouth, and rests a stack of papers on the counter.

"What's that?" I eye the pile with disdain. There's a reason she took over the business and I became Mr. Mom.

"These are the numbers we need to figure out. With Phoenix and Sedona heading to college next year, we need to look at the finances." She saddles up in the stool across from me.

"I thought we'd already set the college funds aside and we were good?"

My dipshit of a brother decided after he graduated that he wanted to risk his life and jump out of planes and fight forest fires as a smoke jumper. Savannah and I told him he couldn't touch his college fund until he was twenty-one. It's a sore subject around here.

"We did, but that doesn't mean there aren't papers to sign. And... I'm not sure Phoenix is going to college."

"She's going."

Another sore subject in the Bailey house.

"We can't force her, and I'm not letting her waste that

money by sending her to college and paying for it when she doesn't even want to be there." She grabs another piece of broccoli but heads to the fridge where she grabs the ranch dip and cracks it open.

"Help yourself," I say.

"Thanks." She smiles with a full mouth of broccoli.

I concentrate on the chicken, knowing Savannah and I are going to argue about Phoenix.

"How is she doing in school?" Savannah asks.

That's the thing with Savannah—she knows how to manipulate. She learned from Grandma Dori, who taught her the ropes at nineteen when she got involved in the family business. We're usually easygoing with our siblings, letting them live their lives the way they want, but Phoenix needs direction and I'm not letting her sit around and do nothing with her life.

"She does okay. But we both know she doesn't put in the effort she should."

Savannah eyes the other room and nods in that direction. "What about...?"

"Sedona has good grades in English, decent in science, still editor of the newspaper. She'll be fine."

Savannah sighs, eating another piece of broccoli. "So before we get down to business, I have to say, I'm kind of disappointed in you. I mean, having sex in the alley behind Lucky Tavern? You had to know you'd make Buzz Wheel." She grins.

I roll my eyes. "When was the last time you were on the Buzz Wheel? Oh, that's right, you don't do anything but work and workout, so not much opportunity."

She cocks her head with a "whatever" expression. "Dodging the subject, I see." After taking a ponytail holder out of her purse, she secures her blonde hair and heads to the sink.

"I'm not dodging. I don't give a shit who knows what I did. I'm a thirty-year-old man who's raising his siblings. I deserve to get laid."

She laughs, wiping her hands on a paper towel and throwing it away. "No one said you didn't. I just thought what with you having twin seventeen-year-old sisters to set an example for, maybe you'd be more discreet."

"I wasn't thinking straight."

Which is the truth. Holly kind of took me by storm. When we left Luckys, I assumed we'd head to her place, or maybe the inn down the street, but she couldn't seem to wait, and hey, again, I'm a thirty-year-old guy who doesn't get laid nearly enough. You do the math. Willing partner plus roaming hands the minute we reached the vehicle equals sex in my Jeep.

"No, you weren't. I think the best part though is the picture of your face when she stepped on stage."

Fucking Buzz Wheel. "Well, imagine it was you."

She laughs, putting oil in a pan. "I tend to get names before I sleep with someone."

I slide the chicken off the cutting board into the pan, and Savannah salt-and-peppers it.

"Next subject," I say, bringing the cutting board to the sink. "Don't we have to talk about our sisters' futures?"

"I'll give you a pass this time." She smiles and puts the broccoli in the pot to steam while I check on the baked potatoes in the crock pot. "We need to discuss Founder's Day too, and there's something I need your help on with Bailey Timber."

"After dinner?"

"Sure." She shrugs.

"Hey, you two." Brooklyn barrels into the kitchen, probably smelling the food.

"What's with the new look?" Savannah asks, because Brooklyn's makeup looks mismatched.

"Oh." She covers her mouth. "I was trying on what makeup I want for the wedding, so Aubrey did one half of my face with a nighttime glamor look and the other with the innocent girl-next-door."

Savannah examines both sides.

"Nighttime," Savannah says at the same time I say, "Girl next door."

"Don't listen to Austin. He doesn't respect a girl enough to give her a proper bed." Savannah winks.

I knew the subject wouldn't go away that easily.

"She's cute. The principal lady." Brooklyn smiles at me, taking over for Savannah stirring the chicken in the pan.

"She seems a tad out of your league. I mean, Yale?" Savannah adds more of her two cents.

I cut up a loaf of bread, ignoring them.

"Look at those pink cheeks." Savannah pinches one and I hip-check her. She stumbles in her heels, Brooklyn catching her, and the two of them laugh in one another's arms.

"One day it'll be payback."

"Please, you gave Jeff the third degree on our first date."

"Because he's an asshole," I mumble.

Savannah straightens and pokes me in the side. "You know, Brook, no one will be good enough for you in Austin's eyes."

I don't argue with Savannah's point because Brooklyn is twenty-five and can decide for herself what she wants. The wedding is happening, and her douche of a fiancé is going to be my brother-in-law no matter how much I try to help Brooklyn see his faults.

At one point, Savannah sat me down for a conversation to tell me to stop before Brooklyn leaves Lake Starlight and we never see her again.

"Yeah, well, he's coming to pick me up and take me to the movies," Brooklyn says.

"What are you seeing?" Savannah grabs the plates, Brooklyn the silverware, and the two of them set the table.

"That new action one with Tom Cruise."

I inwardly roll my eyes. I've never once heard Brooklyn say they were doing something she liked.

"Oh, is he coming for dinner?" Savannah asks.

I turn my back with the excuse of having to stir the chicken, so Brooklyn doesn't have to see my grimace.

"Well, I didn't want to ask..."

"He's more than welcome. Right, Austin?" Savannah says.

I smack on the smile Savannah demands I use when asshat is here. "Yeah." Needing as many reinforcements as possible, I call to the family room, "Jamison, you want to stay for dinner?"

"Aye, let me call me hosts and let them know."

Perfect. A full table where I can talk with Jamison about soccer and ignore Jeff's incessant chatter about himself.

"Smooth," Savannah whispers, taking the bread basket off the counter.

I shrug. I can't wait for one of our brothers to bring home a girl she doesn't like. My phone rings on the counter, and I place the spoon over the pan to grab it.

"I bet it's his girlfriend," Brooklyn imitates a thirteen-year-old's voice, fluttering her eyelids.

I point at her. "Shut it."

"She's probably asking for another round in his Jeep," Savannah says on a laugh.

Sedona enters the kitchen and joins the party. "That thing is so ugly."

"Nah, the Jeep's cool."

I fist-bump Jamison for the compliment as he walks past me toward the table. "Let's remember my business is my business."

"Then keep it private. You know how many girls already fawn over you at school? It's disgusting and now they're imagining you..." Sedona's entire body shudders and her eyes roll back into her head.

Savannah laughs. "When we were in high school together—"

I drag my finger across my throat to Savannah. Sometimes we both forget we're the role models for these kids and not their cool older siblings. She nods, understanding the kids don't need to hear how either of us behaved in high school. Not that we were bad. We were... well, teenagers. It's just different when you *are* the teenager and when you're trying to raise one.

Glancing at my phone, I see a number I don't recognize. I answer in case it's one of the colleges I'm waiting to hear from.

"Hello," I say in my most professional voice.

"Hey, Austin, sorry to call you on your cell phone, but I need to see you in my office first thing in the morning. JP's mother called, and I guess there's a problem," Holly says.

I walk out of the kitchen, reminding me of when I was a teenager and could never talk to the girl I liked in front of my family. "Just a little 4-1-1, JP's mom always has a problem."

She laughs. "I can tell by his file. But I guess she's

concerned about his friend, Elijah. She's making some pretty outlandish accusations, and before I address them, I want to talk with you in person."

"What's she claiming?" I sit in the family room, turning off the television Sedona and Jamison left on. I used to hate when my parents nagged me to turn shit off. Now that I'm the one paying the electric bills, I get it.

"She's claiming Elijah isn't earning the grade he's getting. She said you've been giving him a free ride, so he can get into college."

The phone almost slips from my hand. She's got to be fucking kidding me. After all the shit that woman has done, she's not going to ruin my reputation just because her son got his ass handed to him by Elijah a few nights ago. God, that fucking woman needs help.

"We'll talk about it in the morning. No worries tonight."

Her voice is level and kind, but I can't help but think she probably believes the lie because her whole experience of moving to Lake Starlight has been ruined by my doing. I exposed her to Buzz Wheel, something *I* knew could happen but didn't give much thought to in the moment. *I* embarrassed her at school, which caused her name to once again appear in that stupid anonymous blog. *I* made her cry.

Fuck, my mom always told me not to make a girl cry. I hate that she could be looking down on me with her hands on her hips and her stern, disappointed eyes surveying all the trouble I've caused Holly since she moved to Lake Starlight.

"Elijah earns his grades. The only thing I've helped him with is the tapes to send in to colleges, but that's a coaching thing."

"Did you do the same for JP?"

"No." I want to say it's because JP can barely field a ball

cleanly, let alone hit a ball. He's on the team because he's the best we have, but he's no Elijah. My heart races over Gail Andrew's accusation. An accusation that could ruin my future.

"Well, like I said, we'll get this all sorted in the morning. I'll call a sub to take your first period tomorrow so we can talk."

"Thanks, Holly."

"Oh, and one more thing."

"Yeah?"

"You mentioned you're leaving Lake Starlight next year to pursue a college coaching position. Is that a for-sure thing?"

I blow out a breath. "Yeah."

"Okay," she croaks. "Great. Just wanted to know since she talked about that, but I didn't have any record of official notice or..."

"It's not set in stone yet. I mean, I haven't officially been offered anything yet."

"It's fine. I mean, I'm only here temporarily, but obviously it's something the school board will need to be informed of."

"Holly," I say before she rushes me off the phone.

"Yeah?"

"Please don't tell the school board. I don't have a for-sure job lined up yet. They're looking into me, but I'm still waiting to hear." I tap my foot on the floor, waiting for her to agree.

There's silence.

"Well, JP's mom knows, so my guess is this Buzz Wheel thing will be leaking that news soon enough."

"I'll handle Gail."

"No, you won't. Listen to me, do not call or go over

there. We'll talk in the morning and figure out a plan. I'm on your side."

"Why?" I'll admit I'm surprised. I can usually read people pretty well, and I didn't take Holly for someone who would have my back.

"Because you said you didn't do it and I believe you."

I don't respond, surprised by the resolve in her voice.

"Let's just talk tomorrow. Good night, Austin."

"Thanks for the heads-up, Holly. Good night."

Savannah pops her head in from the kitchen. "Everything okay? Dinner's ready."

"Yeah, everything's great." I stuff my phone into my pocket and head to dinner with a smile, courtesy of Holly.

SIX

Holly

Austin arrives at my office early, before Fay has clocked in for the day. He knocks on the glass window of my office wall, and I wave him in.

"I know it's early, but I brought you a coffee and a blueberry muffin from Brewed Awakenings." He sets them on my desk.

"Thanks, but that wasn't necessary."

My eyes soak him in. He's wearing a pair of charcoal slacks with a V-neck sweater and a white T-shirt underneath. Very uncoach-like, but hot AF as the kids say these days.

"Are you dressed up for an interview I don't know about?" I laugh.

He sits in the chair opposite my desk, opening the lid of his coffee and blowing into the cup. I try not to think of how he blew his warm breath on my wet nipples the night we were together, but I mean, come on, how can I not?

"No, but it's laundry day."

I shake my head. Time to move on. "Well, Gail Andrews is quite the number, isn't she?"

I open JP's file on my desk. Complaint after complaint from his mother rests inside. Everything from school lunches to threatening to sue the school when JP got caught cheating in the ninth grade and was forced to serve detention.

After speaking with Austin last night, I knew I had to investigate before his reputation was tarnished by this accusation.

"She's something for sure, but this is beyond thinking her son is the angel he isn't. She's going to ruin Elijah's chances of a scholarship if this gets out." He sits on the edge of the chair, his legs open, his coffee on my desk.

I look up from the file and study him. He's so gorgeous. I have no idea how he's not taken already. His dark brown eyes, surrounded by thick, dark lashes, look at me, waiting for me to respond.

I clear my throat. "I know. I think we can prove her wrong. My only concern is with the other teachers. I'll need to question them, get Elijah's test results, but if I flag them, one of them might get suspicious. Same as you, my concern rests on Elijah's future."

"What if you ask for all the seniors' results? You mentioned at the assembly that you're going to be meeting with each of them to discuss their futures after graduation. You can say you're reviewing everyone's results."

I lean back in my seat. "That's a daunting task."

He slides closer to the edge of his chair. "I'll help you with whatever you need. After school, I'll go through papers and test scores with you. We can prove that Elijah's marks are in line with his classmates who performed similarly."

I sense that the desperation in his tone is more about

Elijah than himself, confirming my instinct that he didn't do what he's being accused of. Gail Andrews is just a mom who thinks her son is a special snowflake and can't imagine him being anything less than *numero uno*.

"Okay, let's do it. From what I've seen, Elijah has a bright future, and I already have him on the schedule to talk to tomorrow as part of my senior stay-on-track program. But I need you to handle this whole Elijah, JP, and Becca ordeal. I'd ask Vice Principal Ealey, but he's not in any shape to give advice to anyone about relationships."

He nods. "I can handle that."

I figured out what everyone was talking about in the staff room—apparently JP and Elijah are letting some girl come between their friendship and blows have already been exchanged.

"All right, well, I'll call Ms. Andrews this morning and tell her I'm investigating her allegations. Hopefully I can put this to bed in a week and both you and Elijah can rest easy about your futures."

He stands. I forget how tall he is when he's sitting. "Thank you. Honestly, you owe me nothing and the fact you're willing to do this for me—"

"And Elijah," I add.

He nods, stuffing his hands in his pockets. "And Elijah. After everything..."

"It's all right. You might be the class clown, but your heart is in a good place." I stand and walk around the side of my desk.

His eyes fall to my chest. I'd never admit this to anyone, but I purposely wore a tighter blouse today. I have no idea why. I mean, Lake Starlight will be in both our rearview mirrors in a few months.

"Thanks, I think." He smiles. "Okay, so do you want to

meet somewhere or at your place tonight to go over test scores and papers?"

I wave him off and almost touch his arm when I do, but I retract my hand quickly. "Don't worry about it, I'll handle it."

"No." His eyes widen as he steps closer to me. "I'm going to help you. We have baseball practice until six, then I'm free."

"Well, um... okay. Why don't we meet at Lard Have Mercy? Or..." Shit, that damn Buzz Wheel blog. The last thing I need is Mrs. Andrews seeing a picture of Austin and me together. "I'll text you my address. Park down the road."

"I'll run over or ride my mountain bike."

I laugh and shake my head. "This seems ridiculous, like we're two cheating spouses sneaking around."

"Welcome to Lake Starlight." He rocks back on his heels. "I'll see you tonight then."

"Yeah. I could maybe make us dinner, or we can order in?"

He smiles. "You're doing me the favor. I'll have something delivered. My treat."

"You don't have to."

"I want to." His hand is millimeters from touching my upper arm when a knock bangs on the glass door.

Austin tenses, and our eyes search out the source.

"Hi, you two." Fay pops her head in the door and smiles and waves. "There's a situation in the courtyard."

We look at one another, then Austin heads out the door and jogs down the hall. I follow him, my heels making it impossible to match his pace. When I reach the courtyard, I find a crowd of students have formed a circle, and a girl is screeching from the outside of the circle.

"*Stop!* Oh, Coach Bailey, stop them." The petite

brunette weaves back and forth wanting to get in the middle.

Austin pushes through the students. "What the hell are you guys doing?" He grabs JP's sweatshirt and pushes him aside before walking a red-faced Elijah to the other side of the circle.

The students clear a path for me, and I see Elijah's eyes laser-focused on the brunette, who I presume is Becca, staring at the ground. He tries to fight his way past Austin, but Austin holds him in place.

JP straightens his sweatshirt with a cocky grin. "Remember, Elijah, you're the one who went up into that bedroom with Sara."

My attention moves to Becca. She's staring at Elijah with tears streaming down her face. Elijah looks at her. I never believed in finding your soul mate in high school, but whatever is between these two is a helluva lot more than puppy love.

"Stay the fuck away from her!" Elijah screams.

"Relax," Austin tells Elijah. "The rest of you, get inside." Austin points toward the doors of the school.

There I am, standing like an idiot in the middle of it, saying nothing rather than taking control of the situation. "JP, get to my office."

"No way! I didn't do anything. He threw the first punch. He's the one who should be expelled."

"Go," I bite out through clenched teeth.

The crowd disperses and JP follows them inside, but a dark-haired girl lingers.

"Please head to your first period class," I tell her.

"Go, Phoenix," Austin says to her.

Austin has Elijah sitting at a picnic table, where he's

lecturing him about cooling his temper and how he can't do this stuff next year. I approach, and Elijah looks up first.

"I'm going to have to see you too," I say, crossing my arms.

"I might've thrown the first punch, but JP's trying to piss me off. He never wanted Becca. He always used to make fun of her, tell me I was wasting my time, and now that she broke up with me, he's constantly all over her." His hands cover his head and his back heaves from his heavy breaths.

"I'll bring him right in, okay?" Austin asks me.

I nod, shooting him a look to say I can't sweep this under the rug. He appears to share the same thought.

"Five minutes," he says.

"Okay, I'll deal with JP first."

Walking into the school, I find the same dark-haired girl in the hall, staring at me.

"Phoenix, right?" I ask.

She nods.

"You need to get to first period. No worries, we have it all handled." I place my hand out for her to walk with me down the hall.

She glances out the window one more time before reluctantly falling into step with me.

"Bye, Holly," the girl sneers before sliding into a door halfway down the hall.

"Bye." I head to my office, the realization she called me by my first name hitting me just outside my office.

JP is sitting in front of Fay, looking as though he's trying to charm her. That'll do him no good with me.

"JP." I hold my hand out for him to head into my office. "No interruptions, Fay. Coach Bailey will be bringing in

Elijah. Have them sit in Vice Principal Ealey's office. He's sick again today."

She cringes. "Sure thing."

"Thank you."

When I walk into my office, I find JP relaxed in the chair Austin was sitting in moments ago, his feet propped up on the desk and the blueberry muffin Austin brought me half eaten in his hand.

I stop and stare. I've dealt with a lot of assholes, but high school is a whole new level of adolescent bullshit. I grab the muffin out of his hand when I walk by and drop it in the trash.

"Sorry, I thought this was a new thing. You serving breakfast."

"Remove your feet from my desk." I sit down in my chair.

He smirks but lowers his feet to the floor. He remains slouched in the chair like the delinquent he is. "Call my mom."

"I don't need to call your mom."

"Then call the cops. I want to file charges."

"There will be no charges. We're going to hash this out here. Regardless if Elijah threw the first punch, you engaged, which means you'll be getting detention."

He rolls his eyes and sits up straight, resting his elbows on his knees. "Let's just call my mom."

The more he asks, the angrier I become. I lean over the desk, eyes locked with his. "I'm not going to call your mommy for you. You have detention for the rest of the week."

"Coach Bailey isn't going to like that. We have practice." He shoots me a look to suggest I'm an idiot. "We both know how you like to please Coach Bailey. Tell me..." He leans in closer. "Was it your handprint on his Jeep window or his?"

What I'd give for it to be fifty years ago so I could smack this kid over the hand with a ruler. "That's two weeks. Want to go for three?"

"For what?" he yells. "It's the truth. The pictures show it."

Austin and Elijah enter the office, Austin beelining it to my office until Fay directs him next door.

"I am your principal, Mr. Andrews, and I will be treated with respect. What I do after hours is my business, not yours."

"Same here then."

"Fine, then conduct your fights off school property."

He narrows his eyes, clearly upset he isn't getting his way. No way Miranda Miller let this kid use his mother as a threat.

"Fine." He stands. "Expect a phone call in about five minutes. I'm pretty sure this is a black eye." He points at his face.

"Then stop at the nurses' station, but I *will* see you after school today for detention."

He doesn't turn around as he walks out of the room, waving.

"Little piece of shit," I mumble.

Austin comes in, leaving Elijah in Vice Principal Ealey's office.

"They're both in detention for the week. JP is for two weeks."

Austin opens his mouth to interrupt.

"I'm sorry, I know they miss practice, but I have no choice here," I say.

"No, I was going to agree."

"Really?"

He chuckles. "Yeah. I told you I don't give my boys free passes."

My shoulders relax. Since when do I worry about what others think? I mean, who cares if Austin would've been upset that I had to give his two players detentions? "Okay, good. Send Elijah in."

"You got it, boss." He smiles, walking out.

My stomach somersaults as I watch his backside leave. Damn, he's hot, especially when he agrees with me.

SEVEN

Austin

"Francie told me you played the white knight this morning." Jack hits balls to the guys from home plate while I stand off to the side. "No, Jaden, throw the ball to your cutoff man."

Jack shakes his head at me. We're fortunate we have Elijah this year, so we don't have to rely on our fielding.

"Don't believe everything you hear," I say.

"Like I shouldn't believe what Buzz Wheel said?" He raises a brow.

"Fucking Buzz Wheel. I stopped reading it years ago."

Jack tilts his head, questioning my truthfulness.

"I did. I'll take that as you still do?"

He shrugs. "Francie reads it to me at night."

I imitate a woman's voice as I say, "'What a great bedtime story, Jackey.' Does she give you a glass of warm milk too?"

"I'm sure Principal Radcliffe wouldn't mind tucking you in."

I shoot him a death glare and shift my vision to the guys in the field. Luckily they're all razzing Jaden for missing three in a row and not paying us any attention.

"Be professional," I remind him.

"Sorry." He cringes, but I know Jack and he doesn't care. "So, Elijah and JP are in detention?"

"Yeah. I mean, would we have let a chick get in the way of our friendship back in the day?" I drop the clipboard on the bench and sit down. "Let's call practice. My balls are about to freeze off."

"Run your laps and head to the showers," Jack announces, throwing the bat in the bag.

The players pick up their equipment and head to the track to run ten laps apiece.

I laugh. "Don't have to tell you twice."

"My blood hasn't thickened back up yet." He puts on his hat and gloves, sitting next to me. "Back to your question. You know as well as I do this is JP, not Elijah."

"Can't say that for sure."

Though he's probably right. JP walks around like an entitled little prick most of the time. And we all know it's his mom's fault.

"I know. But going after a friend's girl? I mean, could you imagine if you would have gone after Francie?"

I laugh. Francie's a great girl, but she's not really my type. "I would never."

"I know." He smacks my shoulder. "But Coach wouldn't have let us mess up our friendship over a girl either."

"Yeah." My gaze falls to my hands clasped between my legs. Sometimes I feel as though I can never live up to my mentor.

"Come on, Francie's cooking poppy seed chicken

tonight." He stands, eager to get home to his wife.

I'd probably take him up on his offer, but I have more than my two teenage sisters to entertain me tonight. "Thanks, but I have papers to grade."

See what I did there? Jack expects me to tell him everything, but I didn't even have to lie to him to keep my whereabouts tonight a secret.

"You work too much."

I chuckle as we follow the boys into the locker room. "You work seven days a week."

"Nope. I just hired Jaden for Saturday and Sundays."

I smack him on the back. "I sure hope he can figure out the difference between a nail and screw better than he can a curveball and knuckleball."

We laugh, walking into the halls that were ours once upon a time.

My phone rings as soon as I climb into my Jeep. Savannah's name flashes on the screen, so I switch her to Bluetooth.

"Hey," I answer.

"You're never going to believe what that slimeball at North Forest Lumber Company did!"

"Calm down."

"He tried to poach Ventures Housing from us." I hear something smash in the background. Savannah has a little bit of a temper. She wouldn't actually hit a person, but coffee mugs are fair game when she's mad.

"Did he succeed?" I ask, turning a corner.

"I swear I'm going to burn down that place."

"Jeez, Sav, let's hope the line isn't bugged. Now answer

my question."

"I mean, we've been around for how many years? He comes up here from God knows where and thinks he's going to take over our clientele? The clients that Daddy and Granddaddy fished and hunted with? I bet he thinks I'm weak because I'm a woman. Well, he's about to find out that I will not roll over." Another smash echoes over the speakers.

"Sit down for a second." I bring the car to a halt at a stoplight.

"*No!* How can you be so calm? This is our family legacy. The business that affords us what small luxuries we have. It's my future, Austin. I get that you want to hightail it out of this town as soon as the twins cross the stage with their diplomas, but this is it for me." The anger in her voice fades and she sighs. "Sometimes I think I'm disappointing Dad."

The key with Savannah is to let her anger burn out on its own. There's no reason to rush her to come to the right conclusion. She usually will on her own after a good fight with herself. Not that I don't understand her feeling that way. I was just on the bleachers, thinking the same thing.

"You're not. Dad would be so proud of you. Just ask Grandma Dori. Speaking of, have you asked her for advice on this?"

"No. I want her to be assured that I can handle these things on my own. If she's ever going to hand the company over to me completely, I need to be capable."

The light changes and I drive slowly through downtown Lake Starlight. The green-and-white banners with the Bailey Timber Corp logo decorate the light posts for the upcoming Founder's Day.

"Well, here's some good news for you. I'm driving

through downtown and everything is looking good."

"Really?" she asks, a chipper tone overtaking her stressed-out one. "That's one thing, I suppose."

"So back to this other issue. What have you done so far to fix it?"

"I'm having dinner with the Venture reps tomorrow night. They want to renegotiate the terms. Said that asshole Clint's offer was five percent less." The tapping of a pen on her desk echoes through the receiver.

"There you go. Why are you calling me? You've already got this handled."

She laughs. "I needed to vent, and I have no one but you."

"Jeez, thanks."

"You know what I mean." She sighs. "Do you ever think it's sick that we only have each other? Here we are, almost thirty—well, you're already over that hump—we're pseudo parents to our siblings, and we're both single?"

I can tell from her voice that she needs to be lifted up once more.

"You could get a husband if you wanted one," I remind her, slowing for another stoplight.

She laughs. "No one wants to date a woman who runs a company."

"Sure, they do." I slam on my brakes when two guys jump in front of my Jeep before I've come to a complete stop. "*Fuck!*"

"What?"

I look up after my whiplash. My brother Denver and his friend Liam laugh and smack the hood of my Jeep. "Our dipshit brother and his best friend just ran in front of my Jeep."

Denver's been gone flying supplies up north for the past

few months. He must just be back in town today.

"See?" She releases a breath. "Immature. The guys around here can't find their way out of a wet paper bag. What is it about this town and all the men who are incapable of growing up?"

"Hey!" Denver bangs on the window.

"Hang on a sec, Savannah."

"Who are you talking to?" Denver asks me through the window.

I roll it down, and the cool spring air wafts into the Jeep. "Savannah."

Liam hops in the passenger seat without warning and rifles through my glove box.

"Hey, Savannah. Miss me?" Denver asks.

"No," she deadpans.

"Come on. I've been gone a long time. You weren't worried about me?"

"Oh, Denver, I only worry if your health insurance covers STD examinations."

Liam laughs. "Good one, Savannah."

"Oh great, your sidekick is there too. Gotta go." Savannah clicks off before anyone has time to say goodbye.

"She's so uptight. If you weren't her brothers, I'd suggest someone loosen her up." Liam smirks at us.

Denver narrows his eyes at Liam. "She's my sister, dude."

This is where Denver and I differ. Savannah's my sister and I hope she finds a better guy than Brooklyn has, but I don't really give a shit who it is as long as he treats her well and she loves him. She definitely needs a guy who can handle her outbursts of doubt though. We've both given everything to this family, so I would never give her shit for anything.

"Your older and *hot* sister," Liam says.

Denver tries to climb through the window over me, his arms outstretched. Liam laughs, snatching something out of my glove box, and opens the door.

"Hey!" I say.

"I'll return it." Liam yells, holding up my tire pressure stick, turning around.

He pretends to be a boxer in the ring with Denver when he comes around his side. They're twenty-three, but these two will never fucking grow up.

I pull up and off to the side so the vehicles behind me can get past. Then I honk the horn as they test the tires on Liam's 1970 Pontiac GTO. It's his pride and joy and I swear he'd marry the damn thing if he could.

Denver jogs back up to the Jeep and passes me the tire pressure stick.

"Thanks," I say and toss it back inside the glove compartment.

His arms hang in the passenger window. "I was at the house earlier. Sedona's boyfriend was there."

"Yeah." I shrug.

"You need to keep a better eye on her. Remember when I was seventeen?" He cringes.

"They're fine."

"Well, we don't want Sedona to make headlines on Buzz Wheel like you do. I meant to ask you, how is the new principal?"

Liam laughs, coming up beside him.

"Both of you can fuck off." I put up my middle finger, and Denver jumps back as if I'd run over his toes.

I should be used to being at the center of the news in Lake Starlight. Being the oldest Bailey, I feel as though I've lived in the spotlight my entire life.

EIGHT

Holly

"So, you're stalking your dad?" my best friend, Dana, asks over the Bluetooth speakers in my SUV.

"I'm not stalking him, just doing some recon." I sip my iced coffee and settle in to watch the front doors of the building that houses his company's offices.

"You say that like it's normal. Be the woman I know you are. Go in there and tell him you're there and see what he says." Dana chomps down on her dinner before she has to head back to the ER.

"I can't. I'm still adjusting to being here. One step at a time."

"And you still haven't told Karen?"

"No, my mom still thinks I'm in Oregon." Guilt weighs heavily on me. My mom has been everything to me my entire life and I don't enjoy lying to her, but it feels like what's best at this point.

"I'm oddly proud of you for taking this step," Dana mumbles over whatever she's eating.

I sip my coffee. "Thanks?"

"You always play it so safe. Remember in college when that guy dared you to streak at that party and you broke up with him?"

"Why would he want his friends to see me naked? That's just stupid."

"He was a twenty-one-year-old guy who wanted to see your tits. Plain and simple."

I chuckle. "And that's why I'm not with him."

"Ever see your one-night stand guy again?"

I still, even though she can't see me. "Why do you ask?"

"Don't you live in Mayberry now? I'm guessing you ran into him at the one stoplight." She laughs.

"Lake Starlight isn't that small."

"If you say so. I worry that if a polar bear attacks you, you won't have proper medical care. The hospitals there probably don't have trauma units. Have you checked that out?"

I roll my eyes. "First of all, I'm not going to run into a bear, and I'm sure the medical care is fine."

"Whatever you say. Let's get back to hot Jeep guy."

"Funny you should ask."

"Oooh, that sounds promising."

"He works at the school. He's a teacher and the baseball coach."

Dana laughs, and I hear her hand slap on the lunch table. "No way!" More laughing and smacking. "I love it."

"Yeah, my life is a real comedy skit these days. Oh, and get this, they have this blog that reports the local gossip, so *everyone* knows about our tryst. I'm the laughingstock of this place."

"A blog? That doesn't sound very Mayberry-like," she murmurs.

"Nope." I sip my coffee again. Pretty soon I'll have to use it as a pee cup, because I'm not leaving without catching a glimpse of my dad.

"What's the blog called?"

"No way."

"Come on, can I comment on it?"

"Absolutely not!"

She laughs. "I'm due for some vacation time. Before you head back home, I'm coming to visit."

"Just so you know, you will stick out."

"Maybe I'll find some hot guy with a Jeep to screw me in."

"Dana," I sigh.

As always, her response is to laugh.

I spot someone in the lobby, walking toward the front door.

"I think he's coming." My heart beats in my throat as I wait for the man, who is a stranger to me, to walk out the door.

"Okay, I'm here for you. What does he look like? Does he have your auburn hair? Because your mom doesn't. Come to think of it, you look nothing like your mom. Oh, what if you were adopted or Karen stole you? Shit, could you imagine if Karen wasn't even your mom?"

"You're watching way too much of the Investigation Discovery channel." I lean forward, anticipation clawing at my stomach.

"True. But think about it, you and Karen are *so* opposite."

A man with auburn hair sprinkled with gray wearing a striped suit with a tie, and black wingtips emerges from the building.

"I think it's him," I whisper, as if he could hear me.

"Really?" Dana lets go of the whole *Dateline* story she formed in her head. "Does he look nice?"

"I guess so. He's not smiling or anything."

"How can he look nice if he's not smiling?"

"He looks content—oh, oh my." I blink a few times in rapid succession.

"What?" Dana asks. "I've got, like, two minutes left of my break. Hurry."

"It's just... his car..." I squint to make sure I'm seeing it correctly.

"What does he drive? Some expensive sports car because he's a bachelor who doesn't give a shit about his daughter? He probably spends all his money on toys."

"He paid child support," I mumble, still concentrating. He climbs in while looking in my direction, so I slide down in my small SUV. "Shit, I think he saw me."

"Relax, you're probably imagining it."

"Am I total idiot for doing this?" I ask, doubting myself not for the first time since putting this plan into action. "I mean, I left with almost tenure to fulfill some little girl's dream of meeting her father. I lied to the woman who raised me and helped put me through college. I'm an idiot."

"No, you're not. Who doesn't want to know their parents? I told you, I'm proud of you."

A small smile pulls at my lips. I sit back up in my seat, staring at the back of his window. "He has kids. One girl and two boys. And a wife."

"How do you know that?"

"He has those stickers on the back of his window. You know the stick figures?"

"Lame. Great, your father is lame." But her words don't hold much conviction.

"I guess I never thought about him having a family." Especially when he was never a part of mine.

"I'm sorry, Hol," Dana says, and I hear a page coming through the intercom in the background. "I gotta go. There's a code, but I'll call you tonight."

"Okay."

"Just don't freak out, okay?"

"Sure. Go, Dana."

"Love you, chica."

"Love you."

The line dies and I stare at the building for a while longer. It's a huge part of the life he's built here. As is his loving wife and three adorable kids. Too bad he didn't bother to include the little girl he left behind thirty years ago in his nice, shiny new life.

NINE

Austin

I opt to run over to Holly's rather than ride my bike even though having my bike outside her house would be way less obvious than my Jeep. Since she lives a block off Main Street, the chance of someone noticing my bike parked nearby is too high.

I shake my head at how ridiculous this is as I look both ways down the street before climbing the small set of stairs up to her front door. She opens it before I ring the doorbell, shooing me in and slamming the door.

"Whoa," I say.

"I'm not taking any chances of being in that Buzz Wheel thing again."

As I remove my jacket, my gaze falls down her body. She's dressed in a pair of jeans and a long-sleeve T-shirt that reads Florida State. Her auburn hair is pulled back in a messy bun, the strands sticking out every which way.

"Here." Her hand is out for my jacket, a hanger ready.

"You're quick." I pass it to her.

She puts it on the hanger and hangs it up in the closet before closing the door. "Thanks for placing our dinner order. It came a few minutes ago. Nothing better than Chinese takeout."

I follow her into the kitchen, where she's already put the containers out next to some plates and a line-up of a variety of different beverages. I wasn't sure if we'd be eating on cardboard boxes or what since she's only in town for a short time, but I'm guessing she's in a furnished rental.

"I didn't know what you'd want to drink."

"I'm good with water. I have no idea how I'll be able to run back home, but I wanted you to experience Wok For U. It's the best Chinese food I've ever eaten. The Chang family immigrated here from China two generations ago, but it's still in the family." I ramble when I'm nervous and being in her environment definitely makes me nervous.

"Can't wait." She opens a container of rice then shifts over and opens a drawer, from which she pulls some spoons and places them beside the containers. "Do you use chopsticks?" She holds up a pair.

"I don't. You?"

Her cheeks turn pink. "A friend of mine from childhood... whenever I'd go over to her house, you had to use chopsticks if you had Chinese food, so I learned young. Now when I eat Asian food, it's a must."

"Cool." I shrug.

"I'm not one of those people who wants to be cool..."

I laugh.

She presses her lips together for a second. "Sorry, I'm rambling."

"Please, I went on about the linage of the Chang family."

We laugh together.

"If you want me to teach you, I'm happy to try."

"I'm always up for trying new stuff."

She smiles and pulls another set out of the drawer, along with a fork. "Just in case."

"Thanks." I accept both, our fingertips brushing as she passes them over.

Our eyes catch for a moment before her gaze shifts away, and she suddenly seems really interested in opening the orange chicken and rice.

I pile on heaping portions while she meticulously selects four pieces of chicken, a spoonful of rice, one strip of beef, and a floret of broccoli.

"You can see more plate than food," I say.

She shrugs. "Don't worry, I'll be back for seconds." She sets her plate on the table before weaving by me toward the drinks again, grabbing two waters, and placing one in front of where I guess I'm sitting. "I have the papers and test scores from half of Elijah's teachers. I see Elijah tomorrow, although I talked with him a bit already after the fight in the courtyard."

"I thought I was getting a lesson on chopsticks." I hold the two sticks in the air.

She laughs. "Oh, right." She picks up her own and it's clear that she's totally comfortable using them. "Hold them like this. One should stay steady, and you only move the top one up and down. See?"

Her tips meet at the end, but when I try it, mine cross. "No, I guess I don't see."

"Here." Her chair slides out, and she leans over me, her thin fingers manipulating my large ones into position.

Her hands are soft and smooth, her touch gentle but firm, her scent intoxicating. I can't tell you exactly what she smells like because I'm not a perfumist or whatever they're called, but whatever she wears, it suits her.

Oh, and her tits feel phenomenal on my shoulder. What? Last time I checked, I still had a dick. These are things a guy notices.

"Now you try." Her voice in my ear pulls me from my thoughts that were headed down a pretty dirty path. "Try a big piece first."

I lower the chopsticks, my hands cramping from the muscles constricting so hard to keep the wooden sticks in place. Somehow, I manage to grab one, the sticks crossing on the top.

"There you go," she says.

I slowly bring it to my lips, my mouth practically meeting it halfway to make sure it doesn't fly off and hit her in the eye. As my mouth opens, the piece of chicken falls and drops in my lap. "Crap."

I drop the sticks to get the chicken, but Holly's instinct has her reaching to pick it up. Right between my legs.

She doesn't realize the fact her hand is an inch away from my dick until it's already there. Instead of withdrawing, she stills, turns her head, and our eyes meet. Her lips are inches from mine. With her hair pulled up, the slender bend of her neck looks more appetizing than the food.

"Got it," she whispers, picking up the piece of chicken, her eyes still locked with mine.

"Good," I say.

The tension is ripe between us and it's a perfect time for a kiss. Does she want me to kiss her? Probably not. I mean, we're colleagues now, not two strangers in a bar.

She blinks and steps back, heading somewhere behind me. "So, have you always lived in Lake Starlight?"

I hear the trash can lid open and close. "Yep. The

Baileys go back generations. My family owns Bailey Timber Company. It was my great-great-grandpa's and it's been passed down ever since." I attempt the whole chopstick thing again, grains of rice sliding off.

Damn it. Who knew two little pieces of wood could be so fucking irritating?

"Feel free to use your fork." She smiles, sitting next to me.

I guess we're forgetting that almost-kiss a moment ago. I take her cue and decide to roll with it. "Thanks." I drop the chopsticks and pick up my fork, stabbing a piece of chicken with it.

"You didn't want to work for the company?"

"No. My sister Savannah was best suited for that. She's got the cutthroat personality for business." My stomach thanks me as I refuel. No one does Chinese food like Wok For U. I'll miss this place when I move away.

"And you're more of a teacher?" She uses her chopsticks with ease, as if she was born knowing.

"No, teacher by default. I used to see myself as a baseball player, but now I'm satisfied with being a coach."

"Oh, well, you're a great teacher. I mean, it seems like the kids respect you." She takes a piece of chicken between her chopsticks and brings it to her mouth.

"They respect me because they see me as their older brother. Most of them I've known my entire life. I'm not sure I'm good at it though." I lean back and sip my water.

"Elijah loves you."

"Elijah loves me because I understand him. Hell, I was him once upon a time. Minus the whole asshat of a best friend and the steady girlfriend."

She smiles over her mouthful of food. When she

finishes chewing, she asks, "Not really the steady girlfriend type of guy?"

I side-eye her.

She giggles and holds up her hands. "Am I stepping over the line?"

"No." I smile back. This is easy. She's easy to be around now that we've gotten past the awkwardness of our second meeting. "My mind was only on baseball in high school. Everything I did was to get to the next level. High school to college, college to the minors... and so forth."

It all feels like another life now.

"What happened?"

I concentrate on my plate. Does she really not know? I'm used to everyone knowing the tragic story of what brought me back here and away from the future I'd worked so hard for. She's new, but I thought Fay or someone else would've filled her in considering gossip seems to fuel this town.

"Life happened, I suppose." I shrug, trying to play it off.

I could tell her the truth, but I'm not ready for her to look at me differently. Returning home and taking responsibility for my family paints me as a saint to most. I'm not a saint. I'm a guy who stepped up to the plate for the people he loves most. Anyone else would've done the same.

"Oh." Her gaze drops to her plate.

"What about you? Why is a Yale graduate's dream to be a principal at Lake Starlight High?"

She rises from her chair and walks over to her small kitchen island. I swivel in my seat to follow her. She's dodging the question, just like I just did. I should let it go. She did mine.

"You don't have to explain," I say.

"I needed to find a piece of myself."

"Bad breakup?" I ask, because isn't that the only reason someone moves as far as they can from home?

She sits back down with another plate full of five pieces of chicken and broccoli. "Not really. I mean there was a breakup, but it wasn't super serious, like an engagement or anything."

She clears her throat, and that's when I realize I'm staring at her like an idiot, wondering why the mention of some guy from her past irks me so much.

"You mean some guy isn't gonna come up here on a red-eye trying to win you back?"

She narrows her eyes.

"Sorry, just figured a guy would be crazy to..." Where the hell did that come from? I don't say cheesy shit like that.

"Nice line." She puts a piece of orange chicken in her mouth.

We eat in uncomfortable silence before I can't take it anymore.

"I'm sorry," I say, wishing I'd kept my mouth shut.

"Did you mean it as a genuine compliment or are you trying to get me upstairs by the end of the night?" Her eyes sparkle so I know she's testing me. Our banter was what led us to the backseat of my Jeep the night we met.

"Strictly as a compliment. Not that trying out a bed wouldn't be a nice change of pace for us."

She rolls her eyes and shakes her head. "Not going to happen again." She slides out of her chair and heads to the sink with her dish.

"It's not?"

She turns back around from the sink. I close up the containers of food and place them in her fridge. If I was hoping to gain more information about her based on what's in her fridge, I'm out of luck. The thing is empty except for a carton of milk, water, a half-drunk bottle of white wine, and a six-pack of beer. Aren't all chicks into greens and vegetables?

"I haven't gone to the store yet," she says from behind me.

"So, what? You eat out every night?"

"Let's just say I know Rachel down at Lard Have Mercy."

I shut the fridge doors. "You'll have to come to my house for dinner one night."

"Which brings me back to the fact that after we're done with this paperwork, our relationship is strictly within the walls of Lake Starlight High School." She places the dishes in the dishwasher and closes it.

"Why is that again?" I crunch my finished water bottle down until it's half the size and grab another one.

"First of all, we work together. Second of all, I'm gone in three months and I'm not into the long-distance thing. Thirdly, I'm pretty sure your plan is to leave Lake Starlight as well?"

"Yeah, I'm hoping to head to California, but time will tell." The impulse to check my phone rears its head, but I refrain.

"How many more reasons do you need to know that we're not a good idea?"

"It doesn't mean we can't have fun while we're both here."

C'mon. You can't blame a guy for trying.

"I'm not looking for a mess to clean up when I leave here, and I'm not dumb enough to think sleeping together won't get messy." She slides my fortune cookie to me and opens the cellophane of her own.

"Should we see what our fortunes have to say about the situation?"

She narrows her eyes. "No way. You probably had them fixed."

I hold up my hands. "Yeah, before coming over, I hand-rolled and folded fortune cookies and had Li put them in the bag."

She smiles. "On the count of three. One... two... three."

We crack open our cookies and place the cookies on the counter to read the small papers inside.

"'Don't be a dick,'" she says.

"What?"

She holds up her fortune in front of me. Sure enough, it says, "Don't be a dick."

"'Your cook spit in your food,'" I say, reciting the words from my own fortune.

We both laugh, though she seems a little confused.

"It's Li's idea of a joke. We went to high school together."

She nods. "That explains a lot."

We eat our cookies then sit back down at her kitchen table to do what I'm there to do—get myself and Elijah cleared from Mrs. Andrews's claim, *not* flirt with the sexy new principal.

TEN

Holly

L ake Starlight is starting to feel like home. Back in
Florida, other than the late-night cashier at the liquor
store, no one was familiar. Here, Rachel always seems to be
working at the diner, serving me almost every night. Francie's husband, Jack, helped me buy a plunger when my sink
backed up, and he already knew who I was when I walked
into his store.

It's nice to smile and wave and have people ask how I'm
doing. And have them actually care about the answer.

I drive out of the downtown area toward the high
school. A smile pulls at my lips when I park and see Austin
in the courtyard. He's talking to that dark-haired girl again.
Phoenix, the one who called me Holly in the hallway. I
meant to look up her file or ask Fay who she is, but the
whole Elijah-and-JP thing snowballed into a day full of
meetings and phone calls.

Phoenix huffs and rolls her eyes at whatever Austin's
saying. He touches her upper arm, and she flings it back. A

few students look on, some of them laughing, spurring Austin to point in their direction.

I watch from the car. Austin has great relationships with all the students as far as I've been able to tell. Surely there isn't more to his relationship with this girl who sneered my first name at me. Was that jealousy in her tone? No way.

I bring Dana up on my phone. She should be out of work by now and I really need her to tell me that I've watched too many *Dateline* episodes.

"What's up, sugar plum? Still incognito from Daddy Warbucks?"

I hear traffic in the background. "Just out of work?"

"On my way to my car. What an exhausting shift. Not one ounce of sleep in the break room."

"Don't you mean you didn't get a chance to let Doctor Montgomery cop a feel?"

She laughs. "Yeah, he switched shifts, so no more quickies in the break room. I do miss his Dr. Dick though."

"Thanks for *that* reminder. I'd almost forgotten the explicit description you gave me afterward." I sip my iced coffee that Carla had ready for me at Brewed Awakenings. She already knows my schedule. Perks of a small town, I suppose.

"I'm a doctor, not a poet. Aren't you usually sharpening your pencils or organizing your paperclips now?" I hear her opening her car door and shutting it. "Hold up, you're going to sync."

I wait, my eyes trained on Austin and the girl. What is with their dynamic? It definitely goes beyond teacher/student. He keeps touching her arm in a kind way while she looks as though she's giving him a blast of her crazy teenager hormones. He runs his hands through his hair, looking around the courtyard.

"Okay," she says when the Bluetooth kicks in. Then she honks her horn. "One way, asshole!"

I move the phone away from ear.

"Yep, move along. I'm not saving your life today. I intend on twinkling my star until I pass out for ten hours."

"Thanks for that."

"Sorry." She laughs. "The guy would not move out of the way."

"Do you think teacher-student affairs really happen?"

She huffs. "Yeah. I mean, didn't you ever have a teacher you were hot for? Those young ones who just graduated from college? Oh, I had this TA once and damn—"

"Heard the story already. So, you think it's not just something in books and on television?"

"Hello? You see it on the news, don't you? If people are getting caught, there're way more that are getting away with it. Why?"

Austin has turned, and I stare at how rigid his back is now. Phoenix is eyeballing him with a look of teenage rebellion. She did call me Holly. She obviously likes to push the limits...

"Oh no, I get that it's been a while, but even if the kid is eighteen, don't do it."

"*No!*" I yell. "Dana, do you not know me at all?"

"I did, but then you ran off to Alaska. People change." The rumbling of her tires on the highway is a drone in the background.

"I'm still me."

"If you say so."

"Listen, that guy, the Jeep guy—"

"He's really a student? You had it all wrong?" She gasps. "Well, you can claim insanity. Or shit, just come back, I'll totally be your alibi. We can make up that you have an evil twin and she pretended to be you."

I laugh and shake my head. "No, there's this student. Phoenix. He's talking to her outside and it looks heated, personal. Every other time I've seen him with someone, he has a totally different demeanor."

"Oh."

"Yeah."

Another girl comes out of the door, and I blink. Wait, what?

"What's with you always spying on people from your car?" Dana asks.

"I'm not spying. I just happened to pull up and there they were."

"And you didn't announce your arrival."

"Well, you find out more about people from afar than what they tell you." I sip my iced coffee again, taking in the scene. I had no idea there was a set of twins at this school. "Another girl just joined them, and I think she's Phoenix's twin."

"Well, you know how men are with twins. It's a wet dream."

The other girl touches Phoenix's shoulder and looks at her with sweet eyes. Phoenix circles her arm to get her sister's hand off her shoulder and stomps away, middle finger in the air. Her twin stays back and talks to Austin. He's nodding, then shaking his head. Now he's ushering the other girl into the building.

"Oh my god, I'm going to be sick. He just touched the other girl's lower back."

"Gross! You slept with a pervert?"

"I didn't know."

The first bell rings. *Shit.*

"I gotta go."

"To call the police, I get ya. Call me later."

I click End and toss my phone into my purse. *Is he really screwing around with his students?*

The entire way into the school, my mind runs over everything I know about him. He did sleep with me the first night I met him. In his Jeep. He does have a close relationship with Elijah. Maybe...

"*No*," I mumble. There's absolutely no way. I trust my gut. It's never steered me wrong before.

I walk into the office, and Fay is there, her smile contagious.

"Good morning, Holly." She stands as I walk through the half door to head to my office. "Here you go."

I glance at the paper she hands me. Bailey Timber's Annual Founder's Day Celebration. There's the logo I keep seeing on all the lampposts.

Oh, it's Austin's family's company. The entire town celebrates in their honor? Maybe he is a little entitled after all. And usually entitled people don't feel as though they have to follow the rules. Rules like not sleeping with your seventeen-year-old students.

"You have to come. Gary, my husband, is finishing up his float for the union. It's always a great day. The Baileys put up a carnival in the library parking lot, and Main Street is closed for the day. Everyone celebrates, eats, shops. There's an auction at night to raise money for a different charity that the townspeople vote on every year, then the Baileys match the money. They really are the sweetest family."

I stuff the paper into my purse, still distracted by what I saw in the courtyard. "Great. I'll try to make it."

Fay's eyes scrunch up as I head into my office. I didn't

mean to dismiss her, but I need to get to the bottom of this. There're always secrets hidden under any aura of perfection. Add on money and it's the next *Dateline* episode.

I sit in my chair, booting up my computer so I can search up Phoenix's name. She has to be the only one in this school, since it's not a common name.

Fay buzzes me through the intercom.

"Yes, Fay?"

"There's someone on the phone who's interested in buying the building?"

"What? Tell them it's not for sale."

"I did, and they said it's on Craigslist."

I straighten in my chair. "What? I think someone is pranking you."

I watch through the glass as Fay hangs up the phone, then her fingers move a million miles an hour on her computer keyboard. A minute later, just as my computer pulls up the log-in screen, she stands and knocks on my door. As though I don't see her through the glass.

"Come in."

"The guy wasn't lying. It's right here." She lays the ad on my desk.

Commercial property for sale. It gives specifics about the square footage and says, "available immediately if you act fast." The number is mine, telling them to ask for Holly Radcliffe.

"Seriously? This town," I mumble.

"My money is on JP." Fay sits on the edge of the seat across from me.

"I doubt he'd chance it when he's already spending his afternoons in detention." I pick up my pen and tap the desk.

The phone on Fay's desk rings. Fay rushes to stand, but

I hold my hand up to stop her and press the button for the line that's ringing as I pick up the phone.

"Holly Radcliffe," I answer.

A man on the other line asks about the building.

"No, it's a public school. It is not for sale." As I hang up, I log into my computer and pull up Google to find a contact number for Craigslist. "We'll figure out who did this and get it stopped."

Fay smiles and sits back. My other line rings, so Fay leaves to answer it.

Twenty minutes later, the Craigslist guy finally figures out that we were pranked, and although he took the ad off, he won't tell me who placed it. Not that it matters. I'm pretty sure they used a fake name, and it's not as though the high school has the resources to track down an IP address.

"I've never talked to that many people in such a short amount of time." Fay looks winded, standing in my doorway.

"You could've let them go to voicemail."

"I didn't want anyone looking to buy missing out on another building because they think this one is up for grabs."

I swear Fay isn't real.

"This is probably one of those senior pranks, you know?" she says.

"Call a school meeting in the auditorium. Just the seniors. Starting in five minutes. Best to nip this kind of thing in the bud and if they're all confronted together it'll be easier to suss out who did it before they can all get their stories straight."

Fay cringes.

"Whoever did it, needs to be punished."

"Okay," she agrees.

On my way to the auditorium, I pass Austin leaving his classroom. Great.

"Hey," he says, coming to walk beside me.

"Hey."

"What's this about? I heard someone put the building on Craigslist?"

"That they did."

His raised eyebrows tell me he hears the ice in my voice. "You know kids. The senior pranks are starting."

"Senior pranks won't be tolerated. I understand you like to be lenient with the rules, Mr. Bailey, but I do not."

"Mr. Bailey? We're back to being formal, are we, Miss Radcliffe?" He opens the auditorium doors.

I walk through, seeing the students all finding their way to seats.

Fay idles inside the doors, a girl biting on her lower lip standing next to her.

"Principal Radcliffe, this is Lyndsey. She has something to tell you." Fay practically pushes the girl toward me.

I cross my arms. "Do I need to have this assembly?"

"No. You don't," Lyndsey says, her eyes on Austin instead of me.

"You're kidding me, right?" he says to Lyndsey.

She shakes her head and bites her lip some more.

"God damn it!" Austin turns the other way, running right into Phoenix. He grabs her arm and leads her from the auditorium.

"Mr. Bailey!" I yell. "Fay, please close these doors and keep the students busy for five minutes. Bring Lyndsey back to my office when you return." I head out into the hallway and they're mostly clear. "Coach Bailey!"

Austin stops, turning, not taking his hand off Phoenix.

"Let her go," I demand then catch up with them.

He scrunches his eyebrows at me.

"Yeah, Austin, let me go." Phoenix laughs. "You're not supposed to touch the students." She's smirking at him.

He releases her and asks me, "You know who this is?"

"I do. And I have to say I'm shocked." I can feel the anger heating my face.

"I meant to tell you, but—"

"Can I go? I'm not really in the mood to hear some heart-to-heart between the two of you." Phoenix walks back down the hall.

"Stay. You are in so much trouble," Austin grates out.

"Phoenix, let's go to my office," I say with a calmness I don't feel. "If you did call Craigslist, I'm sure it's a cry for help."

"Cry for help?" Austin asks. "It's been nine years."

The air leaves my lungs. "You've been with her for nine years?"

"Yeah. I was twenty-two and you were what?" He looks back at Phoenix. "Eight?"

Phoenix rolls her eyes.

This cannot be real. I have to be on one of those 20/20 "What Would You Do" shows.

"What will her mother think? She probably trusts you..." My hand covers my mouth.

"If you want to ask her, go up to Union cemetery. Though I don't think she'll answer you," Austin says with what I think is restrained anger.

"Your mother is dead?" I turn and ask Phoenix.

"Stiff as a board."

"*Phoenix!*" Austin screams at her.

"What? It's the truth. Our parents are dead! Why are you the only one who can say it?"

Austin's nostrils flare and he clenches his hands at his sides.

"You're related?"

Austin stares at me for a long time, looks between myself and Phoenix a couple of times, then his face morphs into one of disgust. "You thought...? Of me? God, no!"

"*Eww!*" Phoenix's head rears back as though she's been slapped.

"I'm her older brother. Her name is Phoenix *Bailey*!" Austin says.

Oh, God. This is definitely going to make Buzz Wheel, isn't it?

ELEVEN

Austin

Phoenix and I are seated across from Holly in her office to discuss my sister's stupid prank. My knee bounces, and I'm having trouble keeping my anger in check. Both from the stupidity of my sister and Holly. How could she think I'd be some slimeball and do that with a student?

Holly's eyes flash to mine a few times. If she's looking for reinforcements, she's crazy. Phoenix has been acting up for over a year, and clearly I've failed at keeping her in line, so I'm no help here.

"I have to suspend you," Holly says.

"She's not sitting around the house all day," I say.

Phoenix glares at me.

"What? So, you can think of new ways to be an asshole?" I ask her.

"I don't think we should name-call," Holly says in a placating voice.

"I'm calling Savannah, so expect a visit from her today," I say to Phoenix.

"Great." She crosses her arms and looks in the other direction.

"Why did you put the ad up, Phoenix?" Holly rounds her desk and sits on the edge, crossing her ankles.

She's wearing a skirt today, and if I wasn't so mad, I'd envision my hand sliding up between her thighs. Okay, I did. But just for, like, a millisecond. I stopped myself because apparently she already thinks I'm a pervert.

"Because it's funny." She shrugs.

I should tell Holly to give up the fight. Phoenix is Phoenix. I can't even explain her at this moment. She fights me on every single thing these days.

"Do you have any idea how that affected my morning?" Holly asks. "Did you think about Fay or even your brother when you decided to do it?"

Phoenix ignores Holly and turns her head to look at me, raising her eyebrows with an expression of boredom. I nod for her to answer Holly. "Well, it gave you something to think about other than my brother seducing me."

"Out." I stand. "I'm sorry, Holly, I don't mean to override you, but just suspend her. She's deserving."

Holly stares between the two of us. "Okay. It's Wednesday, so you're suspended for the rest of the week."

"Great." Phoenix jumps to her feet and holds out her hand.

"What?" My forehead crinkles in confusion.

"Keys."

"In your dreams." I pull out my phone and dial the only person who has the time to babysit her, though he'll do a crap job of it. "Hey, it's me."

Holly crosses her arms, still eyeing Phoenix and me.

"What's up?" Denver says.

"You still in town?"

"Until after Founder's Day, why?" He sounds as if he just woke up.

"Come to the high school and pick up Phoenix. She's been suspended."

He laughs. "Classic. Why?"

"We'll talk about it on Sunday. Dinner, remember?" I eye Holly. She really doesn't need to know anything else about my life today.

"I'm not coming until you tell me."

"Denver..." I sigh and rub the bridge of my nose.

Phoenix beams at me because she now knows suspension equals fun if Denver is in charge.

"Is that a family member?" Holly asks.

"It's my brother. Do you really know nothing about us?" Phoenix asks.

"Obviously I don't."

I smile at Holly, happy that she can give it back to Phoenix.

"She put the high school for sale on Craigslist," I say into the phone.

Denver laughs again. "I love that girl."

"Listen, no fun of any kind. Take her home, strip her room of electronics, and don't let her out."

"How many of you are there?" Holly asks.

Phoenix sits back down and crosses her legs, eyeing me for a moment before leaning toward Holly. "There're nine of us. And just so you know, there's another one of me roaming the halls. That's Sedona. Then there's Austin, Savannah, Brooklyn, Denver—whose twin is Rome—Kingston...oh, you know who you should meet next?"

Holly smiles at Phoenix, tricked into thinking Phoenix is being earnest. Phoenix is pissing me off, that's what she's doing.

"You should meet my sister Juno. I mean, she is the matchmaker of Lake Starlight. And since rumor has it you and Austin aren't knocking boots anymore, she might as well find you someone who has more respect for you than to screw you in his Jeep."

"Come now!" I tell Denver. "You." I point at Phoenix. "Go out there and wait for him to show up."

"Come to Founder's Day, Holly, and you'll meet the whole gang."

"Phoenix," Holly says before my sister can flee from the room. She turns around slowly, a self-satisfied smirk plastered on her face. "You will refer to me as Principal Radcliffe."

She stands still and stares for a moment, her gaze shooting over to me for a second. Then she opens the door and leaves.

"I swear she was a good kid at one point." I tuck my phone into my pocket. "I better get to class. My brother will be here in twenty. He has to drag his ass out of bed first."

"Okay, I'm sure Fay will enjoy the company."

I glance behind me to find Fay offering butterscotch candies to a smiling Phoenix.

"She can turn it on and off pretty easily. Have a great day." I walk toward the door.

"Austin."

I stop, my hand on the doorknob.

"I'm sorry, I didn't mean to offend you earlier. I let my mind get away from me."

I circle around. "You thought the absolute worst possible thing of me."

"Well..." Her gaze drops to her feet. "You told me nothing about your situation. I thought you were single. I didn't realize you were the guardian of your sisters. When you said you returned home because life happened, I didn't know you meant you'd sacrificed your own future to make sure your family had one. I saw you this morning in the courtyard with Phoenix. Can you understand a little why I thought maybe... after what I saw?"

I cross my arms. "You know what I think? I think you wanted to see a bad side to me. A self-fulfilling prophecy, if you will. I think you don't want to be attracted to me. I think you moved up here to hide from something. Whether it's a guy or your family or life, I don't know. But the fact that you could draw that conclusion?" I shake my head. "You know what? I can't deal with this right now."

I open the door and walk out, shooting Phoenix a death glare before I head back to my classroom to finally start the shittiest day I've had in a long time.

I ARRIVE HOME TO FIND MOST OF THE BAILEY CREW AT the house. All their cars, including my Grandma Dori's Cadillac and Uncle Brian's truck, are parked along the long driveway to the house.

"Great, fucking great," I murmur as I head up the walkway to the front door.

I walk into the house to find them in the kitchen, with the exception of Phoenix, Sedona, and Jamison, who are huddled at the dining room table, doing homework.

I toss a packet of papers on the table. "This is your work from Mr. Layton."

"Thanks," Phoenix murmurs.

"*Austin!*" Grandma Dori spots me first. Her blue eyes sparkle and her wavy gray hair is pulled back off her face in some kind of clip.

Denver has Brooklyn dancing, instructing her how not to step on her husband-to-be's toes.

"Where'd you learn to dance?" I pass them and grab a carrot Savannah's cutting for the salad. "Why are you all in my house?"

"It's our house," Denver says.

"You moved out," I remind him.

Savannah smiles softly at me.

"Here, let me show you how it's done." Uncle Brian kicks Denver out of the way and sways side-to-side with Brooklyn.

He should be the one to show her, since he'll be doing the daddy/daughter dance with Brooklyn at the wedding. He circles her around and around until they leave the room.

"Uncle Brian!" Brooklyn screeches, but I know from her tone that she's amused by whatever he's doing.

Denver plops down on the kitchen stool, stealing a carrot for himself.

"Another one and I'm taking a knuckle." Savannah points the knife our way.

Denver holds up his hands. "Whoa, when did you become so aggressive?"

"Birth," I say.

Denver nods and Savannah narrows her eyes.

"The doctor says I need daily exercise. Walk with me, Austin?" Grandma Dori circles her arm through mine.

Savannah shoots me a look that says she's had enough grandma guidance for the night and now it's my turn.

"Of course."

Ten minutes later, Grandma's got her shoes on, as well as her hat, her gloves, and her parka. To every other Alaskan, it's sweatshirt weather.

"Thin blood," she says. Obviously telepathy is one of her skills too.

"Have fun, you two!" Sedona calls.

One day it'll be her turn to take in Grandma Dori's wisdom.

We haven't even reached our usual path through the trees before she lays into me. "Phoenix is getting out of control. You need to rein her in. It's ridiculous that she's not looking into schools yet. She needs to figure out what she's going to do with her life. Also, I told Savannah to put money aside for Brooklyn's divorce because that fiancé of hers is just... well, I'm a lady, so I won't go on. You still thinking about leaving?"

Typical Grandma Dori. Right from one thing to the next.

I grip her hand on my forearm, just in case there's any ice I don't see. "Not thinking. I am."

She nods. "I suppose it's your right. You coming back here instead of trying your hand at baseball. I have no fight in me to try to stop you."

"Thanks."

"But take this for what's it worth from an old lady who's lived a lot of years on this earth. You might not find what you're looking for down there. The grass sometimes looks greener because you're seeing it through a filter."

"What does that mean?"

She smiles at me. "You'll know what I mean if things don't end well. That's all."

"Thanks."

Sometimes Grandma Dori's wires cross. I'm not sure I understand what the hell she's talking about. I'm hoping to go to California to coach, not play, but maybe she missed that fact somewhere when I announced it to the family.

We walk in comfortable silence through the woods for a bit before she speaks again. "Tell me about this principal lady. She's very pretty."

We reach the small lake hidden on our property and sit down on the bench my parents placed there for Grandma Dori when she started getting older. The water is still half frozen, but it's thawing around the edges where the water is shallow.

"There's nothing to tell." I shrug.

She smacks my shoulder.

"What was that for?"

"I raised you better. Your mama and your dad raised you better than to do that. I was embarrassed when my friends at the center were talking about it."

"They read it?"

She nods. "We're old, what else do we have to do? Lucky for you Viv's daughter rear-ended Father McAlister. Did you read that yesterday? It's made them forget my grandson is wooing women in his Jeep."

"Sorry," I mumble, unbelieving that I'm having this conversation with my grandma.

She hits my shoulder with hers. "But the picture of the handprint on the fogged window was hot."

I shake my head, unable to stop from smiling. It might've been the hottest night of my life, but I'm not telling her that. "Can we talk about something else?"

"Phoenix told us about the misunderstanding."

"Of course, she did."

She laughs and places her hand on my thigh. I stare at her gloved hand, picturing the wrinkles and age spots I know lie under the fabric. She's growing older, and I hate that I'll be leaving her when I know she's going to need more support soon. Will Denver step up? Will Rome return for good? Kingston is only nineteen. I don't want him to sacrifice his dreams like I had to. Savannah will always look out for her; I'm sure I can depend on that.

"I think you need to make it up to this principal. Embarrassing her like that when she was new in town isn't very gentlemanly. Does she even know who you are? What your name means in this city? What you gave up to come back here?"

I shake my head. "She's only here until the end of the year, and I'll be leaving anyway. There's no point."

She huffs, her shoulders falling. "You have now. I'm not telling you to ask her daddy for her hand in marriage. I'm only suggesting that you owe it to her to take her out on a proper date. Let Buzz Wheel print that." She hits my shoulder again.

"C'mon. You know what she thought. I mean, how could she?"

"She's not from this town. She didn't know you had two sisters at that school. You're fairer, like your daddy, and Phoenix looks more like your mom. You don't look related. Cut her some slack."

"Fine," I say begrudgingly. I suppose I can somewhat understand how she could make that mistake.

"Besides, it'll make me look good at the center. Ask for a window seat at the restaurant and maybe take a nice stroll down Main Street."

We both laugh.

"Now, it's damn cold. Get me back to the house."

I stand, holding out my arm for her. She slides her arm around mine, and we walk away from what I think is every Bailey's favorite spot.

"And don't worry, your grandpa always loved the thrill

of a tryst in the most unlikely of places. You probably got your love of adventure from him." She smiles, looking up at the sky as though my grandpa is staring down at her.

To quote Phoenix—eww!

TWELVE

Holly

Main Street is lined with people as floats big and small travel down the road, interspersed with the high school band, fire engines, and police cars. The Bailey Timber's Founder's Day Parade is as big as the Fourth of July parade back home.

"Holly!" Francie waves from the front row, Jack at her side.

I weave through people, a few saying their hellos to me. I smile and wave, although I'm not nearly as familiar with the people of Lake Starlight as they are with me.

"Hi," I say, stuffing my hands in my sweatshirt pocket.

"It's crazy, I know." Francie looks at Jack. "You know Holly Radcliffe?"

He laughs. "I know her and *of* her."

I smile, a tad embarrassed that I'll always be known here for being in Austin Bailey's backseat.

"I'm kidding. How's your sink?" he asks.

"Good. Thank you."

"Come closer. This is your first time here." Francie steps in front of Jack, allowing me to squeeze in beside them.

"Thanks. I wasn't sure if I would stay to watch the parade."

Francie looks at me as though I just said that every man who owns a hardware store is a sexual deviant. "Oh!" Her hand lands on my arm. "It's a must. You know how at Christmas parades Santa comes at the end? For this one, the Baileys come on the last float."

I can't help the chuckle that escapes. "Are they like the town royalty?"

Francie looks at Jack. "Kind of, I suppose. Way back, the town was floundering, then the Baileys started their business. Employed a lot of people, and the town began to flourish. They're basically responsible for Lake Starlight being what it is. Everyone's always looked up to them, but even more so since, you know..."

"I don't. Austin hasn't shared anything with me."

Francie's gaze veers to her husband again. Their smiles falter.

Jack looks my way. "He doesn't like to talk about it." He shrugs as though it's understandable.

"It's really none of my business." I shove my hands deeper into the pocket of my sweatshirt. I notice that the guy next to me is in a long-sleeve Henley. Does blood really thicken depending on where you live? Is that an actual thing?

"It's not that he's sad. I mean, he is, they were his parents, but..."

Francie continues where Jack left off. "This whole town puts Austin on a pedestal for what he did, and although there are men who would love that, Austin isn't one of them."

The crowd's sudden cheering interrupts us, and my eyes shift to the street, where the high school band marches by, playing a song I'm not familiar with.

"What song is that?" I ask.

Francie leans in. "'Sea of Love' by The Honeydrippers. It was Austin's parents' wedding song. The high school does it every year in tribute to them."

Jack tightens his hold on Francie, and they sway with the melody. My eyes scan the other side of the street. Everyone has their arms linked and are swaying back and forth.

The band passes by, and a voice sings along with them. Either Phoenix or Sedona is on the top tier of the upcoming float, wearing a beautiful maroon dress that has multiple layers flaring out from the waist. Her hair is curled and loosely pinned back.

"She has such a beautiful voice," Francie says.

"Is that...?"

"Phoenix. She's always had a voice like that. Like the voice of an angel." Jack smiles, his eyes fixed on Phoenix.

I agree—I can hardly stop admiring her or her voice.

A couple in a wedding dress and a tuxedo dance along the bottom tier of the float, giving the impression that it's a wedding. Melancholy surrounds me as everyone focuses on them. Conversations stop to give their respect to a couple who clearly meant a lot to this town. Tears fill my eyes, and Francie links her arm with mine, as does the stranger on the other side of me.

It's the most beautiful thing I've ever witnessed.

The song ends but starts up again as the float and the band head around the corner.

"How does she sing that over and over again and not cry?" I ask. I suck in a breath and compose myself as the mood shifts with the next spectacle.

The bystanders unhook their arms and clap as a line of muscle cars take over the scene. They're all driven by men, with the logo of the tattoo place I walk past on my way to the diner every day on magnets on the sides of the cars.

"Now this is new." Francie claps as "Born in the USA" by Bruce Springsteen blares from the backseat of the first car, which is driven by a muscular, tattooed man.

A group of girls and guys walk along the edge of the crowd, handing out small American flags while everyone sings along.

"Figures. Liam knows exactly how to get the crowd going after Phoenix's song." Jack raises his hand. "*Liam!*"

The guy in the first car raises his fist and honks his horn. Francie and I wave our flags high, singing along with the rest of Lake Starlight.

"Told you, you couldn't miss the parade," she leans over and says. "Be careful, this town has a way of sucking people in." She smiles and knocks shoulders with me.

I definitely understand the appeal, though I'll keep that fact to myself.

"*Here they come!*" Francie screams.

You'd think it was a float full of A-list celebrities the way everyone leans over the barricades to get a glimpse. The Bailey siblings are all on the float—minus Phoenix—each holding a microphone. Austin stands in the middle, next to a blonde. An older lady sits in a chair one level up.

I don't have a lot of time to take in the scene before Francie prattles on beside me. "Okay, I'm going to go fast, starting from the left." She points at the float. "Brooklyn, Denver, Savannah, Austin—who you know—Juno, Rome,

Sedona, Denver, Kingston, and we already saw Phoenix on the other float. I'm surprised to see Kingston here. He's not around much. They probably had to wrangle him to come and my bet is he'll blow back out of town as soon as the parade is done. Anyway"—her finger moves from person to person—"Denver and Rome are twins, and you already saw Phoenix who's Sedona's twin. That's Grandma Dori. She's the late Mr. Bailey's mom. Got it?"

"*No.*" I laugh and shake my head.

"You will. They couldn't be more different. Well, other than Denver and Rome. Those two are *way* too much alike."

"In a bad way," Jack adds.

"If I Ain't Got You" by Alicia Keys plays over the speakers, and all the Baileys sing along, smiling as they wave to the people on each side of the street.

"Every year one of them gets to pick a song, but it has to be a song that says thank you to the town and all the workers."

"Man, you're an encyclopedia of knowledge," I say to her.

"I'm a Lake Starlight lifer, what do you expect?" She smiles and waves, leaning over the barricade.

Children walk along the edge of the crowd with their parents, handing out seed packets printed with a label that has the Bailey logo and the words, "Thanks for letting us grow with you." I thank the child and the mother smiles, moving down the line.

The siblings look at one another every once in a while, but the majority of their attention is on the crowd. Everyone screams a different family member's name, as if they're One Direction and everyone has their favorite. It's insanity.

"*Austin!*" Francie yells.

Sedona knocks one of her brothers with her elbow, who

knocks a sister, who knocks Austin. They all point in our direction.

"Great," I mumble.

Austin's eyes swallow me, and his smile grows brighter. At least I think it does. Am I hoping it does? How can one parade soften my feelings toward this man?

He nods to Francie, waving.

The sister on his other side follows his line of vision, knocking her shoulder with his.

"That's Savannah. They're close," Francie continues giving me the Bailey intel like she's written an *US Weekly* magazine article about the family.

As the float passes by us, Austin's gaze follows me. My eyes don't waver from his until the float turns the corner. I feel oddly bereft once he's no longer in my sight.

"Come on. We'll meet them at the end." Francie pulls on my arm.

"No, I'm good. I'll just head home."

She tilts her head and studies me while the crowd disperses. "Why would you do that?"

"It's a family thing, and I have some work at home I need to finish."

She looks at Jack then back to me before wrapping her arm around my shoulders and turning us the way the float went. "Sorry, Bailey Founder's Day is a no-work day."

I allow her to lead me down the sidewalk, and Jack laughs as we round the corner.

Francie whispers in my ear, "Please don't fire me."

The parade, Francie, Jack, the Baileys, the town of Lake Starlight, and all its residents have a way of wrapping the softest, warmest blanket around my heart. I hope I'll be able to shed it and say goodbye in a few months.

THIRTEEN

Austin

Savannah leans away from the microphone and says into my ear, "The principal is here."

"I totally would have matched you two together," Juno adds from next to me.

"You don't even know her," I say.

"She looks like your type." Juno shrugs.

I roll my eyes at my sister. The funny thing is, people believe in her matchmaking abilities and pay her good money to find them their soul mate. "You only think that because of Buzz Wheel." I go back to mouthing the words of the song that's playing.

"Look at her look at you. She likes you. Not to mention she gets along with Francie and Jack. Bonus!" Juno says.

"Francie probably manipulated her into standing there. Francie's like you. She thinks fixing people up is fun. Do I have to keep reminding everyone I'm leaving in three months?"

Rome peers past Juno at me. "Did you get an offer?"

"Not yet." I shrug.

Savannah slides her arm through mine. "You will."

I have my doubts, but I smile, acting as if I couldn't care less.

We all continue with the song as the float reaches Holly. My parents taught us to be appreciative of this town and its families. To make eye contact as the float passes by, smile and wave. Juno blows kisses. Denver and Rome give a lot of open palm raises and thumbs-up. Savannah smiles, waving both hands. We each have our thing.

I know the drill, but as my eyes meet Holly's, I can't look away from her. Her smile is infectious, and my pants tighten when her tongue slides out and licks her lips.

All too soon, the float passes by. I close my eyes briefly, drawing in a breath. I smack on the perfect son persona, smiling and waving to the crowd, thinking how different it feels having Holly out there.

When the float comes to a stop, Kingston and Denver help Grandma Dori off. Once we're all off, it heads away to be stored until next year.

"Let's go to the carnival," Juno says.

"Not in the mood," I say.

"I'm going to meet Jamison," Sedona says, already walking away.

"Curfew is still in effect," I remind her.

She rolls her eyes and disappears through the crowd, graciously saying hello to everyone.

"Loved the 'Born in the USA.'" Denver smacks hands with Liam as he approaches.

"Thanks." Liam eyes Savannah. "What'd you think?"

She narrows her eyes at him. "I actually thought it fit perfectly. Dad would've loved it."

Liam rocks back as if she blew him away with her response.

"What?" she asks, staring between Denver and Liam.

"Austin!" Francie's voice draws my attention to the crowd behind them.

I let Liam handle Savannah because let's face it, I want to see Holly again and I'm really hoping she's with Francie. All I'm able to see is Jack's head above everyone else, weaving through the crowd until Francie emerges with him.

Holly didn't come? Of course, she didn't. She thinks I'm pissed at her. I'm still not thrilled over what she thought, but Grandma Dori had a point. Holly knows nothing about me or my family situation.

My friends stop in front of me, and I catch sight of a body sliding out from behind Jack.

Holly nibbles on her lip, and an incredible urge to feel the softness of her lips again races through me.

"Great job." Jack high-fives me. "Were you really singing?"

I shake my head. "Of course."

"Yeah right." He grins.

Jack knows me too well. The women in our family can carry a tune, the men can't. It's almost like Mom lives inside them and Dad is inside us. Before Mom, there was no singing Baileys in the Founder's Day parades.

"*Jack!*" Rome jumps on his back, putting him in a headlock.

"You want your ass kicked?" Jack walks them away from us.

"No below the belt, Rome!" Francie screams, following. "We want kids!"

Holly smiles at me, and there're a million words on the

tip of my tongue, but they won't come out. This woman makes me tongue-tied like an adolescent boy.

"Aus—"

"Is that Principal Radcliffe?" Grandma Dori says.

Oh shit. Not now.

Holly's vision shifts from me to the blue bandit approaching.

"Grandma, this is Holly."

Grandma shoots me an "I'm not an idiot, you know" look and pulls Holly into an embrace. "It's so good to meet you. I've heard so much from Austin about you."

Holly takes a quick glance at me over Grandma's shoulder. I close my eyes and shake my head.

"It's nice to meet you too, Mrs. Bailey."

Grandma lightly taps her shoulder. "Mrs. Bailey was my deceased husband's mother. I'm Dori."

"Like the fish from *Nemo*," I add because it pisses her off and she's doing her best to step into my business here.

"No." She puts her hands on her hips, her eyes throwing daggers my way. "I hate that." She looks at Holly. "I have no damn memory problems, and I was Dori a helluva lot longer than that blue fish."

Holly's gaze falls to Dori's bluish hair, and I snicker. Grandma's eyes bore into mine. I love her. I do. But I can't deny the blue tint.

"Well, Dori," Holly speaks elegantly to her, "I will make sure never to associate you with a fish." She smiles at me and my heart flips.

"Thank you. I knew I liked you." She slides her hand through Holly's. "Walk me to the library?"

Holly glances at me, eyes wide. "Sure."

"I do story time for the children. Once you get old, society tries to shove you in a chair, sit you in front of the

TV, and doesn't want to hear from you, so this is about as exciting as it gets for me these days. No more roller coasters because of my heart." She pats her chest and leads Holly away.

Holly looks back at me over my grandma's shoulder.

Grandma pats her hand. "No worries, Austin won't leave you alone with me. He'll follow."

What can I say? My grandma knows me well. I fall into step behind them, overhearing Grandma telling Holly how Bailey Timber started. At every light, Holly looks back to make sure I'm following, which if I cared to notice would feel nice, but I don't. Notice that is. I can't afford to care.

We reach the library, and Holly helps Grandma inside and into her rocking chair. We say our goodbyes and let the librarian hand her books as the children hurry to get as close as they can to her.

Grandma Dori waves us off. "Now, you two, go have fun. You're young."

All the kids look at us, and the librarian laughs. She's probably a nightly reader of Buzz Wheel.

I look down at Holly. "Want to ride the Ferris wheel?"

She laughs but nods. "Only if I can buy the tickets."

"Sorry, Dori would kill me if I allowed you to pay."

"She doesn't have to know."

"Trust me, Dori knows everything that happens in this town."

I hold out my arm, and she slides her arm through. "Well, I can at least buy you cotton candy."

"We'll see."

I guide us out of the library and down Main Street. I say hello and thank you to the compliments sent my way about the float as we pass the families returning from the carnival with balloons and stuffed animals, their kids' faces painted as butterflies or superheroes.

"Austin," she says when we hit a stretch without anyone around us, "I want to apologize."

"Don't." I slide my arm out of hers and take her hand instead. "Come on. Let's clear some things up before we head to the carnival."

I lead her to the path along river that travels through Lake Starlight. I'm hoping its empty today since everyone is probably enjoying the festivities. I sit her on a park bench, happy that the only other people around us are a few old guys fishing at the edge of the river.

"I should've told you about my family."

She shakes her head. "No. It's really none of my business."

"Listen, that night at your house, I wanted to tell you, but you're the first person in a long time who sees *me*, not some saint who stepped up to take care of his family. The fact you didn't like me, it made me feel like... well." I run a hand through my hair. "It made me feel like myself."

She places her hand on my thigh, and my muscle there twitches. "I know, but still, I thought you were having an affair—"

I laugh. "Well, I'd say you should stop watching investigative shows, but I get it. Why would you think she was my sister?"

Holly crosses her legs.

I slide back on the bench. "When I was twenty-one, my parents died in a snowmobile accident. My mom was a travel writer, and a few times a year, my dad went with her. They were farther north, and it was late, there was snow and ice." I stop. "No one really knows if my dad lost control or whether they swerved not to hit an animal, but they crashed into a tree."

She touches my thigh again. "I'm so sorry."

I nod. "I was finished up at USC and I came home to raise my siblings. Savannah and I made a deal. She'd take over the business, and I'd take responsibility for the kids. I got a teaching job at the high school with my degree, and the rest is history."

"Wow. That was very selfless of you. I can understand why people give you that saint status."

My lips tip down at the corners. "That's why I didn't want you to know. I sacrificed my own dream, sure, but I'd do it again. They're my family and they needed me. I just did what anyone should do."

She slides closer, her hand still on my thigh. "But not everybody would. That's what makes it remarkable. For you and Savannah to do that... I can't imagine it's been easy for you."

I wish I could tell her about all the nights that I lay in bed, doubting that I was cut out for the job, feeling as though I was screwing up each one of my brothers and sisters. Questioning whether I had what it takes to get through. But I don't because here I am, close to the finish line. And though I don't regret my decision to step up when it was needed, it's hard not to sound like an asshole now that I want a life away from Lake Starlight.

I shrug.

"Well, thank you for trusting me. A lot of dots are connecting now."

I look up, and she's smiling at me. "Bet I can't get you to hate me again now that you know all that."

"Well, I wouldn't go that far."

We laugh, and both of us look at the river. The older men are still fishing, paying us no attention.

"Since you opened up to me, it's only fair that you know why I came to Lake Starlight."

I wasn't expecting this, but I can't deny that I'm curious. "You don't have to explain."

"I want to."

I shift to face her. She swallows and sets her eyes on me, looking nervous.

"I came here to find my dad."

FOURTEEN

Holly

"Your dad?"

"Yeah. I was conceived during a one-night stand, and I've never met him. Or at least that I remember. I found a picture of him holding me at the hospital, but he's staring down at me, so it's not a very good picture."

Austin wraps his arm around the back of the bench and slides over, so we're hip to hip.

"It could be worse. He paid child support and I had health insurance, but he never called, never visited. And here I am, a grown woman tracking him down."

"He lives in Lake Starlight?" he asks.

I shake my head. "No, he's in Sunrise Bay."

"That's two towns over."

I nod, picking at my nails. "This job was the closest thing I could find, but there's more..."

His body tenses. "What?"

"He doesn't know I'm here. I haven't confronted him."

He squeezes my shoulder. "Why?"

I huff and concentrate on my hands, afraid to look at him, afraid of what I'll see. "What if I'm not welcome in his life?"

"Well, I have no idea how you feel, but I do know that if someone doesn't want you in their life, you're usually better off. That would be his loss. But you won't know that unless you tell him you're here."

I blow out a breath. "This is way too heavy for a carnival date."

He laughs. "So, this is a date, is it?"

Heat blooms in my cheeks, but he guides my head to his shoulder, his lips pressing on the top. I freeze and he does too.

"Shit, I'm sorry." He removes his hands. "That was reflex. I think because I have sisters, you know. I've had to deal with a lot of broken hearts."

"It's okay. It's fine." I don't want to admit how nice it felt. How in this moment, it feels like maybe he could actually mend my distrusting heart.

Austin hops to his feet. "That's enough heart-to-heart shit. Let's go have some fun."

I glance past the river at the carnival rides and games, the laughs and screams echoing down to us. "Sounds perfect."

We walk over to the carnival without touching one another. When we reach the parking lot of the library, Austin leads me to the food booths, taking us to Wok For U.

"Li!" he yells to a guy in the back.

The man nods, says something to the girl next to him, and wipes his hands on his apron before making his way over. "Austin. Want another fortune cookie?" He laughs.

"Not one of yours. This is Holly." He points at me with his thumb.

The guy puts out his hand, and I shake it.

"Nice to meet you..." He eyes Austin. "Finally."

I shake my head. "Tell me someone else's story will overtake the Jeep one soon."

Li laughs and shares a look with Austin. "No worries there. Something always does."

"*Austin!*" a woman's voice echoes over the crowd.

"Someone's always looking for Austin," Li shakes his head, grabbing a container and putting in some wontons. "Here. On the house."

"Thank you, but I'll gladly pay," I say.

He holds up his hand. "Think of it as a Lake Starlight apology for Buzz Wheel."

I think it's Savannah who's approaching us. She's blonde, but so is another one of his sisters, so I'm not really sure. "I need your help."

"I'm in the middle of something, Savannah."

Her gaze falls to me then to Li. "Hey, Li."

"Always a fire." Li laughs.

"Truth." Savannah rolls her eyes then grabs my arm and pulls. "Oh perfect, you'll be better than Austin."

"Savannah..." Austin sighs, pulling me back by my other arm, the wontons shaking in the container.

"The mayor had cold feet on the whole pie-in-the-face thing," Savannah says.

Austin laughs. "You're dreaming. I do a lot for his family, but I am not letting kids throw a pie in my face. I'm not letting Holly do it either."

Savannah's face crumbles, and she shoots Austin what I guess is her best puppy dog eyes.

"No," he says. *Guess I was right.* "You do it. I'm sure plenty of your employees would love to throw a pie in your face."

"You know as well as I do that it's mostly kids who throw the pies, not adults. Sorry, Mr. Educator, but you picked the wrong field." She puts her hands on her hips.

I pull a wonton from the carton and bite into it while I enjoy their sparring. I give Li a thumbs-up.

"Good, right? I swear, I'm a god in the kitchen."

"Not compared to me." Another one of the Baileys approaches and does some weird handshake with Li.

"Rome, heard you were back! Bring it on, fancy pants European chef."

Rome hops over the table to join Li, and the two of them head over to check out some of Li's produce.

I swear I'll never get all the Baileys straight.

"Please, Austin." Savannah has her hands in front of her now in a prayer pose.

Austin shakes his head. "I promised Holly a Ferris wheel ride. Sorry."

Savannah sets her eyes on me. "Please, Holly? Or Principal Radcliffe—what do you prefer? I'll do anything if you help me out. I only need someone for an hour. It's our biggest event every year and it makes the most money. The money goes to a local charity and the families depend on it."

"She's pulling on your heartstrings. She'll find someone else." Austin snags a wonton from the container and pops it into his mouth.

Savannah's head falls back. "What do you want? Name it."

"I want you to straighten Phoenix out, that's what. But maybe we can negotiate a deal for you not to guilt-trip me for leaving," Austin suggests, raising his eyebrows.

I watch these two, wishing I had my own sibling. It was always just Mom and me.

"I'll do it," I say.

Austin glares at me. "No, you won't. I'm not letting her guilt you into it."

I stare at Austin. "I'm doing it to help the families who rely on the charity. Where do I go?"

Savannah claps. "You're the best. Come on."

Savannah nods in the direction to head and thanks me profusely the entire way there, as Austin grumbles behind us. The booth is set up with a cut-out to put my face through. There are racks and racks of pie pans filled with whipped cream, along with a station of girls continuing to make them.

"All of those?" I ask with wide eyes.

Savannah laughs. "Once the first one hits, you'll barely notice the difference."

"She's lying. She has no idea because she's never actually done it herself," Austin adds.

"*Coach Bailey!*" A few teenage boys amble over.

"I'll take him." One of the boys places a twenty in front the of the girls. "Remember when you benched me for chewing gum?"

Austin rolls his eyes. "Sorry to ruin your day, Sullivan, but my face isn't going through the hole."

I tug at his arm. He looks at me with an expression that clearly says no.

"I thought you were fun?" I ask and poke his stomach. Actually, his set of rock-hard abs.

A half-smile tilts his lips. "You were mistaken."

I raise up on my tiptoes and whisper in his ear, "Really? Because I think the guy who picked me up that night was *a lot* of fun." I drop down to my regular height.

"Nope." He rocks back on his heels.

I narrow my eyes, my smile unable to stop growing. "What if I let you clean me up after?"

Savannah laughs.

He raises a brow. "What do you mean by clean up?"

"Play and find out." I shrug in a coy way, and his gaze falls down over my body.

"Fine." He stomps over to the cut-out. "One hour, Savannah, then find another duo of suckers."

Savannah releases a long breath. "Thank you."

"Not much of a choice," Austin deadpans.

She touches my arm but steps closer, enveloping me in a hug. Her expensive-smelling perfume surrounds us. "You're the best. Sure you don't want to be my sister-in-law?" She laughs it off before I can respond.

"I better go before Cranky makes a run for it," I say with a chuckle.

"Great, and I'll find someone for the next hour. I just have to think of whose face I'd want to throw a pie at."

I laugh, heading back behind the cut-out, and smack Austin's ass when I pass him.

"Watch it, sweetheart, otherwise I'm taking a can of whipped cream back to your place with us."

"I don't recall asking you over?"

"You said I get to clean you up. As much as I enjoyed our time in the Jeep, this time I want more time to explore."

I shake my head. "Dirty mind you have there, Coach Bailey."

"Only when it comes to you, Principal Radcliffe."

We both grin then stick our heads through the cut-outs. Austin talks shit to the players as we get nailed by pie after pie.

"These kids have way too good of aim," I murmur before licking the whipped cream off my lips.

"Just remember this was your idea," he says from beside me.

"Not really my idea."

"Might as well have been."

"Your sister needed our help," I insist, relieved when the pie that was just thrown falls short of its mark.

"Let me give you a little advice when it comes to the Baileys and Lake Starlight—the word no needs to be in your vocabulary."

"Are you suggesting I should tell you no?"

He turns to me and I side-eye him, my smirk proud.

"I'm the exception."

"I had a feeling you were going to say that." I laugh, a light, buoyant feeling filling my chest.

An hour later, my face is covered in whipped cream, including the front of my hairline.

"Have a nice day, Savannah," I say.

Austin grabs my hand and pulls me away from the booth. I think Denver and that guy Liam are next in line. I heard him razzing Savannah about not wanting to get dirty.

I stop walking. "Where are we going?"

"To your place to clean up?"

"I said you could clean me up, not that we were going back to my place." I toss him the dishtowel Savannah gave me. "Here you go."

He catches it and stares blankly at me. I laugh.

"Really?" he asks.

"Really."

His shoulders sag, and he walks over to me with the towel. Starting at the tip of my forehead, he slowly runs the towel down the side of my face. He takes half a step forward, and my chest meets his. When his labored breaths hit my face, I'm back in that Jeep again, his scent and gentle hands surrounding me. I close my eyes while he wipes cream away from my eyes.

By the time he's reached my lips, a moan slips from my mouth.

"If you think this is good," he whispers, "you should let me take you home."

"Then you'd have no respect for me."

A soft chuckle escapes his tempting lips. "You're going to make me work for this, aren't you?"

"Well, I did give in pretty easily the first time." I open my eyes. His stubbled cheeks are in my line of vision, and I can't help but want to feel the rough hairs on my skin. "Austin," I sigh.

"Yeah." He runs the towel down the other side of my face.

"I'm only here for three months."

"Good, so am I."

"I'm probably going to leave here with a broken heart because of my dad. I don't want to leave with a shattered one." I speak my worst fear out loud.

He blows out a breath. "I get it."

"So?" I say, disappointment flaring in my stomach.

He tosses a towel onto a nearby table. "So, I think I promised you a ride on the Ferris wheel."

My forehead falls to his shoulder, and he wraps his arms around me.

"Let's just have fun," I whisper.

Besides that one night with Austin, fun doesn't seem in my vocabulary lately, and it sounds nice coming off my lips. Why can't I give myself three carefree months before I let my feet touch the ground again? I deserve to push my worries away.

I draw back and look at the big smile overtaking his face. "No sleepovers, no dinners, no lunch dates, no flowers. Pretty much you can't do anything nice for me."

He laughs, and his dark eyes sparkle like melted chocolate. "How can I argue with that? But only if you agree not to send me flowers either." He winks, and his hand slides down my arm to link with mine.

I retract my hand. "We need to keep it private. No one can know."

He stuffs both hands in his pockets. "Okay."

"I don't want to be on that Buzz Wheel thing again."

"Well, I don't have a lot of control over that, but I'll try to be as stealthy as a thief."

"Okay then."

He nods. "Ferris wheel?"

"Ferris wheel."

We walk down Main Street with whipped cream drying in our hairlines, a few inches between us and our hands in our pockets. My stomach dips as though I'm already on the Ferris wheel, because I can only imagine how thrilling this ride Austin and I are about to embark on will be.

FIFTEEN

Austin

The sun is setting, leaving an orange glow in the sky. A lot of the families with younger children have left, headed to the Veteran's Hall for snacks and drinks. We climb aboard the Ferris wheel, and a few kids lingering nearby snap pictures with their phones.

"I don't think your wish regarding Buzz Wheel is going to come true."

"Guess not. As long as they don't see us kiss or anything, we're good."

"I really want to kiss you," I mumble, sliding my hand between us and running my finger over her thigh.

"Austin." She picks up my hand and places it in my lap.

I move my hand back. "No one can see us."

She laughs. "I have a feeling you're going to have a hard time adhering to the secrecy thing."

"Me? I'm great at taking direction. Or don't you remember?"

Her cheeks pinken and my dick stirs. It's the first thing I

remember noticing about her at Lucky's—she embarrasses easily.

Our cart reaches the top of the circle.

"This would be a great place for a kiss," I say.

She shakes her head and we miss our opportunity, falling back down the other side. When we get into sight, I remove my hand from her leg. Both of us sit there like two thirteen-year-olds, our hands on the metal bar, facing forward.

"Go, Coach Bailey!" someone on the ground screams.

She raises her eyebrows.

We go around and around, my stomach dropping with each fall. Each rotation, I slide my hand onto her thigh until we get in view of others. My hand inches closer and closer to the space between her legs, and she spreads them an inch wider each time. The thread of sexual tension between us tightens with each dip and rise of our cart.

When they stop to let off passengers below, we're a few spots from the top. I inch my fingers closer to her center.

"Austin..."

My name is a soft plea on her lips.

"I really want to kiss you," I whisper, tucking my head into the crook of her neck.

"We can't." She lets out a long breath, her legs parting for me even more.

Sliding my finger over the seam of her jeans, I press in. My lips kiss her neck. "No one can see us up here."

Her hand falls to my hand. "But..."

"Turn to me," I beg, her smell just as intoxicating as it was that night in my Jeep.

She turns her head. Her eyes are hooded, her lips moist, and her cheek soft as it runs along my nose.

"Holly?"

"Uh-huh," she says, her eyes closed.

"I'm going to kiss you," I whisper as our chair stops in the top spot. If this guy running it knows what's good for him, he'll leave us here for a while.

I don't wait for a response, taking her lips with my own. I taste the sweetness of the whipped cream as my tongue slides into her hot, waiting mouth. She meets me halfway, her tongue gliding along mine. I press my finger against her center, and she squeals into my mouth, rising up off the seat. When she falls, I plunge my tongue into her mouth and my hand covers her center for more pressure.

The chair falls down a notch and she pulls her mouth from mine.

"I guess I'll buy you cotton candy another time?" she pants.

"I knew we were in sync."

She laughs as the chair continues down. I notice the slight flush of her cheeks, the shyness of her actions. Her gaze skitters to me then away.

Watching her step out of the Ferris wheel chair, I hope that we can stick to the plan. I'll already be hurting my family when I leave. I can't take crushing someone else's heart on top of it. Regardless of what happens, I'm leaving Lake Starlight in three months. It's about time everyone understands nothing is keeping me here, not even a gorgeous auburn hottie.

WE WALK THE TWO BLOCKS TO HER HOUSE, AND because I'm a gentleman, I walk her up the stairs.

"So, this is where we part?" She smirks as she unlocks her door.

I smile in case anyone happens to be watching. In towns like Lake Starlight, there are eyes everywhere. "I'll come to the back door in twenty minutes."

"Sounds good. I'll leave it unlocked."

"Perfect." I nod.

"Well, good night, Austin," she says in a louder voice than she needs to.

"Night, Holly."

I jog down the stairs, watching her get into the house. We wave goodbye, and I walk back toward downtown so I can be seen without her before sneaking back to her house.

Of course, once I reach Main Street, I run smack-dab into Mrs. Andrews.

"Austin," she sneers.

"Hello, Mrs. Andrews. Have a great night." I attempt to slide past her, but she places her hand on my upper arm.

"May I have a word?"

I blow out a breath. I have about one hundred words for her, none of which I think she'll appreciate.

"Sure." I deliver a fake smile because I'm a Bailey and that's what we do in this town.

"I just wanted to say that JP talked to me about his detention, and although I think it's very unfair since Elijah punched him first, I don't want him to lose that friendship."

I blink to make sure those are actually tears forming in her eyes.

"I'm not sure... well, Mr. Andrews says I protect JP too much, but he's my baby and after..." She inhales a deep breath and composes herself by repositioning the purse hanging off her forearm and blinking a few times. "After we lost Vivian, I suppose I spoil him, but it was good friends who got me through losing her and I don't want JP to lose a good friend like Elijah. So..." She stops again, straightening her back and looking across the street. "I'm asking if you could help to mend that? It's the least you could do, what with not getting recruiters to come look at JP for college."

She was doing so well until that last line.

She holds her head up, her eyes briefly making contact with mine.

"Sure. I'll do what I can."

She nods. "Thank you, Austin. Have a good night."

"You too."

She walks down the street, stopping briefly in front of the toy store before glancing back at me and walking into Lard Have Mercy.

Figuring Mrs. Andrews saw me on the street without Holly and that I'm good, I circle the block and walk through the backyard to Holly's back door. I open the door, the distinctly female scent of her house reminding me of her.

A can of whipped cream sits on the counter with a small note. I pick it up.

I DID PROMISE YOU COULD CLEAN ME UP. I'M UPSTAIRS waiting. ;)

GRABBING THE CAN, I DITCH THE NOTE, TOE OUT OF MY shoes, and walk up the stairs.

My hands move to the hem of my T-shirt as I walk into her bedroom, admiring her lying on her bed, even if she's fully clothed. "For some reason I thought you'd be naked?"

"Half the fun is undressing one another." She gets up on her knees, moving toward the edge of the bed. She's washed the dried whipped cream off her face.

"Especially the first time." I quirk an eyebrow, and she laughs.

"It was dark, and we were suffocated for space."

"True, I've been reliving it through the memory of touch more than sight."

She falls back to sit on her ankles. "You relive it?"

I step forward, drop the can next to her on the bed, and take her face in my hands. "Are you kidding? Will you think less of me if I say it was the hottest sex I've ever had?"

She playfully pushes my chest, her cheeks flaming red. I love that look on her. "I'm here, willing and waiting. You don't have to use lines."

I grab the hem of her sweatshirt and pull it up her body. She helps me by raising her arms, and when I see another layer of a long-sleeve T-shirt, I groan.

She giggles.

I reach for the hem. "There better not be another shirt under this one."

When I slide it up her body, her bare skin is revealed to me inch by inch. The T-shirt and my hands move up and over her breasts, my thumbs grazing her black lacy bra. She sits back on her ankles, letting me soak in the vision of her. I'm committing her body to memory because that's going to come in handy every morning in my shower.

"I'm on the fence about these things." My hand kneads her right breast, and she bites her lip, squirming.

"This *thing* is a bralette." Her fingers dive under the bottom to free herself from it, but I stop her.

"I thought that was my job."

"Okay," she says sheepishly.

Sliding my fingers under the elastic edging, I pull up. Her tits bounce down, and I throw the fabric on the floor.

"I think there should be a zipper or something."

She tilts her head. "Are we going to talk about bras all night?"

She raises up, her fingers latching onto my jacket zipper and slowly pulling it down. Her hands splay on my chest, up and over my pecs to my shoulders, to slide my jacket off me. I toss it on the chair in the corner of her room. She wastes no time reaching under my T-shirt and splaying her hands on my bare stomach. With my shirt rising, her plump lips cast small kisses up my abdomen.

I grab the back collar and pull off my shirt.

"Hey, that's my job." She stares up at me with her chin pressed to my stomach and her lips a millimeter away from my nipple. Without warning, she latches on, biting it.

I retract in surprise, not pegging her as that type.

She laughs. "Don't make me tie your hands behind your back."

Her fingers manipulate the button and zipper of my jeans. Pushing them down, she doesn't take my boxers with them. I think because she loves the process of undressing. Not that I'm complaining. It's been years since I took time like this before sleeping with a woman.

My dick tents my boxer briefs, and she rubs her palm over the long length, squeezing it. She sucks on my nipple as my cock twitches in her hand, and I thread my fingers through her auburn hair. Fuck, going slow definitely has its perks.

I step out of my pants, fling off my socks, and lightly push her down on the bed. She slides up to the pillows, her breasts prominently on display for me to admire. I swallow the excess saliva pooling in my mouth. I haven't wanted something this badly in a long time.

I lift one of her legs, dramatically taking off one of her socks before my hands slide up her jean-clad leg. Slowly, I lower her leg back down and take the other leg, doing the same thing.

"You sure are taking your time with this undressing thing."

"Well, I kind of owe it to you. At this point last time, your shirt was around your neck and your pants in the driver's seat."

"True." Her fingers play with the comforter underneath her.

It's impossible to stop admiring her body as my knee presses to the edge of the bed and I climb between her legs. My gaze glides along her bare stomach, over her breasts, right to her eyes as my fingers unbutton and unzip her jeans. She lifts and wiggles as I strip them from her body.

Black lacy underwear that matches the bra she was wearing makes my dick grow harder, eager for relief.

In the truck, I slid her panties over, but this time, I want to feel our bodies with nothing in between us.

Well, nothing except a condom.

Shit. I wasn't exactly thinking I was going to get laid tonight.

"Condom?" I ask, sending up a small prayer that one of us is prepared.

Her body slackens into the mattress, with an expression that says *nope*.

"Fuck, this isn't good. I can't go to the drugstore in town because people will talk."

She sits up in bed. "Well, that's crushing."

It is. But necessity is the mother of invention, as they say.

"It doesn't mean I can't do other things." My fingers slide under the top of her panties, and she wiggles back down on the bed. Grabbing the bottle of whipped cream, I say, "I gotta get you messy before I can clean you up."

I spray a mound of whipped cream on her nipple and my mouth descends.

"It's possible by the end of the night, I'll be happy we don't have a condom." Her hand falls to the back of my head, and I start the very long, but pleasurable, task of making Holly as dirty as possible.

SIXTEEN

Holly

Austin's mouth is incredible. I remember it well from the night in the Jeep, but his slow, languid licks, and the way he groans when his tongue circles my nipple, makes this time even better.

His hands haven't stopped roaming. His hard length presses into the side of my thigh as he bucks each time I do. He sprays a dollop of whipped cream onto my other nipple and ditches the can, his fingers slipping up my thigh and dipping under the edge of my panties. My stomach tightens as he runs his finger through my wet folds, and I squirm into his palm.

A moan rings out of me right before his mouth latches onto my breast.

Never in my life have I been this tightly wound before an orgasm. His thumb strums against my clit and I sigh, my fingers unable to leave the back of his head. My reaction spurs Austin on, and he presses one finger deep inside me.

My body squirms, my hips lifting up off of the mattress.

I need him. I need to feel the weight of him in my hands. I slide down, making his mouth pop off my breast. He stares at me with furrowed eyebrows until my hand reaches under his boxers and wraps around his swollen length. His eyes roll back into his head and his own sigh falls from his lips.

I never really had a chance that night to see Austin or truly take the time to feel him. By the time he got me off, much like he is now, we were frenzied animals lost in sensation. I squeeze and tug, rubbing his pre-cum around the tip of his cock. He buries his face in the crook of my neck, his labored breathing increasing my own arousal.

"You're so fucking wet," he murmurs, curling his fingers inside me, drawing me closer to him.

I slide my leg over his, panting in his ear, and his dick swells even more in my fist. I stroke him harder and faster with each thrust of his hips. He matches my pace, my hips falling against the plunge of his palm between my legs.

"Fuck, Holly," he groans. His eyes roll back into his head and he buries another finger inside me, stretching me even more.

His labored breath rings in my ear. I clench around his fingers, trying to push off the inevitable, wanting to live in this state forever. Austin's manly scent in my bed, his fingers magically ruling my body, his rock-hard length in my hand. It's all perfection.

I push back my body's demand for relief until he smashes his lips to mine. Have we really not kissed since the Ferris wheel? I shiver when his tongue meets mine. His lips are firm and insistent, and my body has no chance of staving off my climax with the hunger between us.

Our kiss is messy and sloppy and holds enough desire to knock me senseless. Our mouths ravish one another as his hips drill his cock into my hand. He moves faster, fucking my palm, while I do the same, fucking his fingers.

"I'm gonna come," he says.

Seconds later, warmth coats my hand as I cry out, my pussy spasming when his thumb rolls my clit. For a full minute, I'm in orgasmic bliss until I shudder and fall back to the bed, exhausted.

"I guess we didn't need a condom." He kisses me once more before climbing out of bed and heading to the bathroom.

He shuts the door and I lie there, in awe of what just happened. I've never felt satisfied after being fingered. I mean, I've come before, but never without still wanting to have sex after. Until now. I don't have time to think more about it before Austin comes back out, naked.

"Next time, I promise to have a condom." He laughs, grabbing his pants and pulling them on.

Here I am, lying naked on my bed as though I have no shame in the world. I sit up and grab my shirt and pull it over my head, ready to throw on a pair of sweats to see him out.

He hops on the bed. "You hungry?"

I shake my head. "No."

"Oh, right. The agreement." He says it as though it doesn't need to be in place.

"Yep. So, I guess I'll see you Monday morning." I slide off the bed and dig a pair of sweats out of my drawer.

"Really?" He puts his arms behind him and leans back on the mattress. I'm choosing to ignore the way it bunches up the muscles in his arms and his abs. "I don't think having a post-orgasm snack is going to lead either of us to heartbreak."

I pull on my sweats and cross my arms. "Bye, Austin."

A part of me wants him to stay. My mouth, for instance, which is salivating at the thought of running my tongue over the ripples of his abs. But thankfully my brain is in full-on protection mode and knows it's best to keep the lines clearly drawn between us.

He grumbles something, grabs his clothes, and puts them back on while I watch. "Try not to miss me or anything." He winks and steps into me with a kiss.

I should've said no kissing. He's way too good of a kisser. I'm going to miss that. "You either."

He taps his temple. "I've committed all of you to memory."

My hands land on his shoulders, and I turn him toward the door. He laughs, eventually stepping out, and we make our way down the stairs.

"Oh, I almost forgot." He turns at the bottom step. "I saw Mrs. Andrews. I think she'll be retracting her allegations."

"Why?"

He slides his arm around my waist. This man is so comfortable with affection. "She said she's worried about Elijah and JP's friendship. She wants me to try to help mend it."

I roll my eyes. "I don't get it. She's a little crazy."

He shrugs, an empathetic look crossing his face. I get the impression there's so much in this town I still don't know. "Well, I say it's a win. Now we don't have to act like I'm only here to look at papers and test scores. We can get down to studying each other's erogenous zones."

I playfully push his shoulder. He steps back.

"I'm glad she's not causing trouble for Elijah or you anymore."

"Me too." He steps in, his lips firm on mine, taking me by surprise.

"Go!" I nudge him.

He opens up the back door to my house and slides out with a smile while I try really hard to remove my own.

After Austin leaves, I feel restless. I clean up the house, although with only me, there isn't much to do. Then I read for a bit and flip through the TV channels but nothing catches my interest. When I'm finished, my gaze falls to the microwave clock. Dana's just finished nights so she should be up.

I pick up my phone and dial her number.

"You are aware it's Saturday night, right?"

I laugh. "I am."

"Are you calling because you're at the police station and you're being charged with stalking?" She chomps down on a piece of food. Every time I talk to her, she's either eating or driving, or sometimes both.

"Whatever, I knew you'd just come off nights and would still be up. I called to tell you I found out more about Austin and there's been a change in our status."

"Oh, do tell! Look how interesting your life has become since moving up there with the polar bears." She giggles.

"I'm going to ignore that."

"Okay." *Chomp. Chomp. Chomp.*

I fill her in on everything Austin told me about his family situation.

"Really?" Dana asks when I'm done.

"Yeah."

"So, you thought he was a pervert trying to sleep with a

student, but really the student was his sister who he gave up everything for to come home and raise?"

"Salt in the wound."

"You should pitch a reality show."

"You're ridiculous."

Chomp. Chomp. Chomp. "Now tell me about the change in your status."

"We've kind of agreed to sleep with one another." I bite my lip, remembering his hands and lips on me and feeling my sex clench.

"How very proper of you."

"Dana!"

She laughs as though she's saying *okay, okay, I'll behave.* "I just think it's funny that you discussed it before actually doing it. Where's the wild girl who had Jeep sex?"

My shoulders fall as I sink into the couch. "I had to have an agreement between us. I'm here short-term and so is he. Knowing what I know now, there's no way we'd ever work out. He's sacrificed his entire adult life for his family, and now that his sisters are graduating from high school, he's free to fulfill his own dreams. I'd never want to take that away."

Dana's silent. She's only ever quiet like that when she has something to say that she knows I'm probably not gonna like.

"What? Say it."

"All right. You're thinking about *his* needs and wants and forgetting your own again. All I heard is he, his, and him. Where is the I and me? You should make up the agreement because *you're* leaving in three months and because *you* have a life to return to. A best friend who is terribly lonely except when she's reading the *Lake Starlight Buzz Wheel* every night."

"What?"

She laughs. *Chomp.* "I'm a doctor, Hol, did you really think I wouldn't be able to find it? I'm only sorry I found it after they took down the picture of the Jeep with the steamed-up windows."

I raise my hands in defeat. "Okay, enough." I get up from the couch, needing a glass of wine. "Back to the whole 'you thinking I'm doing this agreement for Austin' thing."

"Come on, convince me otherwise." *Chomp.*

"I know I'm leaving here too, and so part of it is to protect me. A part of me doesn't understand why Austin would want to leave. I can't even explain this town. He's like a god here. He's looked up to by every person, and not just because he returned home to care for his siblings. He's just an all-around great guy."

"Well, if I had to raise eight siblings, I'd run away when I could too."

"Seven."

"Seven what? You said there was nine of them." *Chomp.*

"Savannah, his sister, was nineteen when their parents passed, and she took over the company."

"There's a company?"

"Are you even listening to me?" I swear I told her about the company.

"Sorry, I'm distracted."

"By? I thought you finished binge-watching *Friends* already."

She laughs. "Oh, what's distracting me is so much better than *Friends*."

"Is it a new show? I'm in desperate need of watching someone else's drama."

"Oh, well then, this isn't for you." *Chomp.* "But it's good. My entire night staff is obsessed with it."

"Dana, what is it?" We're getting off-track, but I'm all for a new show to binge.

"I don't think you'll like it."

My annoyance grows, and I scowl even though she can't see me. "You're acting like a cockblocker."

Chomp. "That's insulting. I've never cockblocked you. You on the other hand..."

"You should thank me for that. He ended up being on the Florida State Police's Most Wanted list. Now just tell me what has you so amused."

She laughs. "Your mind really is somewhere else these days, or you would've figured out what I'm talking about by now."

I roll my eyes.

"You want to know what's keeping me entertained?"

"*Yes!*"

"Fine. The *Lake Starlight Buzz Wheel,* and you only have about five minutes to read it before it disappears forever."

"*Dana!*"

"It's a wonderful article with lots of pictures of you and a strapping young male. You failed to mention how dreamy his dark eyes are."

I groan, reaching for my iPad on the coffee table. "What does it say?"

"Just go read it," she says. "Too bad we can't save these for your wedding."

"Oh. My. God. I just told you about our agreement!"

"Yeah, I heard you, but you need to read the article."

"Just give me the gist of it."

"Oh shit, Barney! Gotta go, he just tipped over the plant." She hangs up.

She must think I'm a moron. Her dog, Barney, is so well-trained, there's no way he tipped over a plant.

I focus on the iPad on my lap, with what feels like a spotlight over it. "Screw it."

I turn it on and open up the Buzz Wheel blog, glancing first at the time. Three minutes. But I don't have to read it at all. The title and pictures say enough. "Principal Gets Dirty with the Coach."

SEVENTEEN

Austin

The entire time I'm prepping Sunday dinner, Holly is in my head. The feel of her grip around my shaft, the silkiness of her desire, the soft cries that left her lips when she was close. For the thousandth time this afternoon, I push images of Holly and me in her bed last night from my thoughts.

Since the Founder's Day party was yesterday, all my siblings are in attendance for this week's Sunday dinner, which means that by the end of the night, each of us will probably be pissed off at someone. Big families, gotta love them.

Phoenix walks into the kitchen and flops down on a stool. "What are you making?"

"These are called vegetables." I hold up a cucumber. "Cu-cum-ber." She rolls her eyes, but I hold up a tomato. "To-ma-to."

"You're so annoying." She walks over to the fridge and

opens it to find all the meat I'm barbequing. "Eww, you need to warn me." The fridge door slams shut.

"I can see why that might disgust you, you know, what with you becoming a vegetarian last month and all." I chop the lettuce and put it in the bowl. "Funny that you don't eat meat *or* vegetables, so what do you eat? Surviving on bean burritos down at Taco Bell?"

"Why do I even bother with you?" She rolls her eyes and goes to sit back down on the stool.

"Because you love me." I slice the cucumber, eyeing her on the other side of the breakfast island. There's a reason she's lingering. God only knows what it could be.

"So, you're going to Cali after this year?" she asks after a minute of silence, as though she had to work up the courage to speak the words out loud.

"Why do people keep asking me this? I told everyone I want a college coaching position. California would be nice, but I'm willing to go anywhere."

"To get away from us?"

I drop the knife and look at her. She studies the island, her fingernail moving into the groves of our wooden countertop.

"I'm not getting away from anyone. I'll come back for holidays and vacations."

She nods.

"I know it's upsetting—"

"Are you and Savannah locking up my money if I don't go to college?"

Just when I thought the girl had a heart.

"You need to go to college." I pick the knife back up and cut into a tomato.

"I don't. There's nothing there for me to learn."

"We've been over this. It's not all about learning, I

mean, it is, but you need the experience and the education. You know how many kids can't go because they can't afford it? Here you have the money and you're fighting us on it." I drop the tomatoes in the salad, then I grab the onion since I need to do something with my hands.

"Kingston didn't go."

"And he'll get his money at twenty-one."

She blows out a breath. "Why do you and Savannah get to control everything?"

Savannah steps into the room, grocery bags hanging off each arm. "Because we're the coolest Bailey kids."

"Oh great, never mind." Phoenix stands.

"What's going on?" Savannah asks.

"Our youngest sister doesn't want to go to college."

Savannah drops the bags on the kitchen table, pulling out all the items I asked her to get. She shoots me her "we talked about this and you need to ease up on her" look. "Why are we talking about this now?"

"Ask her." I point at Phoenix, who is already half out of the room.

"It's not a huge deal. You make it sound like it's some natural disaster if I don't go to college."

"I'm starting to think you should go into the army. Maybe a drill sergeant can get you in line." I raise my voice, which I promise myself every time I won't do. Letting my anger rule the conversation gets nowhere with Phoenix, but she tests the limits so much, even a priest would go ballistic on her.

"Oh nice. Send me off to war and maybe I'll die just like Mom and Dad!"

My knife pauses mid-slice. Savannah holds a box of cornbread mix suspended in the air.

Savannah is the first to respond, in a kind gentle voice.

"Phoenix."

If my eyes were shut, I'd think my mom was standing ten feet away from me.

As always, Savannah shoots me that look, the one that suggests I'm the evil one.

"Never mind. I'm going out."

"No, you're not!" I call.

Savannah lets out a breath, places her arm over Phoenix's shoulders, and sits her down on the breakfast stool. "Okay, give us a reason why you don't want to go to college."

Phoenix shrugs. "It's a waste of money. I don't know what I want to study. Nothing that can be taught at college is what I want to do."

"What is it you want to do?" Savannah leads the conversation while I continue chopping.

Phoenix shrugs. I blow out a frustrated breath. Phoenix glances at me, rolling her eyes.

"Do you have any ideas? Ones maybe you don't want to tell us?" Savannah asks.

Phoenix hesitates before speaking. "I was thinking if Austin was going to California for a job, maybe I'd go with him and pursue singing?" Her voice is so small, so unsure.

You've got to be kidding me. I look at Savannah, who nibbles on her lip.

"Singing? That's what you want to do?" Savannah asks.

Phoenix nods.

"All right. Well, let us soak in this new information, and we can talk about it and come up with a plan."

I stare at Savannah. She's got to be kidding me. My life is finally about to start, and the most deviant of Bailey children wants to tag along? A girl who seems like she can't stand to be in my presence most days? I might as well slap the words "Bodyguard" and "Missing Person Locator" on the back of my T-shirt.

"Austin, would you be willing to take me with you?" Phoenix asks.

"I don't even know where I'm going to land yet. That takes priority. But if singing is what you want to pursue, we'll talk." I blow out a breath. "Just so you know, there *are* schools that let you study music."

I throw it out there, but all three of us know that Phoenix wants to be an entertainer, not a classical musician. She wants to be the next big thing, complete with an entourage and adoring fans. I'll say one thing about her— she's always dreamed big. Even though she makes me nutty, I'm not sure I can be the one who crushes those dreams for her.

"I know," she says, obviously unconvinced.

Savannah runs her hands through Phoenix's hair. Our relationships with our siblings are such a tangled web between nurturing parents and older siblings. "Let's talk about it after dinner."

"Okay." Phoenix nods.

This is the first time in the past year or so she's seemed like the old Phoenix, and that gives me hope.

Savannah goes back to pulling groceries from the bags. "Phoenix, you might be on the cover of *Rolling Stone* one day, but our older brother is going to set the record for how many times he appears on Buzz Wheel."

I continue mixing the salad, rolling my eyes.

"It was sweet," Phoenix says.

"Did you see that Holly cried while you were singing?" Savannah eyes Phoenix, silently praising her for a great job.

"I also saw Austin cleaning up her face." Her head falls to the side and she clasps her chest. "It was so adorable."

I pick up a cucumber slice and throw it at her. "I'm going to hire a PI to figure out who the hell runs that blog."

"Good luck with that." Savannah raises both eyebrows, and the three of us get on with prepping dinner.

***

NOT LONG AFTER THE FIRST BATCH OF CORNBREAD IS done baking, another sibling rises from the depths of the house. Rome saunters in, his dark hair sticking straight up on one side. He's shirtless, with low-hanging pajama pants on, and looks to me as though he may still be drunk.

"Good afternoon," I say.

"Damn, jet lag is kicking my ass." He runs a hand down his stubbled face.

"Thanks for that whole speech yesterday about making dinner for everyone." I stare at the meat I just finished placing on a platter to take out to the grill.

He laughs. "Shit. Well, I'm man enough to admit you probably make better ribs than me. I've been in Italy with pizza and pasta."

Savannah pats his stomach as she walks by. "Too many carbs."

Rome looks down, rubbing a circle around his flat stomach. "Hey now, that's body-shaming."

Savannah nods, rolling out more biscuit dough on the kitchen table. "Touché."

Rome heads over to the coffee pot and fills a mug, a soft sigh escaping him after his first sip. He pats me on the back. "You make good coffee."

"Thanks."

"So." He slides onto the stool across from me.

I'm working on skinning the potatoes for yet another

salad. I loathe Sunday dinners at this point. I'm in the kitchen the whole fucking day. But Mom would be proud that we've kept up the tradition.

"So?" I ask when he says nothing further.

"I heard you and the principal are..." He makes a circle with his finger and puts his other finger through it.

"What are you, ten?"

He laughs.

"What did you do?" Savannah asks.

Rome swivels his stool to show Savannah, who laughs.

"Yep, Austin is the hot news around here," Savannah says.

"Yoohoo!" Grandma Dori's voice rings from the front of the house.

"Grandma Dori!" Rome leaves his cup on the counter and heads out of the kitchen to greet our grandma.

They join us a minute later, Grandma's arm linked in Rome's and his loving eyes set on her.

"You're way too thin," she says to him.

Rome takes her bag from her and gently pulls out the pies she made.

"All they serve you is pea-sized portions over there."

Rome smiles as if she's his idol. "Well, I worked a lot, but"—he peeks under the foil of the pies—"I'm here to stay. I'm thinking about opening a restaurant."

Silence envelops the kitchen as everyone stops what they're doing.

Rome used his college education money for culinary school and to do apprenticeships throughout Europe. He hasn't lived at home for years.

"Jeez, I thought after Austin's announcement that he's leaving, maybe you'd be excited to have me back."

Grandma pinches his cheek. "Of course, we are."

"Where are you getting the money?" I ask.

"Investors. I have people who think I'm worth investing in." A proud smile splits his face.

"Rome," Savannah sighs.

"You'd better get up a lot earlier than one o'clock on a Sunday," I say.

Rome's icy glare lands on me. He can't argue that he's ever been one for responsibility, and owning a restaurant is one hell of a responsibility. "Man, what a great fucking welcome home."

Slap. Rome holds his arm, where I can see Grandma Dori's handprint.

"Don't come home using those words," Grandma says sternly.

"Sorry," he mumbles.

"Fine. We'll talk about it later. Everyone out. I need to speak to Austin."

Savannah looks at the biscuits and throws up her hands.

"I'll do it." Grandma Dori holds out her hand for the round cutter.

Savannah and Rome leave the room with clenched jaws and wide eyes in my direction.

"Leave that and come sit." Grandma Dori pats the spot in front of her with floured hands.

I drop the potato and knife, wash my hands, and sit down at the table with her. She rolls the dough so much better than Savannah. Not that Savannah sucks, but Grandma Dori has made these biscuits a thousand times more than her.

"I read the Buzz Wheel. Did you?" Her eyes sparkle.

I say nothing, crossing my arms and leaning back in the chair.

"I loved the way she teared up with Phoenix, and then

you staring down at her as the float passed by? So romantic."

I'm laughing on the inside. Grandma wouldn't think what we did after those pictures were taken was so romantic.

"Then the whipped cream, where you're wiping it off her face so tenderly." She looks at me. "You remind me of your grandpa."

The heat pooling in my pants from remembering my night with Holly dissipates. Eww.

"Smooth move on the Ferris wheel. Waiting until you were up on top."

"Thanks, Grandma. Good to know I'm making you proud."

She smiles. "The women at the center couldn't stop texting me this morning."

"Texting?"

She frowns. "Yes, you know I'm not *that* old."

I shrug. "I'm assuming that means I'm off the hook for taking her on a real date?"

Not like it matters. I plan on sneaking over there this week and storing a box of condoms at her house. I just have to figure out when I can get out of the city limits to buy a box. Or worse, steal some from my brother. Shit. What has my world come to?

I remember Holly's red-rimmed eyes that day in the bathroom at school. She's the reason I'll drive my ass twenty miles.

"I understand why you're heading to California but that girl..." She's quiet for a moment, nodding to herself. "She would fit in with us. Here. In Lake Starlight."

I can't deny that I haven't had the same thoughts, but this is my chance. I can't forgo it because of some girl who's going to fly out of town as fast as she flew in.

EIGHTEEN

Holly

Fay walks into my office Monday morning, a smile on her face. Seems to me everyone thinks I'm Mary Poppins this morning, the way they're all smiling at me with their eyes lit up.

"Today's seniors coming in are Phoenix and Sedona Bailey. Do you want me to call Austin, or maybe pencil him in during fourth period? I didn't know, since you said you wanted the parents to attend whenever possible." She taps the tip of her pencil on her notepad as though she'll need to write this down to remember it.

"Um…" I think for a moment. Austin in my office. Not a good idea. Especially after the Buzz Wheel article and the fact he hasn't left my mind all weekend. I kind of hoped for a text last night saying he's got the condoms and he's ready to roll, but one never came. "See if he's available, but if not, no worries. I'll still keep my appointments with both girls."

Fay tilts her head and smiles as if I just told her she's

getting paid by the board through retirement. "Okay." She taps her pencil again and rises from the chair.

"Fay?"

She turns around before she reaches the door.

"Is there talk? I mean, are people..."

Fay rounds the chair and sits back down. "People are talking. This is the thing." She looks behind her. "This town..." She glances over her shoulder again then stands and shuts the door before coming back over. "I'm sure you could tell on Founder's Day that this town loves the Baileys. But Austin has always..." She blows out a breath. "I don't want to take away from the other Bailey children, but when Austin returned home..."

Tears well in her eyes and she takes a moment to compose herself. "It was as though he saved everyone and helped us all put the pieces back together. You can imagine what an accident like that does to a town. The Baileys employ a lot of people around here. That, and all their charity work? They're a driving force in our economy and social structure. Add on the fact that, though these people have money, they aren't rich and snobby. They're kind, generous people. Everyone knew Doris Bailey could run the company until they found someone to take over. Not that I want to downplay what Savannah has done over the years. But someone had to take care of those kids."

She wipes a tear from her eye, and I grab a tissue for myself.

"But now he wants to leave, and although everyone understands, they're sad to see him go. That's where you come in." She shoots me a small smile. "The reason you're in Buzz Wheel is that you're giving everyone the hope that Austin will fall for you and stay in Lake Starlight. Everyone thinks this is where he belongs. That he might be chasing a dream that's already passed him by."

"And what do you think?" I toss the tissue in the garbage bin beside my desk.

"I think Austin is an amazing young man with a lot more potential than being a high school teacher and coach. That's not to say I don't selfishly want him to stay here, but what this town doesn't realize is that he's not theirs for the keeping."

I lean back in my chair, absorbing and cataloguing all the information I've obtained about the Baileys in the past week. I don't like it, but it makes a little more sense why the town is treating us like some prince and princess. Could you imagine our wedding? Pfft. The whole town would probably come.

I cover my mouth. Did I really just think that?

"Thanks, Fay. I just wondered."

"You know, he fought to take responsibility for those kids. His grandma and uncle were ready and willing to step up, but he fought them on it. Wanted to return home and raise them. Wanted them to be able to grow up in the family home with him as the patriarch. Not many twenty-one-year olds would do that." She wipes her eyes again.

"No, they wouldn't," I say quietly.

She smiles and rises from the chair. "So, should I still see if he's available?"

"Sure, let's stick to the original plan."

She smiles and tucks the pencil behind her ear. "You got it."

"So, you want to be a travel writer?" I ask Sedona when she's in my office. I flip through her file.

"Yes. My mother was one before she passed away."

"I'm sure there's no better way to see the world than to get paid to do it," I say with a smile. It's sweet that she wants to follow in her mom's footsteps.

Sedona nods. "I don't remember that much, but from what everyone tells me, she loved writing and seeing the world. Hence our names."

I scrunch up my forehead. "What do you mean?"

Sedona seems like a sweet kid, but she still gives me the teenage "are you serious?" look. "Haven't you noticed our names?" When I sit there with a blank expression, she carries on. "We're all named after the cities we were... you know... conceived in."

Her cheeks turn pink, and I feel heat in my own.

"Oh, no, I didn't notice actually." Now that I think about it, I wonder how I possibly missed it. "What about you and Phoenix? And the other set of twins?"

"Layovers." She shrugs.

"Gotcha. Okay, well, getting back to business... I assume you're going to major in journalism?"

She shrugs again. "Kind of."

"What does 'kind of' mean? Do you have another major in mind?"

She's looking at her lap and playing with her hands. "I want to go to college, but I was thinking of going in Europe."

"Europe? Well, you could definitely do a study abroad program."

"Yeah, well. You know Jamison?"

I rack my brain for who I've seen Sedona with in the halls. It's hard, since I have yet to figure out any difference between Sedona and Phoenix. I once knew a set of twins where the one twin had a birth mark by her eye, so we called her Lisa with an I. But Sedona and Phoenix look exactly the same. They even style their hair alike.

"I'm sorry, I haven't met him yet."

"He's my boyfriend and a foreign exchange student from Scotland. I was thinking about going back with him after the school year."

"Okay... but you'd still attend college, right?"

"No." She shakes her head slowly and sucks in her bottom lip.

"And have you talked to your brother or another family member about this?" My heart is in my throat. From everything Austin's ever said about Sedona, she's the golden child.

"Not yet."

Damn it. Why would she choose me to confide in? I'm really wishing Austin had been able to make this meeting.

"Well, I'd advise you to do so, since the end of the school year is approaching."

Sedona glances at me through her long, dark lashes. "I heard you call the parents after the interview if they couldn't be here. My friend Kali said you told her parents about her not wanting to go to her dad's alma matter. She said it lessened the blow when she got home."

I tap my pen on the desk. She's kidding me. She has to be. "Well..."

How do I politely say, "I'm not screwing Kali's dad behind closed doors"? I don't give a shit if Kali's dad hates me. Sedona's brother on the other hand...

I smile. "Well, I will touch on the subject of your wishes at my meeting with Austin, but I'm sure your brother is not going to be okay with it just because it comes out of my mouth."

She smiles and grabs her bag off the floor, thinking our chat is over. "Yeah, he will. You're her."

"I'm sorry, what? I'm who?" The pen drops from my hand onto the desk.

"My sister Juno—did you meet her yet?" She waves me off before I answer. "She's the matchmaker. It's been passed down to one family member or another since our great-great-grandmother. Well, Juno has the gift, and she said one look at you, and she knew. You're the woman who will open Austin's eyes to love."

I huff, my lungs constricting. "I can assure you, I'm not."

She swings her bag over her shoulder, smiles, and heads to the door. Right before she opens the door, she turns back, and I try to appear as though a boulder isn't stuck in my throat.

"Thanks a lot. Do I call you Holly or Principal Radcliffe?"

"Principal Radcliffe."

"Okay. See you." She breezes out the door.

My forehead falls to the desk. The bell rings for the period to be over. I groan. These Baileys are exhausting.

"Well, this isn't a good sign."

I look up.

"Sedona's the good twin." Phoenix walks in, shuts the door, and stands on the other side of the chair.

"Please sit." I motion in front of me.

"No need. I've already informed my brother and sister, although she doesn't really have a say except for the money aspect, that I'll be heading to California after school to pursue a singing career."

"Great, well, we can still chat about it. Maybe you want to attend college down there while pursuing it?"

She shakes her head. "Nope, and I only really need one thing from you."

I tilt my head.

"I need you to stay away from my brother."

I should really page Fay and ask her to get me a strait-jacket. It'll make the process of losing my mind go a lot faster. "As I just informed your sister, there is nothing between your brother and me."

She rolls her eyes, something I've noticed she has perfected. "I'm not stupid. He came home late Saturday, and if I had to guess, he was at your place."

"Don't jump to conclusions. Not to mention that what I do in my private time is my business."

She laughs. "You banging my brother is *my* business, because if he stays in Lake Starlight, I'm screwed."

"Well, I can see we aren't going to get anywhere today. Please head back to study hall."

"Great. That was easy. You're definitely not like my siblings. Always wanting to talk it out." She leaves my office with a small wave, looking quite pleased with herself.

I swivel my chair and look out the window at the forest across the athletic field and the mountaintops far off in the distance. There're still a few small patches of snow dotting the brown grass. Even at its ugliest, when winter has caused Alaska's beauty to lay dormant, it's still beautiful. Why does my kinship to Alaska feel so strong when it's the polar opposite of my real home?

My dad comes to mind. Maybe because he's here. Which is a ridiculous thought, since I don't even know the man.

"Knock, knock."

I swivel back around in my chair. Austin's standing in the doorframe, wearing his million-watt smile.

God, my body hums from that alone. Or maybe it's the way his muscles pull at his shirt in the perfect way.

"Is it already fourth period?" I ask, trying to keep my voice neutral.

"Sure is." He steps out for a second and says to Fay, "I'm shutting the blinds because we're working on an end-of-the-school year surprise, okay?" He steps back in.

"Don't do it," I warn.

He winks, shuts the door, and draws the shade. Continuing around the glass walls of my office, he closes them all, secluding us. The rational side of me is screaming *bad idea, bad idea,* like a warning light, but my body is saying *hurry up, work those hands faster.*

"There we go." He wastes no time in rounding my desk and delivering a knee-weakening kiss, tongue and all.

He takes my hand, pulls me up, and my body is flush to his. His smell is intoxicating, almost overriding any thoughts in my head other than letting him take me here on the desk.

"I have some really good news." He rests his forehead to mine.

"What is it?" Automatically, I think, *I have some really bad news.* My fingers fiddle with his shirt buttons.

"I have tonight available. My brother Rome is back in town, so he's at the house and he's going to take care of the twins."

"Do they need watching?"

"No, but Sedona and her boyfriend are getting close and we're all scared someone's going to walk in on them doing the horizontal mambo one day. And Phoenix... well, you know Phoenix."

I nod. Boy, do I.

"So, am I invited?" he asks, and I forget the question.

He must notice my furrowed brows. "To your house tonight to rock your world."

I laugh, lightly smacking his chest. "I'm not sure. You come in here and shut all my blinds, eliciting rumors all over this school no doubt, and now you want to come over tonight?"

He chuckles, his fingers running circles on the back of my neck. "I'll make it worth your while…"

I slide my hands over his strong chest and around his neck. "Give me another kiss and I'll think about it."

"Well, I guess if I have to."

His lips crash to mine and I'm transported somewhere else, maybe I'm floating above our kiss. All I feel is *him*. His hands. His lips. His thigh between my legs. As our tongues slide along one another's, a moan slips past my lips, pulling a groan from him. His fingers tighten around my hair. My hand glides down his hard chest until I rub his length through his jeans. His hands venture to my ass, squeezing, making me grind along his thigh.

Knock, knock!

We break apart, panting.

"Fuck, okay, maybe keep it out of school until I learn to control myself better." He looks down at the large bulge in his jeans. His lips are red and swollen.

I touch mine, but I already know they are too. "Who is it?"

"Phoenix."

Austin's head falls back. He opens his mouth, but I place my hand over his lips.

"What do you need?"

"I think I left my book in there."

"Is Fay there?"

Austin shakes his head, annoyed that I'm even putting up with this.

"No, she must have stepped out."

I throw up my hands, and Austin presses his lips together to stop from laughing. "Well, I don't see anything. I'll have someone deliver it if it shows up. Maybe look in the lost and found."

"Ugh. Fine."

Austin leans into me, but I lay my hand on his chest. "No way, Romeo. No more in-school make-out sessions. They're too risky."

The smile on his face tells me he'll be sure to test that theory.

NINETEEN

Austin

I'm gathering my shit to head outside for practice when my phone rings. Seeing a number that's not programed in, I try to remember the area codes of all the schools I reached out to.

Sliding my thumb over the screen, I answer, "Austin Bailey."

"Austin, this is Dick Freeman from USC. How are you?"

I fall back into my chair, my heart nearly beating out of my chest. "I'm good. Thank you."

"Good to hear. So, an acquaintance of yours dropped your resume on my desk. You're doing great things up there in Alaska. Not exactly easy to make a winning team with your limitations in weather and practice time."

"Well, we do tend to have thicker blood than you lucky people down in the lower forty-eight."

He laughs. Thank God he has a sense of humor. "True.

True. I went to Iceland once—you know, the wife wanted me to go—and I nearly froze my balls off."

"Man, but a happy wife..."

"Yeah, that's one piece of advice I give all my players. Happy girlfriend, happy future. Some of these kids aren't afraid to lay it out there. I mean, they take pictures of every-thing. Aren't afraid to profess their love on all these stupid apps they use nowadays."

From what I know of Dick Freeman, he's in his sixties and might retire in a few years. He's been trying to find a protégé who could take over for him someday. Getting in there would be a tremendous opportunity.

"True."

"You married?" he asks.

"Nope."

"I'd say stay that way, but in about five years, your life is going to be lonely as hell."

I laugh. My eyes aren't on a wife and family right now. They're on getting this damn job and finally starting my own life. "I'll take that advice to heart."

He slaps something, but it echoes over the line. "All right, let's get to the point of my call. You're looking for a coaching position at the college level, right?"

"I am, sir."

"And why do you want to leave"—paper crinkles through the receiver—"Lake Starlight, Alaska?"

"Well..." I stop myself from telling the real story. "Coaching college is a dream of mine, and as you're aware, they just don't have the teams up here."

"But why now? I mean, you graduated nine years ago. I'm surprised you haven't already gone down this path. Shit, nowadays they hire guys your age as head coaches. And just so you're aware, I don't agree with that line of thinking. It takes years to know how to coach a winning team."

I nod, though he can't see me. "I had some family commitments up here, but I'll be done with those by the end of this year."

"I understand family commitments. Well, let's do this..." More papers crinkle and my heart feels as if it's knocking against my ribs. "Let's bring you out here for an interview. Our season has started, so you can grab a game, see my coaching style, we can chat, and we'll move forward from there."

"Perfect." Excitement feels like electricity humming over my skin.

"Let's do a Friday through Sunday. I don't want you sacrificing your job for anything that's not promised yet. So how about three weeks from now?"

"Perfect. Done."

"Great! You're going to hear from our guy Zeke. He manages all the travel, and if you wanted to bring your... oh, I forgot you're not married." A knock echoes from his end of the call. "I've got someone at my door. It was great talking to you, Austin. Look forward to meeting you in a few weeks."

"You as well, Mr. Freeman."

"Dick. Call me Dick."

"Okay, thanks, Dick."

I press End Call and drop my phone on my desk, staring at it in awe. I think a part of me didn't think he'd actually call, that no one would want a washed-up high school coach from Alaska. A smile breaks across my face.

"You're happy," a sweet voice says from my doorway.

I look over to find Holly leaning on my doorframe, watching me. "Hey, I thought we were off-limits at school."

"It's the end of the day, but I'm on my way to detention."

"Shut that door and come here. You'd be surprised how comfortable my desk is." I pat the wood top.

She shakes her head. "No way. You'll put me in a trance and some kid will walk in and then my breasts will be front-and-center on Buzz Wheel."

"Well, they'd make a good headline. They are spectacular." I laugh, leaning back in my chair and admiring her long legs. I cannot wait for them to be wrapped around me tonight.

"So, who was on the phone that brought out that smile?"

I look at the phone again and at her. She knows the drill. I'm leaving. She's leaving too. But I don't want to bring that up right now. I want to enjoy this feeling a little longer without the repercussions it brings. "I'll tell you tonight. Now, you're going to be a softy?"

I stand and stalk toward her. She shakes her head the entire time, but I swing my arm around her waist and pull her into my room as I grab the doorknob and slam the door. She giggles in my arms, and my lips fall to the crook of her neck.

"I can't wait to explore you tonight," I murmur against her soft skin.

"How are you going to sneak over?" she asks, her hands weaving through the hair at the back of my head.

"My bike. I'm not running back home at five in the morning." I draw back and wait for her reaction.

"No sleepovers, remember?"

I laugh, trailing my tongue up her neck to her earlobe. "Yeah, I remember. But if we're not sleeping, it doesn't count."

She shakes her head, and my teeth latch onto her earlobe, my hand running up and down her hip. "You're trouble."

"Only the best kind," I say.

She pushes at my shoulders, but I shift our bodies, so I have her locked to the counter that runs the length of my classroom.

"Tell me how much you want me right now?" I whisper.

She blushes like I knew she would, and I slide my hand down the back of her skirt, feeling the soft silk of her panties.

"You keep doing that and I'm going to get fired, then this thing between us will stop before it even starts."

I remove my hand. "True. I need to feel you come around my cock at least one more time."

She inhales a quick breath. "You're too much."

I kiss her lips. "Go to detention and I'll meet you at your place. In the meantime, just remember this."

I place my lips on hers and take what I want, what she's so willing to give. My fierce kiss shows her how much I want her. By the time I pull away, she's gasping and clutching her chest.

"See you later. You can spend your time in detention guessing how I'm going to deliver your first orgasm of the night." I wink.

She shakes her head again as though I'm amusing. "Fine, but remember, at midnight you're gone, otherwise you turn into a pumpkin."

I laugh, opening the door for her. "Noted."

I watch her walk down the hall and around the corner to detention.

Damn. I'm man enough to admit that she'll be a hard one to walk away from.

After practice, I catch Elijah and JP leaving detention.

"Hey, guys," I say as they walk in opposite directions. "We need to talk."

They glance at one another before looking at me.

"Fuck that." JP turns and walks toward his truck.

"Get over here." I pat the picnic table in the courtyard.

Elijah walks over because he follows the rules, which will do him good when he lands on a college team.

"JP!" I yell.

He stops mid-stride in the parking lot. "What? I don't need some lecture, okay? I'm in detention already, so let it go."

I tilt my head. "Just come."

He blows out a breath and treks back over to us. Yeah, I figured he was acting like a tough guy, but what he really wants is to mend his relationship with Elijah. He drops his backpack on the picnic table and sits down.

"Listen. You two have been friends since kindergarten. What's happening is ridiculous."

They remain silent. No surprise there.

"You know Coach Jack?" I ask.

They nod.

"He's been my best friend since third grade. Have we had fights and disagreements? Hell yeah, but nothing like this. Nothing where we let a girl come between us." I turn to JP. "Do you really want Becca?"

He shrugs. Elijah huffs.

"My guess is you don't, but something is making you want to stick it to your friend. I get jealousy."

"I'm not fucking jealous!" JP spits, the first reaction I've seen from him.

"Then why?" Elijah asks. "Why are you fucking with my life?"

JP glares at him, silent for a minute. "Because you're the fucking golden boy."

"No, I'm not."

JP rolls his eyes. "You are."

I'm wondering if I should've had this conversation with JP by himself.

"Well, I don't feel like it," Elijah says and looks off into the distance.

"Whatever, man, you're getting out of Lake Starlight next year to go to some fancy college and play baseball. My baseball days are over after this season. Becca will probably follow you. You have everything."

"No, I don't," Elijah bites out.

The two stare at one another for a minute and seem to come to a silent understanding.

"Still. I have a dad who doesn't really give a shit about me and a mom who's so wrapped up in her grief that she'd Saran Wrap herself to me if I let her. I'm going to community college next year because my mom can't stand to have me far away." JP runs his hand through his dark hair and stares at his lap.

All these years of JP being a little asshole, I never once thought of what it was like for him after his sister passed away. And that's fucking sad of me, since I know grief. I know how the loss of a family member can change your life. I've failed this kid.

"I know, but I told you to stand up to her. To fight her on it," Elijah says.

"I can't. You have no idea what it's like. I can't destroy

her like that. If I leave, it will crush her." He takes a deep breath and his jaw clenches.

"Why fuck with my life?" Elijah asks.

"Because I'm pissed. For the first time in twelve years, I won't see you every day. You're going to move on, and I'm stuck here."

"But you're ruining our last months together. It was inevitable, us parting."

JP nods in my direction. "Look at Coach Bailey and Coach Jack."

"Actually, I went to school in California and Jack stuck around here after high school. But he came down to see me, and I saw him when I was home on holidays. If it wasn't for my parents dying, I probably would've never come back here."

JP nods, seeming disappointed by my answer.

"You know what?" I dig out my wallet and drop a twenty on the picnic bench. "You two are going to the cages and dinner on me." I drop another twenty.

They look at one another, assessing if the other wants to. I roll my eyes. They're acting like teenage girls.

Don't go getting all offended at that. It's common knowledge that girls hold grudges, guys don't. We air our shit, then get over it.

They continue to sit there silently.

"Don't make me tell you that you don't have a choice."

They stand, and each of them shrug.

"Thanks, Coach." Elijah fist-bumps me, and I hold my fist out to JP.

"Thanks," he mumbles and knocks his fist to mine.

I head to my truck, watching the boys follow one another out of the parking lot in their vehicles. Holly walks out as I'm about to pull out, so I stop and roll down the window.

"Want to start our secret rendezvous early?" I ask.

She stops at the passenger side of the Jeep. "I wish. I have to take care of something first." Her smile is dim and doesn't meet her eyes.

"Okay then, I'll see you in a bit."

"I'll be waiting."

She says all the right things, but something's amiss. As I wait for her to climb into her small SUV and start it, my stomach churns. My mind tells me it's none of my business though. Because if it was, that would imply there's something more between us, and we both know that won't end well.

TWENTY

Holly

I sip my iced coffee, waiting in the last row of the parking lot, tucked between two work trucks.

"Will you please turn off your car and walk in there?" Dana says through the Bluetooth speaker in my SUV.

"No. I'm not ready."

"Three months isn't a long time." I hear sheets rustling.

"Were you sleeping?" I ask.

"Not really. There was a five-car pile-up a while ago, and the adrenaline is still rushing through me." Her voice lowers. "I'm warning you, I'm going to fly up there and drag you kicking and screaming into that man's office if you don't make yourself known soon."

My eyes focus on the company sign again. He had time to start a company, but never to call me or send me a card or a gift. Not even write me a letter. He had time to start a family.

"I will. I promise."

"Uh-huh."

A lump lodges in my throat as my father steps out of the building with a woman. They say their goodbyes, her venturing in the opposite direction of him. I didn't even know if he was here because that car with the stick figures on the back window isn't in the parking lot.

"Distract me and tell me more about Jeep man."

"Later. He just left the building."

"Good. Now follow my directions. Open the driver's side door, step out, walk over to him, and introduce yourself to him as his daughter."

"Dana." I sigh.

"Is he driving the family mobile again?" Her voice holds more than a note of distain.

"No, a sports car."

"What kind of Alaskan drives a sports car?" Dana asks.

"I guess him. Maybe the minivan was borrowed?"

Dana blows out a breath.

A man who drives a sports car—which makes no sense in Alaska—this is who I expected my dad to be.

He starts the car and pulls out of the parking lot. I wait for the woman's car to follow him out before I do the same, remaining a little behind him so he doesn't get suspicious.

"We're on the move."

"Good times," Dana deadpans.

"Do you want me to let you go?" I ask.

She yawns. "No. Just keep me up and tell me about Jeep-boy Bailey."

His name stirs the butterflies in my stomach.

"He's coming over tonight." I wonder if I should pick up condoms since I'm already far away from Buzz Wheel's eyes and ears.

"So, you made a plan for him to come over?" She asks this as though it's a bad thing.

"Yes."

She laughs. "Only you, Holly."

"What?" I turn right, following my father's car, the other woman's car still between us.

"The fact that you're having a fling but scheduling it. It's just so you, that's all."

"It's spontaneous, okay?"

"No, spontaneous was the Jeep. This is not."

"Hey, he came into my office this afternoon and kissed me."

"And?"

"And we got interrupted."

"Before or after you told him to stop?" She chuckles.

My dad's car slows to a stop at the red light, and the woman's car between us heads into the turn lane. The two of them wave goodbye through their windows, and suddenly there isn't the buffer between us. My fingers tighten around the steering wheel.

"I can't fuck him in my office. It's all glass."

"Hey, relax. I'm just joking with you. It's you, so it fits, and that's exactly why I'll have an extra tub of ice cream for you when you return."

"What's that supposed to mean?"

There's a knock on Dana's end.

"It means I'll have to piece you back together when you get back."

Her words resonate, but she's wrong. It won't be because of Austin. It'll be because of my dad.

"Yeah?" she calls. "Hold up, Hol." I hear someone come into the room. "Yeah, give me five. I'm on the phone."

The door shuts.

"Do you have to go?"

"Nah, it was just Caiden looking for a quickie between

patients. He'll come back after he's done giving his patient a rectal exam."

"Eww!" The light changes and I follow him, keeping a safe distance behind him.

"It's not like he goes in there bareback or something. We wear gloves and—"

"You can just stop there."

"Fine. But see, that's how a fling should work. I didn't tell him to meet me in the break room on Friday at nine."

"Well, you have the luxury of sneaking off at work."

My dad turns down a residential street and pulls up to a huge brick house. He parks in the driveway, exits, and rings the doorbell.

Huh.

"Maybe, but after my orgasm, I don't think 'when can we do it again?' I just go back to work, and when the feeling washes over me again, I seek him out. I have a feeling that's not the case with you and Austin."

"Enough about all that. My father just arrived at a house and rang the bell. I'm driving by, trying not to be suspicious, but the mailbox says Edison. His last name."

Is this a family house? An aunt or uncle I don't know about? What about grandparents? I never had any since my mom's parents died when she was young.

"Big house?" Dana asks.

"Yeah."

"Mansion size?"

I shrug. "It's definitely big, but not a mansion."

I turn around in a court and park on the other side of the street, one house down, before turning off my car.

A woman opens the door. She has dark hair and doesn't look much older than me.

"The bastard has another daughter my age."

"Now this is getting juicy. What if he's one of those people who has, like, five kids by different women?"

He wraps his arm around the woman's back and kisses her.

"Okay, never mind, it's not his daughter. I think it's a girlfriend or something."

"Why?"

"Because he just squeezed her ass and kissed her."

"Gotcha."

A young girl, maybe six or seven, comes to stand beside the woman, wearing a puffy princess-style dress and carrying a little girl's purse. He bends down and hugs the little girl.

Two boys barrel out the door and jump on his back. The dark-haired woman who answered the door pries them off of him, laughing the whole time.

After hugging the two boys and kissing the woman one last time, my father walks the little girl, hand in hand, away from the house.

My stomach knots. "Oh my god."

"What?" Dana asks.

"It's his family. He has a family."

"I thought we already established this."

"I thought maybe since he was driving a sports car and he rang the doorbell that I was wrong, but they're here. They're real."

He opens the back door of his sports car and ushers his daughter in. I guess he was pretending to pick her up like a daddy/daughter date.

She hops in, a huge smile on her face, and he shuts the door.

"So, say something. Go now so you don't regret it."

"They're already leaving," I say.

"Do not follow them. Go somewhere else. Call Austin or that Francie girl."

I start my car.

She must hear the ignition because she blows out a breath. "Come on, don't do this to yourself."

"I have to see. I'll call you back, okay? Have fun with Caiden."

I click End Call as she says my name in desperation. I appreciate her trying to keep me from being hurt, but it's too late. The minute I saw the perfect family he's made here, my heart broke.

A text comes through. I assume it's from Dana, but I don't bother looking since I'm driving.

I follow them to a small downtown area, much like Lake Starlight's but a tad bigger. My father parks along the side of the street, and I park four spots over with the hope he hasn't figured out that I'm following him. The father-daughter duo walk into a diner similar to Lard Have Mercy, and they slide into a booth by the window.

It dawns on me for the first time that I have half-brothers and a half-sister. The little girl and I look nothing alike—her with her mother's features of dark hair and dark eyes.

He's silly with her, making faces and acting goofy. They color or play something on the paper placemats with crayons. They share a sundae, but he only takes one spoonful, leaving the rest to her. At one point he leans over the table and kisses her cheek. His love and affection for her is obvious, and it tightens the noose around my heart.

I start my car, having seen enough.

TWENTY-ONE

Austin

"What are you doing?" Rome asks as I rifle through his nightstand.

"I thought you were with Denver and Liam?" I look over my shoulder for a second then get back to what I'm doing.

"I was, but you said you wanted me home with the girls." He plops down on his bed. "Which seems ridiculous, because they're seventeen and about to graduate."

"Well, Phoenix is testing the limits these days and Sedona and Jamison are getting closer, so it's a precaution. You've been gone for years. You should appreciate a little family time."

He rolls to his side and props up his head with his hand. "Why are you in my drawers?"

"When you were gone, I thought I left something in here."

His forehead crinkles, but he doesn't call me out on my

shit. Since I'm coming up empty, I'll have to point-blank ask him anyway.

"So, you're really leaving, huh?" he asks.

"Yes." I open the bottom drawer and move a bunch of papers out of the way. Still nothing.

"I'm kind of surprised."

"Why?"

"I don't know. I just figured once you came back all those years ago that you'd left that life."

I blow a breath, close the drawer, and flop down into his desk chair. "Of course, you did. You were a self-centered fourteen-year-old."

He shrugs. "It's just, is it really something you still want to do? I thought you were happy in Lake Starlight."

"It's not that I'm not happy. I just want more."

He nods as though he understands. Maybe he does, but Rome didn't sacrifice his dream like I did. "I can understand that. We'll miss you, but the family isn't going to say anything to try to stop you. We owe you and Savannah enough." He sits up and gestures to the corner of the room. "Condoms are in my suitcase, front pocket."

I chuckle. Little asshole knew the whole time.

"So, you're heading to the principal's office, huh?"

I get up off the chair and walk over to the suitcase that lays open in the corner of the room. "Don't say anything, okay? It's nothing serious, and I don't want to have to deal with everyone's questions when it'll be over soon anyway."

He shakes his head. "Your secret is safe with me, but you know you're playing with fire, right? I just want to make sure you can see how this will go terribly wrong."

I throw my hands in the air. "Fucking hell. Why does everyone think they can predict the future?"

He tilts his head and gives me a *duh* look. "Because it's you, and I'm pretty sure she's not like the girls I pick up."

"What're you talking about?"

He lies back down on his bed, lacing his hands behind his head. "The girls I pick up aren't the serious types. They're not looking for a future husband. I'm selective with the people I sleep with."

"Really?" I raise a brow. With the number of women he's slept with, I find that hard to believe.

He holds up his hand. "Not to mention half the time I'm Denver Bailey." He laughs. "Best thing about being a twin."

I toss a condom from his box onto his chest. "Do me a favor and make sure you're using one of these, every single time."

He sits up, sliding the condom around in his fingers. "Don't worry, you gave a good birds-and-bees lecture back in the day." He laughs again, and I leave his room, flipping him off.

I head to the garage to grab my bike. When I hop on, something feels off, so I look down and see both tires are out of air.

"I just rode it into town two days ago," I grumble, climbing off and searching for the air pump. I scour the shelves and the locker with all the athletic equipment, then I search the basketball bin. Nowhere to be found.

I head back into the house. "Has anyone seen the air pump?"

Rome is the only one who answers. "No."

I let the door shut behind me as I go for option two—my Jeep. Screw it, I'll park on Main Street, and if anyone asks I'll make Jack be my alibi.

Climbing into the driver's seat, I turn the ignition, but it doesn't turn over. What the hell?

I get out and open the hood. Everything looks fine, but it's dark outside, so who knows? I go back to the garage to grab a flashlight to have a better look.

I search everywhere, but it's not where it's supposed to be. Can no one put anything back where it belongs in this house?

I swear Phoenix probably did this herself out of spite. I'll deal with her later.

Entering the house again, I scream, "Anyone have a flashlight?"

"No," Rome is the one who answers—again.

The door slams behind me, and I push a hand through my hair. "Fuck it. I'll run."

I grab my headphones from my truck, hook them up to my phone, and stretch a little before heading off. The problem will be coming home tonight, but I'll figure that out after Holly's out of my system.

I'm panting on the back porch, waiting for Holly to answer since the door is locked.

She opens the door, and my gaze flows down her body. She's stripped of makeup. Her hair is up in the messiest bun I've ever seen, and I've practically drowned in estrogen my entire life with all my sisters. Her sweatpants have paint stains on them. And yes, I notice the way her nipples poke through her oversized T-shirt.

"What are you doing?'" she asks, not moving from the door.

"We had a date."

She stays put. "I texted you to reschedule."

"No, you didn't." I pull my phone from my sweatshirt pocket, and sure enough, there's a text from her ten minutes ago. "Sorry, I had to run. There was no air in my tires and my Jeep wouldn't start."

"Oh, I'm sorry."

"Are you gonna let me in?" My hands are on my hips and I'm doing my best not to bend over to breathe.

"It's really not a good night. It's just... something personal."

"Can I grab a water and call Jack to get me? There's no way I can run back right now."

She's apprehensive for a moment but steps aside.

I'm surprised that worked. I walk in with no plans of calling Jack. Holly did me a huge solid dealing with JP and his mom. She looks as though she needs a friend, and since she doesn't have any locally, I'll step up.

"Thanks." I walk into the kitchen and point at the cupboard with the cups. "Mind?"

"Help yourself."

I take one of her cups and fill it with cold water from the fridge. "So, what's going on?"

She stares blankly at me. "Did you want to call Jack?"

I pull out a chair from the kitchen table and sit down. "Nah, let's chat." I pat the chair next to me. "I'm a super good listener."

She smiles. "I'm sure you are, but I'm good. I'm redoing a table. That's my therapy."

I stand, her outfit making more sense now. "Where at? I'd love to see you redo some furniture."

I step out of the kitchen and look around the living room, but then I figure she's probably using the garage or basement. I open the garage door only to find her small SUV parked inside.

"Basement?"

"Austin, please, this just isn't a good night." She follows me down the basement stairs, and there sits a dresser with sanding tools on top of it, like she was just getting started.

"This looks like fun. Not at all what it sounded like when I read it on your bio." I finish my water and set the glass on what I assume is her tool table.

"It's not really. And we're not supposed to do anything fun, remember our deal?"

I tilt my head. "Um, I'm pretty sure *all* we're supposed to do is have fun."

A small giggle escapes her and a little of the light returns to her eyes, making my stomach stir. "Yeah, but only when we were... you know. Not by refinishing furniture together."

I pick up the sander. "Well, we could modify the agreement. It's not like we put it in writing."

She sits on the bottom step. "Austin," she sighs.

I'm being pushy, I get that, and maybe it's the pseudo parent in me, but I hate seeing people upset. And just because we agreed to a mutually beneficial sexual relationship doesn't mean I can't be her friend too.

I sit next to her on the step. "I can be your friend."

She shrugs.

"I promise not to get attached." I make a cross over my heart with my finger, spurring another giggle from her.

"It's not you I'm worried about," she says, and I ignore the way her words make my heart beat faster.

"How about this? After I listen to whatever is bothering you, I'll treat you like shit." She knocks her shoulder with mine, and I laugh. "What? I'm not sure there's another solution here. I'm not going to leave you looking the way you are, so should I settle in for a long night of sanding?"

She glances at me from the corner of her eye. "Fine, but do not be all sweet afterward. No touching."

"Sure. Okay." I hold up my hands and stand, backing away from her.

"And we're doing it while we sand. It's good for my furniture if I'm frustrated." She walks by me and picks up the sanding tool.

"You know, I kind of like this bossy side of you."

She rolls her eyes, smiling, and pulls her phone out to start music. "No One" by Alicia Keys sounds through her Bluetooth speaker.

I meet her eyes.

"What can I say, the parade reminded me of how much I love her."

Savannah picked "If I Ain't Got You" this year to sing on the float. The girls in the family always pick sappy songs, whereas the guys pick more upbeat, "get your heart going and get the crowd involved" ones.

She hands me a sander wedge. "You need to be gentle and not change the structure, but we have to get it down to the wood."

"Okay."

She places her hand over mine, sliding it and demonstrating the amount of pressure I'm supposed to use. I look at her after a few moments when she hasn't removed her hand.

"I feel a *Ghost* moment coming on," I say.

She drops her hand and shakes her head. Her smile says she liked the joke though. She walks to the other side and picks up her sanding wedge. "There you go. That's how you do it."

"So, what's bothering you?" I ask.

"I told you about my father and why I took the job."

I nod, pretending to concentrate on the sanding when really I want to listen to every word coming out of her mouth.

"I have yet to actually reach out to him." She glances at me for a reaction, but I don't give her one. "I've stalked him. Sat outside his work, and today I followed him home." She cringes and looks at me once again.

"And?"

She waits, but I'm not judging her. I can't imagine it's easy to go up and introduce yourself to the father who wanted nothing to do with you.

"He has a whole family here. A wife and three kids. I watched him take his little girl on a date to a diner."

I stop the pretext of sanding and watch as she inhales and closes her eyes.

"Back home, I thought he was a selfish prick who didn't want a kid—ever. But from outward appearances, he seems like a thoughtful dad and a good husband." She bends down on the other side of the dresser so I can't see her, but I hear the sander meeting wood.

I don't want to push her, so I remain where I am, pretending I don't understand how hard she's hurting.

"It just hurts, you know?" Her voice cracks. "It brought up all those feelings of abandonment. All the daddy/daughter events I went to with my mom, all the Father's Days that passed when I had no one to give the craft we made at school to, all the times I wished I had a man in my life to ask for advice about teenage boys. I thought I'd made peace with it, but after seeing him with his daughter, I realize I haven't." She sniffs.

Fuck this. I drop my sander and round the dresser to

find her sitting on the hard basement floor, her hands covering her face. I drop right in front of her, taking her hands. "He's an asshole."

She looks at me with tears falling from her eyes. "That's just it! I desperately want a relationship with an asshole who wants nothing to do with me. Why? Am I that desperate?"

Her honesty makes a lump form in my throat.

"Then you call your own number if he's not going to." I squeeze her hands.

"What?"

"It's a sports term. It means your time is now, and if he's not going to take the opportunity, you take it for yourself."

She shakes her head. "I can't."

"You can. Call him. There could be a million reasons why he hasn't reached out. You came all this way and you only have so long. Do you want to waste this opportunity?"

"What if—"

"What if nothing. Don't even think about it, and I'll promise you something." I hold up my hands in a placating gesture. "I'll be here for you."

She tilts her head.

"Just as a friend."

Her lips tilt down in a frown.

"Jeez. You're a hard person to be friends with."

She laughs, and a smile replaces her frown.

"But, Holly, you got to do it. I know it sucks but do it. You have nothing to lose. At least then you'll have some answers."

She nods and inhales deeply. "Okay. I'll call him tomorrow."

"I'll come with you."

"No." Her hand covers my cheek, and she stares into my eyes. "You've done enough."

Neither of us looks away from the other, and the energy in the room shifts. Maybe she was right, and I should've turned around on her back porch and left. But there's no turning back now, so I lean forward and my lips land on hers.

TWENTY-TWO

Holly

Austin hasn't said anything I haven't already been telling myself these past couple of weeks, but somehow hearing it from him, it rings true.

I thought I knew how Austin Bailey kissed. He's usually hungry for me, and I feel it from my head to my toes. His eyes scorching, his tongue searching, his hands frantic on my body. That's the way it's been.

Until now.

His hands cup my cheeks as he lowers his head to mine. My phone shuffles, and James Arthur's "Can I Be Him" plays from the speaker. Our kiss consumes me. The gentle slide of his tongue along the seam of my lips, his hands moving to the back of my head, the soft sound of satisfaction from the back of his throat.

I straddle him, and his hands free my hair from the messy bun, the strands cascading over my shoulders. As he runs his fingers through it, I rise up and the kiss deepens. There's nothing rushed about his exploration of my body.

He's yet to strip a layer of my clothes, but still, the feeling of vulnerability is present.

He grows under my center and I grind against him, spurring him to tighten his grip on the back of my shirt.

"Jesus, Holly."

We break apart, his lips traveling down my neck, my T-shirt in his fists, tightening and making it clear that I'm not wearing a bra. His gaze falls between us, flashing with desire, and my heart thumps so loudly I swear he must hear it. Seeing myself through Austin's eyes has that effect on me. His desire is laid bare, and he hides nothing. That I'm the reason for that reaction is electrifying.

"I need you," he whispers before his teeth latch onto my earlobe.

A shiver runs down my body and centers at the apex of my thighs. I wrap my hands around his neck, keeping him there as my body pushes against his strong chest, my core grinding along the tent of his athletic pants, my nipples peaked and rubbing on the cotton of my shirt. Intense need sets every nerve in my body on fire. Our bodies have minds of their own and can't stop grinding against each other while he casts open-mouthed kisses across my neck and collarbone.

I ache for his touch. Everywhere. And I'm desperate to touch him.

The friction and heat of his body is no longer enough. I need him inside me.

"Now, Austin. Please."

He manages to get us to stand, and I groan when I no longer feel him between my legs. He walks over to the old couch in the corner and flops down on it, stripping off his T-shirt. The sight of his rippling abdomen and strong arms is almost too much for me.

I follow his lead and strip myself bare. Eager doesn't even describe me.

He kicks off his shoes, takes off his socks, and lifts to remove his pants. His eyes feast on me and I find I welcome it, unafraid that he won't like what he sees. Having lost all patience, I take the condom from his hand, rip open the foil, and slide it down his length.

He takes my hand and leads me to the other side of the couch, nudging me to my back. In seconds, he's over me, pressing at the entrance between my legs. Without preamble, he slides inside. My back arches off the cushion and I struggle for breath, adjusting to his size.

"You okay?" he asks.

"Yeah," I say, pulling his mouth to mine.

Our mouths mesh together, our hot and heavy breathing finding a common rhythm and sounding in one another's ears.

He circles his hips, taking his time and sliding in and out at a pace that draws me closer and closer to orgasm. He's giving me just enough to pull me to the edge and not enough to push me over. It's the sweetest form of torture I can imagine. I drown in everything Austin Bailey gives me, and he doesn't hold back. He's giving me his whole self in this moment.

"Open your eyes," he says, his fingers brushing my cheek.

My eyes flutter open, and he's staring at me. Those dark brown eyes with gold flecks are shining and weighted with something I don't want to examine. Some kind of emotion that's outside of the agreement we made. It's not only want and desire I find there. There's so much more, and I ignore the piece of me that wants to come alive.

"Austin," I plead, my pending orgasm pushing all of

those thoughts away. There's not enough room for them when I'm this close.

"I know, baby. I know," he murmurs. His lips crash to mine and his pace increases.

The word of endearment, one he shouldn't be using, it sends me over the edge.

I tighten my thighs around his waist and grab the couch cushion, clenching around his length. Stars burst behind my eyelids as pure pleasure and bliss lights my body on fire. He rises up on his elbows, plunging into me until he pumps a few times and stills.

"Damn," he says, nearly breathless.

His eyes flash open, and for a split second, I see relief, then all the emotion that filled them moments ago transforms into anxiety. Awkwardness fills the silence in the basement.

He rolls off me and stands. "I'll be back."

He heads upstairs, and I grab my clothes, rushing to put them on so I'm dressed before he returns. By the time his footsteps barrel back down the steps, I've already turned off the music.

Fail number one for sure. Don't set the mood for love-making when you're with your supposed fling.

He looks at me and smirks, grabbing his own boxers and pants. "So, I take it I'm kicked out?"

I bite my lip and look at him. Do we talk about what just happened or ignore this? "Probably best that you leave."

He sits next to me, pulling his shirt over his head. "You're skittish."

"Austin." I sigh.

"I know. I know." He looks around. "Maybe we alter our agreement?"

"No!" I walk back over to the dresser and grab the sander to get back to work.

He huffs but lets it go. "So, I have news." He leans back, his arms extended across the back of the couch.

It dawns on me that I never asked him about his good news. "I'm sorry." I stop the sander and turn to give him my full attention. "I forgot to ask."

"USC called. I have an interview."

A smile breaks out on my face. "What? That's great."

"Nothing's for sure. It's in three weeks, so..."

I sit down next to him. "You must be so super excited."

He nods. "I am, but I don't want to get my hopes up until it's a done deal."

"That's great, Austin." I grip his knee. "I'm super happy for you."

He gives me a funny look. "Super."

I laugh. "Sorry, I'm emotionally and physically exhausted now. My vocabulary is currently operating at a teenager's level."

He smiles and squeezes my hand that I just realized is still gripping his knee. "Thanks. I haven't told my family yet, but..." His jaw clenches and he swallows.

"What?" I shift to face him better and use the opportunity to remove my hand from his leg.

"They aren't really happy about me leaving. They all support my decision, but I can tell it saddens everyone. Everyone but Phoenix."

"Oh, I'm sure she'll miss you."

"She wants to move to California with me." He raises his eyebrows. "She wants to forget college and try to be a singer."

"Oh." I play stupid about what Phoenix told me, but it brings what Sedona mentioned to mind. Austin side-tracked me with that kiss, so we never got around to discussing it. "That reminds me, I forgot I have to see you tomorrow to discuss their interviews."

He settles into the couch. "Well, let's forget the elephant in the room then and talk about the *Shining* twins."

"I think we should do it in a professional setting."

He shrugs. "Okay. If that's what you want."

"I think it's more appropriate."

He cups my cheek like he did before, meeting my gaze. "You think too much."

I lean into his strong hold because his touch feels good.

I'm so screwed.

I'll leave Lake Starlight a complete mess if I don't put an end to this.

"Then you're not going to like what I have to say."

"What?" His forehead wrinkles.

"I think we need to stop this."

He smiles at me, leans in, and kisses my lips. "Sorry, baby, not happening."

I'm stunned for a second and don't know what to say because, really, who says that? "It's not your choice," I manage to get out.

"True." He drops his hand and walks over to retrieve the sander, getting back to work. "You can't stay away from me any more than I can stay away from you at this point. So what if I didn't nail you from behind? It was still sex, and you're thinking too hard about it."

The sander along the wood is all I hear as I sit on the couch and think about what he said. He's right. It felt emotional in the moment, but that doesn't mean we're emotional about each other outside of the sack. I can still walk away once our time is up. He was helping me feel better, distracting me like a good friend would do. That's all.

I hop up from the couch and grab the other sander. "You're right. We got this." I smile over the dresser at him before turning on my music but choose something that isn't romantic.

He grins back. "Definitely."

And if you believe that, you're as stupid as Austin and I are in this moment.

TWENTY-THREE

Austin

I walk into Holly's office at the start of fourth period. She's rounding her desk, giving me a chance to admire her perfect ass in her snug gray skirt. Once she's on the other side, my eyes focus on the dip of her teal blouse. I never really thought blouses were sexy until Holly started walking the halls of Lake Starlight High.

She leans forward on her desk to grab the girls' files, and I inhale a quick breath.

"Do me a favor? Don't do that when any of the dads come in to discuss their kids, okay?"

She looks at me, tilting her head.

"They'll enjoy the view like I am. Now I have a hard-on and we're about to talk about my sisters." I shake my head.

She giggles. I love that sound. I didn't realize how much until right now.

Let's just put it out there—I made love to her two nights ago. There I said it. "Damn it" was my immediate reaction afterward, but she was so sad. No way could I have grabbed a fistful of hair, bent her over, and fucked her. She deserved loving caresses and feeling special after what she found out about her asshole father. Since the bit of awkwardness right after, we've been back on plan.

"Okay, well, this should get rid of that thing right away." She glances between my legs. "Sedona wants to move to Scotland with Jamison."

"Mission accomplished." I sit up straighter, the thought of Holly's tits in my mouth now a distant memory. "Sedona doesn't want to go to college?"

She shakes her head.

"What the hell did I do wrong? Her *and* Phoenix *and* Kingston? All three of the youngest kids don't want to go to college. My parents would be so fucking proud." I lay my head in my hands.

I hear Holly's office chair sliding and her walking around her desk. Next thing I know, her hand is on my thigh and she's crouched beside the chair I'm in.

"I don't think it's anything you did. I can't speak for Kingston, I don't know him, but as for Phoenix and Sedona, it's not uncommon for kids not to have their entire future mapped out at their age. They might see college as confining and keeping them from starting their lives. I had lots of students who were older either because they waited to start college or because they changed their mind about what they wanted to pursue. And what Phoenix wants to do doesn't need a college degree."

I blow out a breath.

"Sedona wants to follow in your mom's footsteps and be a travel writer. I don't think your parents would think badly of that, right?" Her hand runs up and down my leg.

I huff. "My mom went to college. That's where she learned to write."

"Maybe instead of laying the hammer down, you try to negotiate. She goes to Scotland, but she attends college there."

Holly's so naïve, and I want to kiss her right now because of it.

Fuck, I have all this shit going on and I want to kiss her? What the hell is wrong with me?

"Dinner tonight?" I ask to distract myself, because I'm about ready to let my sisters do whatever the fuck they wanna do.

My dad's voice is in my head, replaying when I told him I wanted to try to go into the farm system instead of going to college. That conversation didn't go well. He's probably up there shaking his head in disappointment that I let Kingston skip college.

She smiles. "Let's stay on track. There needs to be a firm line here. We said no dinners."

"Have you called your dad?"

She stands and heads to the other side of her desk, her eyes scouring the courtyard outside her office. "Not yet, but I will later today."

I sit back in my chair and rest my ankle on my opposite foot. "We have about a half hour before fourth period is over."

Her gaze shifts to me. "I'm not doing it while you're in the room."

"Do you have his number?" I ask, ignoring her protest.

She glares at me as though I'm an idiot. She's been stalking him, of course she has his number.

I hold up my hands. "Hey, I'm just asking."

She sits in her chair and wheels closer to her desk. "I had it before I came to Lake Starlight." She opens her desk drawer, pulls out a piece of paper, and stares at it.

"Then let's call him."

"Stop being so pushy." She taps her pen on the desk, glancing away from me. "I know you mean well, but what if he doesn't want to hear from me?"

I refrain from speaking the truth that there's a high probability he *doesn't* want to hear from her. If he hasn't had a relationship with her up until this point, I doubt he's been on eggshells, waiting for her to call. But she needs to discover that herself. Just like all the people telling me I need to stop chasing a dream that died nine years ago—I have to go to California and experience it for myself. Just like Holly, I'm praying everyone else is wrong.

"Come on. I'll hold your hand while you call."

She scrunches her forehead. "I can't do it while you're in the room."

I stand. "Then I'll wait outside, but I'll stay by Fay. That way if you need me, all you have to do is look out the window and I'll be there."

"Austin," she sighs, because that's what she does when I push her into an uncomfortable position.

I head to the door. "I'd give you a big good luck smooch, but you'd probably frown upon that, so..." My hand lands on the doorknob, but I turn around and wink. "You got this."

I walk out without letting her argue.

"Hey, Austin," Fay says after I close Holly's office door. "I've been meaning to talk to you. The parade, Phoenix's singing. It was all too much to handle." She grips her chest and tears well in her eyes. "I felt like I was at their wedding again. And"—her hand covers mine on the counter—"your eyes in that picture on Buzz Wheel were just like your dad's when he looked at your mom that day."

I retract my hand, my gaze shooting to Holly's office. "Fay..." I say, irritation thick in my voice.

She waves. "I feel like it's my job to do what your mom would've done. Stop playing games and admit that you like that girl." She thumbs in the direction of the office.

"Holly's cool."

She shakes her head, her eyes boring into mine.

"What?"

"Austin." She looks around. Vice Principal Ealey's office is dark again, so it's just me and her.

Holly picks up the phone and puts it back down, her gaze shooting to mine. I nod at her to pick up the phone, and her shoulders sag.

"Will you please stop acting like you're not the caring boy I've known you to be your whole life? It's my favorite quality of yours." Fay puts her hand on mine again. "Your heart is triple the size of most men's."

"Did you just call me the Grinch?"

Fay laughs. "I'm serious. Your mom would love Holly. She's a perfect fit for you."

My eyes search out Holly, and I smile. She is perfect. I can't deny that fact. A different time, a different place, hell, maybe even a few years ago, I would've jumped at the chance for something serious with her, but like the old saying goes, timing is everything. And in this case, time is not on our side.

Holly picks up the phone and presses some buttons. She bites her lip and circles her chair so her back is to me.

"Thanks for the advice. I do appreciate it, even if I'm not taking it."

Fay shakes her head and taps her fingers on the keyboard. "You kids today are so selfish. You all lose sight of what's really important with the whole me, me, me that's on repeat in your heads."

My eyes widen. I've never heard that judgmental tone from Fay before.

"What?" She must notice my shocked expression. "It's true. You're so hell-bent on leaving Lake Starlight but let me ask you a question. How bad is this town that built you? It was good enough for your entire family and you act like it's a prison cell. These people love and care about you and you won't get that in California."

Her words are like a slap in the face, and I swear my cheek actually hurts. Is that what people think? That I loathe Lake Starlight? That I don't appreciate the help they gave my family after our tragic loss? Just because I want to leave doesn't mean I don't love this town and everyone in it. Jeez, Fay sounds like a jealous fucking girlfriend.

Anger bubbles in my veins the more her blunt words register.

I lean forward, ready to lose my cool. The words in my head are dying to come out. *Let me ask you, Fay, when is it my time? I raised seven of my siblings. I got a teaching job. I learned to cook. I learned to do laundry. I learned how to budget. To coupon clip. I've lived for everyone but me over the past nine years. When my buddies were out picking up girls and partying until all hours of the night, I was helping kids with their homework. When they were all making mistakes and figuring out who they were in their twenties, I was forced to become who I needed to be, not who I wanted to be.*

Her eyes meet mine and I lean backward, inhaling deeply. I have too much respect for Fay to let loose on her.

"Thanks again for the advice." I reach for a butterscotch candy off her desk.

She smacks my hand. "No butterscotch for you."

"Whatever."

I look to Holly's office as she swivels her chair and hangs up the phone. She's not smiling. *Fuck.*

"Do me a favor, Fay, don't turn around and don't let anyone in this office for about five minutes." I knock on the top of her desk.

"And why should I do you a favor?"

I smile at her. "Because I'm your godson."

She shakes her head, her smile small at first, but eventually she loses the fight.

I kiss her cheek. "I'm sorry, Fay."

"Me too. I know you've sacrificed, it's just..."

I nod, trying to get her not to say what I think she will. That everyone is this damn town wants Holly Radcliffe to save them by being enough to keep me in Lake Starlight. As much as I hate to disappoint people, I won't let that stop me this time around.

I enter Holly's office, not stopping until I pick her up off the chair and wrap my arms around her. "I'm so proud of you."

Her arms grip me around the neck. "You don't even know what he said."

"It doesn't matter, you called him. That's a huge step." I kiss her right under her earlobe.

"Austin!" she whisper-shouts.

"Relax, Fay's doing me a solid." I draw back. "So, what did he say?"

"We're going to dinner Thursday at some steakhouse." She nibbles her bottom lip.

"That's great... isn't it?"

She nods. "Yeah, I'm just nervous. He said he's wondered about me."

"All good news." It is, but she still looks so scared and unsure that I blurt out my next words without really thinking about them. "Do you want me to go with you?"

She shakes her head. "No, that'll just make it more awkward if I bring my boy... I mean, friend."

I laugh, not at all upset about her slip, though it should probably bother me. "Okay, but I'm coming to your house after."

"Fine." She tries to say it begrudgingly, but I can tell that she's actually glad I'll be there.

"Now we have about three minutes to make out like teenagers without anyone seeing."

She glances around.

"Trust me." My hands cup her cheeks, and I press my lips to hers.

She must trust me, because this time her tongue slips into my mouth. I'm reminded of another perfect quality of Holly's—with just one kiss, she can make me forget all the reasons we won't work.

TWENTY-FOUR

Holly

I drive through downtown Greywall, not surprised that my dad picked a restaurant in a neighboring town—his family probably doesn't know I even exist.

After parking, I glance at the clock on my dash and pull my keys out of the ignition. Early is better than late.

The steakhouse is classy with dim lighting, linen table-cloths and napkins, and a nice atmosphere. A water glass and a wine glass are both set on the table, and as I take a quick glance at the menu, it's clear that my mom couldn't have afforded to eat here on her best night.

My phone dings in my purse, so I dig it out, reminding myself to breathe. I'm so nervous, I'm not sure I'll be able to eat anyway. When I have the phone in my hand, I see a missed call from my mom. I'll call her back later. There're also a couple of texts from Austin.

Austin: *You're an amazing person. You can do this!*
Austin: *I'll show you how amazing I am tonight. ;)*

Austin must have sent those earlier, because the most recent one is from Dana. I tap on her message.

Dana: *Karen's on the hunt.*

What the hell does she mean my mom is on the hunt? I message her back.

Me: *What are you talking about?*
Dana: *She tracked me down at my apartment. She said you've been acting weird. She called the school you told her you were working at.*
Me: *WHAT!?!*
Dana: *My question is why did you give her a name of a school? If you're going to lie you need to be vague not specific.*
Me: *Because it's my mom and she doesn't let those kinds of things go.*
Dana: *Then you should've stopped having so much sex and called your Mama more often.*
Me: *This is not funny. What did she say?*
Dana: *She threatened me and she's kind of scary when she gets going...*
Me: *What did you tell her?*
Dana: *I told her that you wanted to get away.*
Me: *And?*

Sweat breaks out at my temples. I need to call Dana then my mom, but this isn't the type of restaurant you have a conversation on your phone in. Plus, I want to be here when my dad arrives.

Dana: *She wanted to know where?*

Me: *And?*

Dana: *I caved and told her that you went to Lake Starlight, Alaska.*

Dana: *I'm sorry!*

Dana: *But you know Karen! She'd spank me or worse. And she's really intimidating when she's digging for the truth.*

Dana: *I really am sorry! Please don't be mad.*

Dana: *Maybe this is a good thing.*

Dana: *She can be the one to reach out to your dad.*

The phone rests in my hands, vibrating every half second. I sit there stunned and unable to respond to my best friend as I try to assess what this means.

"Holly?" a man's voice asks, drawing my attention away from my phone.

He's here. Right in front of me. Staring at me with a small smile.

I ignore the messages from Dana and push my phone into my pocket.

"Hi," I say, teetering in my chair, unsure if I stand or not. Do we hug? I'm a stranger who happens to share half his DNA. Maybe he doesn't even like hugs. He liked them with his new children though.

I don't have to worry about making a decision because he slides into the chair across from me. "You're so grown up." He looks me over, a little unsure.

"It's been thirty years," I sneer then regret it. I want answers, not to run him off in the first sixty seconds. "I'm sorry."

"That's okay. I deserve it." His silver watch sparkles

from the overhead lights as he runs his fingers through the light auburn hair that matches my own.

"So..."

He picks up his menu. "Maybe we order and then we can talk?"

I nod, picking up my own menu, happy for the distraction so I can gather myself. As I glance over the dishes and the prices again, I can't help but wonder if this is a place he visits regularly or is it a place for special occasions? Is he always this lavish? There's so much I don't know.

Deciding on the chicken, I place my menu on the table in front of me.

A waiter comes over, and my dad orders a bottle of wine.

"Do you drink red?" he asks.

I nod.

"Go ahead and order, Holly."

"I'll have the chicken carbonara and a Caesar salad please." I hand the menu off to the waiter.

"Oh no, you have to get a steak. They have a bone-in filet here."

The waiter smiles at me.

Does he think a sixty-dollar steak is going to make up for thirty years of his absence?

"I'm fine with the chicken but thank you."

"Holly, I insist. It melts in your mouth. You have to get it."

I stare at him for a moment and watch his face cave a little.

"But if you'd rather the chicken..."

"No, the steak is fine." I look at the waiter. "Medium please and thanks."

The waiter smiles, making a note while telling me how much I'll love it, then he shifts his focus to my dad.

"Ribeye. Rare. No potato and a salad." He hands the menu back, dismissing the waiter without a thank you.

Maybe it's the fact my mom has been a waitress her whole life, but that gnaws at me. Then again, maybe he's nervous and distracted like me.

"So, tell me about yourself. The call that came into my office said Lake Starlight School District. Are you working there?"

I nod, my throat constricting and not allowing me to talk. This was a bad idea. I feel awkward and unconfident and unwanted. Why do I need to know this stranger sitting in front of me? I got this far in life without him.

"Excuse me for a second." I slide out of my chair and grab my purse, bolting for the restroom.

Behind closed doors, my phone vibrates in my purse, and I pull it out to see my mom's number. I shake my head. I can't deal with that right now too.

There's a string of text apologies from Dana, but I'm not mad at her. I should've never lied to my mom in the first place or put Dana in the middle. I glance at Austin's message from earlier, and I smile.

Me: *I think I made a mistake.*

The three dots appear instantly.

Austin: *No, you didn't.*
Me: *How do you know?*
Austin: *Because you moved five thousand miles away to*

find him. No matter what happens, you obviously had to do this.

Austin: *Want me to meet you somewhere?*

Me: *No, I'm fine. Just trying to figure out why I wanted to meet him now that I am.*

Austin: *Because you wanted to know him. You might not get the answers you want, but it's your right to ask them. Just remember, you're the strongest woman I've ever met.*

My heart flips over. If he wasn't so supportive, it'd be so much easier to deny my growing feelings for him.

Me: *Thanks.*

Austin: ;)

I tuck my phone back into my purse and head out to the table. My dad is on his phone, but he hangs up when he sees me crossing the restaurant.

"You okay?" he asks.

"Yeah, sorry." I place my purse on the back of the chair and sit down.

The waiter must have come and poured the wine while I was in the restroom. I take a small sip.

"Are you living up here now?" he asks, ignoring the fact that I abruptly left the table.

"Yes. It's temporary though. I'll be leaving in two months."

"Oh, that's not a lot of time," he says.

Is that disappointment I hear in his voice?

"I'm here to replace the principal while she's on maternity leave."

"I had no idea. After you turned eighteen, your mom stopped sending me any updates."

My breath hitches. "My mom sent you things?"

He smiles as though they were treasured moments. "Yeah, every year, she sent me five or six photos and a letter of what you'd been up to. I was so proud when you got accepted to Yale."

But not proud enough to call me. "I'm sorry. I have to ask this…"

He leans back in his chair, his arms on the armrests.

"How could you be proud of someone you didn't even know?" I ask.

His jaw clenches. "You're half me. I'd like to think you got those qualities that led you to that kind of success from me. Did your mom tell you I graduated from Notre Dame? It's not Yale, but considering your mom didn't even go to college—"

Rage zaps through me like lightning, and I purse my lips, counting to ten before I embarrass both of us. I throw my napkin on the table. "I'm sorry, Clint, but I think this was a very big mistake on my part." I grab my purse and stand from the table.

"Holly," he calls, but I put up my palm to stop him.

I weave through tables of people laughing and enjoying their dinners. At the front door, I bend over at my waist and catch my breath while tears prick my eyes.

"Holly?" a familiar voice says.

I look up and run right into Austin's arms, letting his large frame swallow me up as the tears burst from my eyes.

"It's okay. It's okay." He runs his hand down my hair and my back, and I soak in the feelings of comfort and safety.

"Austin?" A female voice behind him alerts me that we're not alone.

I move out of his arms, though he takes my hand before I can pull away completely.

"Rome, Savannah, go ahead and take my Jeep. I'm going to drive Holly home." He gives the keys to his brother, who looks like a younger version of himself.

"Sure thing," Rome says.

"Come on."

He drags me toward the door, and once we're out beside my car, he digs through my purse and finds the keys. He helps me into the passenger seat, rounds the SUV, and starts the car.

"How are you here? Why?"

Austin starts the car then shifts to face me. "My brother is a chef, and he was looking at a restaurant that's for sale. He wanted Savannah and me to have a look with him."

Embarrassment scorches my cheeks. "Oh, I'm sorry. You go do what you have to do. I'm fine."

He tucks one lock of hair behind my ear. "We're done. The place wouldn't pass inspection, and he'd prefer a place in Lake Starlight anyway. We were just going to grab something to eat before heading home." He pauses. "Why are you in Greywall? I thought your dad lived in Sunrise Bay?"

"He wanted to eat here."

Austin's eyes close briefly, obviously understanding without me having to explain it. "Let's get you home."

He backs out of the parking spot, and I tell myself that it's okay to let him help me feel better tonight, given the circumstances. If there was ever a time to go against the rules we set for ourselves, it's now, right?

TWENTY-FIVE

Austin

The entire ride home, I stop myself from turning the car around, strolling back into that fancy-ass restaurant, and knocking Holly's dad on his ass. She hasn't revealed what has her so upset, but I can't say I didn't think this would happen. A man who can stay away from his daughter her entire life isn't deserving of a relationship with her.

I pull into her driveway and park in the garage. "Did you eat?"

She shakes her head, grabbing her purse and climbing out.

"I'm going to run to Slice of Heaven Pizza. I'll be right back."

"I'm not hungry," she says, looking sad and vulnerable.

"Maybe not now, but just in case. You can always heat it up later."

I meet her at the back of her SUV before she heads to the house, and I wrap my arms around her waist, pulling her into me. "I'll be right back." I kiss her temple, and she nods. "Get dressed in your pajamas, okay?"

She nods.

By the time I knock on her front door with a pizza in hand, the lights are on in her house. I don't give a crap about Buzz Wheel. I'm over that shit.

She opens the door, grabs my arm, and tugs me into her house. "Austin."

"I don't care anymore," I say as she slams the door as though the paparazzi are snapping pictures on her front porch.

"Well, I do."

"Why?"

She blows out a breath, takes the pizza, and walks into the kitchen. "Not now. I don't want to talk about us."

"Can I ask you a question?" I grab a water from the fridge, but my gaze shoots to the bottle of white wine on the counter, so I exchange my water for one of the six beers in her fridge.

"No." She pulls two plates from the cabinet.

"Have you ever thought about going to California?"

She stills for a second then glances at me. "Don't. Not tonight."

"So, you're up for this conversation another night?"

She rolls her eyes and plops a piece of pizza on a plate.

I know we had an agreement, but after my conversation with Fay, my mind kind of went crazy. I'm not staying here, but neither is Holly, and she'll be unemployed, so technically she'd be able to move wherever she wanted. Is it crazy to ask her this, since the two of us haven't been together that long? Probably. But I'm not ready to give her up yet. That much I've been able to admit.

"Okay, fine. We'll put that conversation on the back burner—for now."

She probably doesn't feel the same way. Maybe I'm good as a friend and a fuck buddy to her, but that's all. My chest feels tight at that thought, but I push it aside, knowing she really does need someone in her corner right now.

"So, what did your dad say?" I ask.

She shakes her head. "I don't much want to talk about that either."

"Okay. We could talk about the weather, or if you want, we could read Buzz Wheel." I take our plates to the table, and we both sit down.

She lets out a frustrated breath. "He actually said that I got into Yale because he's smarter than my mom."

I cringe. "He said that?"

"Not in those exact words, but that was the gist. Can you believe it? He takes me to that expensive restaurant my mom would have to work an entire week to afford and then says that." Her head falls to the table. "Add on that I lied to my mom when I came here and she just found out where I am, and it has not been a good night." She looks at me. "What have I done to my life?"

I slide my chair out and open my arms. "You've done nothing except try to connect with your dad. That's not a bad thing." My phone buzzes inside my pocket, but I ignore it.

She gets up from her chair, sits in my lap, and puts her head on my shoulder. Her usual vanilla scent makes my dick stir. Would it do that if I had her with me every day?

"I feel like an idiot, and my mom is probably so sad right now."

I cup the back of her head with one hand and rub her back with the other. "Why don't you call her?"

I feel a little out of my element here. I hugged Phoenix and Sedona when they were eight and crying because they missed our parents. I would whisper promises of how much our parents loved them and were watching over us. This time, I don't have a clue what to say to make Holly feel better. How do I comfort someone whose parent doesn't want her in his life?

"I probably should get it over with." She turns to check the clock. "She should be off work by now."

She climbs off my lap, but I yank her back down and hug her, kissing her neck below her ear. "I meant what I said. You are an amazing person, and your father is a jackass for not seeing that."

A small smile crosses her lips as she slips from my lap and heads into the living room.

I pick up my pizza when my phone buzzes again, reminding me of the text. Holly is talking in the other room, so I figure I'll answer it while I have the time. There's a missed call from Rome from a half hour ago and two text messages, so I slide those open.

Rome: *I need you to come back and head to the Greywall Police Department.*
Rome: *Never mind. Forget I messaged you.*

What the hell? I dial his number, but Holly walks back in with the phone clutched in her hand, so I end my call.

"What did your mom say?" I ask.

"I got her voicemail. She's probably so mad at me that she's decided to forget I exist, so I left a message."

I open my arms, meeting her halfway across the room.

"A little dramatic?" she asks, leaning into my arms, her own at her side.

"Maybe a tad." I chuckle, and the feeling of her back vibrating from her own laugher warms my heart. My phone rings and I pull back to take a look. Rome's name flashes on the screen. "Sorry, let me just grab this quick."

She nods, and I head into the living room, sliding my thumb over the screen.

"What's going on?"

Rome laughs. "Sorry, it was a prank."

But the loud noises behind him and the walkie-talkies I can hear says it wasn't.

"Rome," I say through gritted teeth.

He sighs. "Okay, it's not, but damn it, you should've told me how crazy Savannah gets over this Clint Edison guy. She saw him in the restaurant and went crazy."

Shit. I pinch the bridge of my nose. With everything going on, I forgot to follow up with her on the issue of him trying to steal our client.

"But I got Liam coming," Rome says, trying to assure me.

"Liam? He'd usually be the one joining Savannah in a cell, wouldn't he?"

"Well, he's the only one I knew who'd have the bail money. I didn't want to call grandma."

"Bail?" I shake my head.

Holly comes into the room, and my stomach turns as all the events from this evening unfold. Rome, Savannah, and me heading to Greywall, finding Holly there after meeting her father, and now Savannah has been arrested because of a confrontation with Clint Edison.

I stare at Holly for a moment. How did I not put this together?

"What did Savannah do?" I ask, admiring Holly's auburn hair. It might be a shade more orange than Clint's, but Clint is graying already. Maybe I'm wrong. I blink, but still, I see some of Clint's features in Holly.

"She picked a coffee mug up off a table and threw it at him. It hit him in the nose, and he filed charges."

"You're shittin' me, right?"

"Nope. It was funny. I mean, except for the police being involved. But that man does something to her. Who is he anyway?"

I shove my hand through my hair. "Long story. About five years ago, he moved his operation to Sunrise Bay, and he's been trying to poach our clients ever since. He's been successful more than once. He plays dirty—lies, cheats, who knows what else—and he's trying to take down Bailey Timber Corp."

"Fuck him. If I'd known, I would've used my fist, not a damn coffee mug."

Holly puts her arms around my waist and rests her head on my chest. She has no idea what I just figured out, what it means. If she did, she'd never be cuddling up to me right now.

"Rome? I gotta go. Tell Liam I'll pay him back." After I hang up, I nudge her chin up and place a chaste kiss on her lips with the fear that I'll never do that again. "Let me ask you a question."

"Okay." A crease forms between her eyebrows.

I savor this moment between us before it all changes. She looks at me as though she never wants me to leave, and I see her only as Holly Radcliffe, the woman who's slowly weaseling inside my heart every day, not the daughter of my family's sworn enemy.

"How is..." I steal one more kiss, savoring the soft touch of her lips and closing my eyes. "Clint Edison?"

Holly's eyes widen.

Fuck, this is one time I wish I was wrong.

I stuff my phone into my pocket.

"Austin." She steps back. "What happened?"

"If I'm right, then my sister threw a coffee mug at your dad's face, and now she's in jail and he's pressing charges."

Her hand covers her mouth. "No."

"Is your dad Clint Edison, owner of North Forest Lumber Company?"

She nods.

Son of a bitch. Or bastard, as it were.

"Why? Why would Savannah...?"

"Because your dad is a fucking asshole and is doing his best to kill Bailey Timber. Shit." I pace, pushing a hand through my hair. "This is crazy."

Her phone rings. "Seriously, we need to shut off our phones."

"Answer it. I need time to think anyway."

She heads back into the kitchen. All I hear her say is, "How did you get this number?" She continues on. "Yeah, okay... yeah, me too. Okay."

I sit on the couch, getting dizzy from circling the small space.

"Sure... yeah, that sounds good. Talk to you then. Bye." She walks back into the living room and sits next to me on the couch. "That was my dad. He apologized and said he wants to start over."

I glance at her, my fingers itching to thread through her hair. "Magnificent."

Her hand lands on my leg. "This doesn't change anything, does it?" Her small voice tells me she knows it does.

"No, because we're only fun, right?" I smack on a smile.

She doesn't smile.

"I'm going to head out. I have to deal with this situation with Savannah." Rome and Liam have it handled, but I need some time to think. Thinking clearly with Holly in the room is near impossible because all I see, all I smell, all I want is her.

"Okay. Thanks for tonight," she whispers.

"Sure." I walk to her front door.

"Do you want to take some pizza with you?" She points behind her to the kitchen.

"Nah, I'm not really hungry anymore." I look at her one more time. Clint's conniving face masks the beautiful woman I've come to... I shake my head. Don't even go there.

"Okay."

"See you tomorrow."

I leave without looking back and head past Main Street for a mile until I walk up the sidewalk to a two-story house with a flowery wreath on the door and a welcome mat on the stoop. I ring the doorbell and hear voices approaching on the other side. The door opens.

"Austin," Jack says. "You look like hell."

"I need a drink." I walk past him while Jack glances at Francie with concern.

TWENTY-SIX

Holly

I pull out my laptop after Austin leaves, searching Bailey Timber Corp and North Forest Lumber Company. There it is. A rivalry that's existed the last five years, ever since my dad moved his company here, documented in the local online newspaper.

I sink into my couch, reading the horrible things my dad has done to them. Poaching customers with promises of lower prices and then not sticking to it. Bailey Timber accepting the customers back at the lower cost my dad promised when his company couldn't deliver. Spreading lies about Austin's family's business to make it seem like they were shutting down and workers were going to lose their jobs. One article implied that my dad's company might have something to do with a fire that destroyed some of Bailey Timber's harvesting land, causing them to miss an important delivery date for one of their largest customers.

My eyes close, unable to read the nasty words about my dad any longer. He can't be that bad, can he?

Moving my search to California, I look up teaching jobs. Maybe I could go there with Austin. Was he serious when he asked me? If he was, would he still want me to join him now? I scroll through a few listings then shut the laptop, my mind a complete mess. What am I doing?

Dialing Dana, I wait, praying she's on break.

"Figured you'd call," she says.

"I think I'm in trouble."

"Well yeah, Karen's probably calling the authorities and telling them you escaped a mental asylum." She laughs, but I can't find it within myself to do the same.

"No. I think I really like Austin." I throw the words out there fast, as though they'll be less true the faster I say them.

"I know," she says nonchalantly.

"How do you know?"

"Because you're you."

I don't even know what she means by that. "You're never going to believe what happened."

"What?"

I picture the meme of Michael Jackson eating popcorn, because I'm sure that's what she's like on the other end of the phone right now. "My dad owns Austin's family's company's biggest competitor's company."

"Sorry, say that again?"

"Austin's family owns Bailey Timber Corp."

"Yeah, I got that from Buzz Wheel."

I roll my eyes. "My dad owns North Forest Lumber Company."

"Okaaay."

"They hate one another. I just googled it, and my dad has done some unthinkable things to try to ruin their business."

"Can't say I'm surprised. He left you when you were a baby. Not exactly a stand-up guy."

"Well, we just figured it out because Austin's sister threw a mug at my dad and—"

I'm interrupted by Dana's laughter. "These Baileys are awesome. I want to be an honorary Bailey when I grow up."

"Okay. Focus. What do I do? He just left, and the look on his face said I disgust him."

Her laughter seizes. "Oh, isn't this so much more fun than when you'd go to those knitting classes?"

I roll my eyes. "Once. I went once because I wanted to knit you a hat."

"I live in Florida. I don't need a hat."

"One day you will, and you'll say, 'Thank goodness Holly was so nice and knitted me this gorgeous hat.'"

She guffaws. "Whatever. Anyway, who the hell cares who your father is? The two of you don't work there. And besides, you don't even really know your dad. It's not like you had any part in his evil ways."

"You don't understand."

You'd have to be in this town to see and understand what Bailey Timber Corp means to this place. You'd have to have seen the devastation in Austin's features when he fit all the pieces together.

"The better question is what are you two going to do when you both have to leave?" she asks.

I fall back onto the couch. "I don't want to broach the subject, but before all this happened tonight, Austin brought up the idea of me going to California with him, and I shut the conversation down."

She laughs. "Then why are you calling me to tell me you really like him now?"

I massage my temple with my free hand. "You know the whole 'take it away and you want it more' thing..."

She laughs again. Good to know my disaster of a life is amusing to someone. "Gotcha. Now that you think he's not going to come back, you realize how much you love him?"

"I didn't say I was in love with him. I'm just saying I like him a lot and I could maybe want more than..."

"His dick. You can say it. It's me you're talking to."

My doorbell rings.

I groan. "For fuck's sake, someone's at my door." I paddle over and stare out the peephole. "I'll call you back."

"I knew I liked—"

I hit End and pull open the door. Austin steps in, kicks the door shut, and his hands are on my hips, lifting me as he smashes his lips to mine without a word. I match his pace, my hands running through his hair.

Eventually he rips his lips away from mine. "It doesn't matter who the hell your dad is." He kisses me again then pulls away. "To hell with my family. They won't care, and even if they do..." He stares into my eyes, and it's there. What I'm feeling is staring right back at me. "I don't."

Now it's me smashing my lips to his. He walks us to the couch, lowering me as his lips sprinkle kisses down my neck and his fingers fumble with the buttons of my blouse.

"You're so beautiful," he says, his palms pushing the silk off my shoulders.

He places open-mouthed kisses to my collarbone while fiddling with the button and zipper of my slacks. I sit up, helping him as my hand grips the edge of his T-shirt. He takes his neckline and tugs it over his head, then my back is on the couch and he's on top of me.

I place my hands on his face and pull him down, not

wanting to ever let a day go by again when his lips aren't on mine. He smiles through our kiss and I melt into the couch, feeling as though I have it all with him in my arms. To hell with the world falling apart around me. This is all I need right here.

TWENTY-SEVEN

Austin

The television illuminates the dark living room, and Holly's breathing is steady and low, her chest rising and falling next to me. Neither of us had the energy to make it up to her bedroom afterward, so we settled into the couch. As I gaze down at her, I wonder if she looks in the mirror and sees the gorgeous woman I do?

I wasn't in Jack's more than a couple of minutes before Francie pointed at the door and told me not to come back until I'd fixed it.

I'm still shocked that she's Clint Edison's daughter. The undercurrent of worry that spurred my initial reaction is still there, but I refuse to let it have power over me. Savannah's going to flip. Not that it's Holly's fault. If anything, she's a bigger victim than we are—the bastard abandoned her at birth.

The cutest purr sounds from her throat and she nuzzles closer to me, her hand running down the front of my bare chest.

"Why couldn't you have come into my life years ago?" I whisper, my knuckles dragging down her side. "We could have been something more."

"Hmmm," she mumbles and flips around so her back is to me.

My dick responds to her ass pressing against it, and I'm struck again by how easy she would be to fall for if I let myself.

I'm not some romantic who believes our life would be as easy as it is right now. Hardships come. Life puts rockslides in your way to force you to change lanes. We might only fit now because there's no pressure—we don't have kids, mortgages, in-laws. Not to mention Holly would be going from a family that consists of her mom and herself to my crazy family. There's sure to be obstacles.

My head falls to my bicep, and I turn off the television. Wrapping my arm around her and pulling her flush against me, I try to push it all from my head and live in the moment. If my parents' accident taught me anything, it was to enjoy the moment you're in because there may not be another one.

That's my only excuse for why I asked her to come to California—I was living in the moment. What was I thinking?

The annoying twenty-one-year-old who still lives inside me answers my question—you think you can have it all.

Then my thirty-year-old brain schools its younger self on the truth—no one gets to have it all. Take the baseball and run.

As the two versions of myself argue, Holly's little noises become my lullaby and I fall asleep.

KNOCK.

KNOCK.

"Holly!" a woman screams from the other side of the front door.

Her phone rings on the table.

KNOCK.

KNOCK.

KNOCK.

"What the hell?" I open my eyes and squint at the light streaming in.

Holly's still passed out in front of me on the couch.

I nudge her hip. "Holly, someone's at your door and your phone is ringing."

She moans and flips over, putting the pillow over her head.

"I guess I'll get it." I laugh, standing up, and realize I'm naked.

KNOCK.

KNOCK.

"*Holly!*" The voice grows more impatient, and her phone rings again.

"Coming," I say.

How in hell is Holly sleeping through this? I pick up my pants from behind the coffee table and shrug them on before walking to the front door. I peer through the peephole and spot a short woman with blonde hair, a phone to her ear, staring back at me.

I open the door. "Can I help you?" I run my hand down my face, trying to fully wake up.

Her eyes widen. "You can put on a shirt for one." She steps past me, rolling a suitcase behind her. "*Holly! Get up!*"

"Ugghhh!" Holly throws the pillow.

The woman catches it. "She's been like this since birth." She smiles back at me then points at my bare chest. "Shirt?"

I blink out of my daze and hurry across the room, where I pick up my T-shirt off the floor.

"Who are you?" she asks.

My gaze flicks to Holly who's somehow rolled over, so her face is pressed into the back of couch. "Austin."

Her gaze flows down my body and her jaw clenches. "I guess it's safe to assume…"

Our attention moves to her naked daughter on the couch, nothing but a blanket covering her.

"Well." I shrug.

"She's thirty, it's not like I think she's a virgin, but… are you the one who pushed her to come here?"

"What?"

"Sorry. Not sure why I would assume that." She throws the pillow at Holly and steps over to me with her hand out. "Karen Radcliffe, Holly's mother."

I figured, but the confirmation makes my face heat. "Austin Bailey, Holly's… friend."

Her mom smiles at me. "A good friend, I hope. My daughter is not some hussy who sleeps around."

"We've developed a friendship," I answer.

"*Holly!*" Her mom screams one more time.

Holly jerks and turns around, her dazed eyes searching the area.

"Like I said, she's been like this since birth. I mean, she slept all the time, which was awesome for a single mother, but scared the heck out of me a few times too."

"Mom?" Holly rubs her eyes and sits up, the blanket falling to her waist and exposing those delectable tits I feasted on last night.

My dick stirs and I force the thought of morning wood

aside, turning around so I can one, adjust myself in my pants, and two, not ogle this woman's daughter's tits with her as a witness.

I hear Karen pick up Holly's blouse and toss it to her. "Here."

"Thanks."

I turn back around to see that Holly's still half asleep as she buttons one button and then falls back down to the couch.

"You've not seen her like this before?" Karen asks me, her eyebrows raised.

I shake my head. "I haven't."

Karen sits on the couch, placing her hand on her daughter's arm. "Holly, sweetie, your mother is here with your boy..." She looks at me. "Friend. I'm fairly sure you don't want me telling him embarrassing stories."

Holly's head turns to me. I wave.

Her eyes widen and shift to her mom. Her mom waves.

She cringes. "This is a dream, right?"

"Nope. Although I appreciate the early morning eye candy, it's time for some answers," Karen says.

Holly slowly slides up the couch as her eyes soak in what's happening. "Oh."

"I should let you two have some time alone." I slide on my socks and shoes.

"It's okay," Holly says, and her eyes are begging me not to go.

"Holly's mistaken. I need a little time with my daughter," Karen clarifies.

"I understand." Picking up my coat on the chair, I look at Holly. "I'll see you at school."

She nods. "Yep."

I put my hand in front of Karen. "Nice to meet you. Maybe we can have dinner one night while you're in town."

She shakes my hand. "I plan on being here until Holly returns to Florida with me, so I'm sure we can arrange that."

"No, Mom, why would you stay?" Holly asks.

"Because..." Her motherly lecture voice starts, but then she smiles sweetly at me. "Have a good day, Austin."

I wave goodbye and step out onto the streets of Lake Starlight.

Let's hope that doesn't make it onto Buzz Wheel.

TWENTY-EIGHT

Holly

My eyes follow Austin as he winks goodbye before closing the door.

I smile. We broke the agreement and slept together all night, but I don't think I've slept that soundly since college.

A pillow smacks me in the head.

"Mom!" I scream.

"Get that look off your face. We need to talk about the fact that you lied to me."

I flip my legs to hang off the couch. "Can I get dressed first?" I stand and secure the blanket around me.

"Fine. I'll make us some coffee."

"What time is it?" I look for my phone and find it on the table. "It's six in the morning."

"I took the red-eye."

"You didn't have to do that." I head over to the stairs.

"When my daughter lies to me, I do."

"I have to get ready for work." I climb the first two steps. "This will have to wait."

"It will not. I'm making coffee, hurry up. We're having this conversation." She disappears into the kitchen and banging around commences.

I groan and head up the stairs, my mind far away from my father and on the fact that Austin spent the night and my mother is now here.

When I'm in the shower, I close my eyes. Austin never far from my mind as I wash my body, remembering his hands exploring me last night—both times we had sex. The way his thumb lightly strummed my clit, or when he slowly inserted one finger, then another, surprising me. His magical tongue that sent shivers up my spine every time he licked me. His deep groan when he sank into me. The dilation of his pupils. How soft his hair is.

KNOCK!

"Stop daydreaming and get out here," my mom yells from the other side of the door.

I miss how peaceful it was, living by myself.

I step out of the shower, dry myself off, and rub lotion into my skin, the same thoughts plaguing me. By the time I'm dressed and heading downstairs, I'm preoccupied with wanting Austin and his mouth, hands, and dick again.

"Finally," my mom says, pouring my coffee and setting it in front of me. "I'm going to the grocery store today." She opens the fridge. "How do you survive on white wine, beer, and leftover pizza?"

"I go to the diner a lot," I mumble over my coffee cup.

My mom makes the best coffee in the world, and I exhale in satisfaction after my first sip. I guess when it's the main thing you serve at a diner, you master it.

"I told you, diner food is so unhealthy."

"You work at a diner," I argue.

"Exactly. Mother knows best." She sits down, shooting me a smile.

I raise my eyebrows. "Maybe in this case."

My relationship with my mother is the easiest relationship in my life. She's my friend when I need her to be and my mother when I need her to be. She can weave the two roles masterfully, and when I become a mother, I hope I'm as good at it as she is.

She shakes her head, but a smile plays on her lips. "I did miss you, sweetie." Her hand covers mine on the table.

"I missed you too."

"I thought we didn't lie to one another?"

I look at the table, circling my coffee mug with my hands. "I didn't want to worry you."

"So, you'd rather have me charge a last-minute ticket to Alaska and worry about you for twelve hours?"

"Mom," I sigh.

"Hol, I get the fascination with your dad. I wouldn't have liked you coming up here, but I would've understood your reasons."

"I just... I didn't want anyone to know because..."

She squeezes my hand and nods. "You were afraid if he pushed you away, you'd have to tell people."

I nod, a tear slipping down my fresh layer of makeup. "It seemed easier to face the disappointment without seeing it on your face."

She squeezes my hand again. "I understand that, but I'm your mom, and my disappointment comes from seeing you hurt."

"It's embarrassing. Having a dad who really doesn't give a shit whether he knows me." I swallow back a sob. "I mean, you should've seen him last night. There was no remorse."

She exhales a deep breath. "I can't say I'm surprised."

"Why doesn't he care whether he knows me or not?"

"I wish I could answer that, but..." She places her hand on my cheek, meeting my gaze. "Don't let your father's faults devalue your worth. You are the best thing that ever happened in my life. You are the light I find every morning—my sun rising in the east." She repeats the mantra she's told me since I realized I had a father who didn't want to be a part of my life. "I know he's your father, but... he's an asshole."

I laugh.

"I'm serious, and not just because he doesn't care for you like he should. That's just him. He thinks only of himself."

"Did you know he's married with three kids?"

The widening of her eyes answers my question.

"Did you really send him pictures and a letter every year?"

"He told you that?"

"Yeah." I sip my coffee.

"I'm surprised. Thought he'd play the victim and try to tell you that I'd denied him visitation and kept you from him or something." She leans back, bringing her coffee cup to her lips.

"I followed him for a few nights before I reached out to him. He took his young daughter on a date." I stare at the table, the mug warm between my palms.

"Oh, Hol."

I nod. "I thought I was well-adjusted, but I'm starting to think I'm messed up."

"You're just still that little girl who wants a daddy to take her to the dance. Maybe I should've tried harder to find another man. One who would've stepped into his place."

I look at my mom. She's always been independent.

There have been men, a few serious boyfriends for a while, but no one she ever wanted to settle down with.

"Are you scared to love?" I ask.

She chuckles. "No. I just have high expectations, and when you were little, I didn't want to sacrifice any time with you. I'm selfish." She shrugs like who the hell cares.

"I'm glad you were selfish," I admit.

"Me too."

We sit in silence for a moment. Just like when I was a little girl, there's nothing she can do to change the situation. You can't force someone to care about you. You'd think since I've always known my dad didn't want anything to do with me, I wouldn't still seek out his love.

"Are you going to tell me about Austin?" My mom smiles over the rim of her coffee mug.

My head falls to the table. "That's a whole other dilemma I don't need in my life."

"Didn't look like much of a dilemma when he answered the door half-dressed."

I laugh, sitting back up.

"He's definitely a cutie, and although I'd prefer never to walk in on my daughter's sexual escapades again, I do want the details about the boy."

"It's a long story." I check the clock.

"Well, I have nowhere to be."

I nod and tell her everything, minus the fact her daughter made the Buzz Wheel blog. Some things are best kept to yourself.

TWENTY-NINE

Austin

Once school is dismissed, I drive over to Bailey Timber Corp. Savannah needs to be the first to hear the news about who Holly's dad is.

I walk down the hall toward Savannah's office. All the employees are in their last couple hours of work, trying to finish everything before they go home. I get a few waves and a couple heys, but no one stops to talk to me, which I'm thankful for. Right now, my mind is set on getting this out of the way.

I stand in front of Savannah's assistant's desk. "Hey, Sabrina."

She looks up over the rim of her black glasses. "Austin!" She stands and rounds the desk. "Savannah didn't say you were coming in today." She hugs me and steps back, smiling.

"Yeah, she doesn't know. Is she busy?"

She shoots me a look that suggests Savannah is always busy.

"Just ten minutes," I say, thinking this conversation will probably go longer than that.

"She's with your grandma. Let me buzz in and see what's going on." She rounds her desk and hits the speaker button.

"Yeah, Sabrina?" Savannah answers over the speakerphone.

"I have Austin here."

Sabrina's voice is so chipper, I wonder how she keeps up with it when Savannah's her boss. Not that my sister's a terrible person to work for, but her work persona and the one she has with the family are very different.

"Okay, tell him to give me... what, Grandma? Send him in, Sabrina."

Sabrina smiles and motions for me to go in.

"Thanks." I walk in.

Savannah's obviously had a hard day. Her hair is up in a messy bun, and her blouse is untucked from her pants.

"What's going on?" I ask, closing the office door.

Grandma Dori pats the couch cushion next to her. "Just business. How are you, dear?" She leans in, and I kiss her cheek as I sit down.

Savannah plops into the chair adjacent to us. "It's that dickwad again. Just so you know, I'm almost ready to go to jail for arson."

"What happened now?"

"He's actually going to press charges on me!"

Savannah sounds surprised, but I'm not. She did hit him with a mug. Knowing everything I do about the guy, I'm not surprised that he'd use this opportunity to his benefit.

Grandma Dori nudges me. "You and the principal weren't even in Buzz Wheel last night. It was all about my granddaughter." She looks at Savannah with a proud glint in her eyes.

"You get upset with me because I was in my Jeep with a woman and Savannah gets arrested and you're happy?" I ask incredulously.

She pats my sister's knee. "I'm proud of her. I wish her arm was stronger and she would've broken his nose, but it was the effort that counts." She winks at Savannah, who rolls her eyes.

"So, what's it going to mean for you if he presses charges?" I ask, looking between my sister and grandma.

"Fines, community service, maybe anger management classes. It's ridiculous. If I'm going to pay for this, I wish I would've broken his nose." Savannah stares out the window.

"I think it's about time I go talk to him," I say.

Savannah whips her head in my direction and narrows her eyes. "*No!*"

"Why not?"

"I don't need some man to come in and save me. I'll do it myself." She walks over to her small bar fridge and grabs a water.

"I'm not trying to save you. I'm trying to help."

"No, Austin. I can handle it."

Grandma Dori pats my thigh. "Your sister is tough. She can handle this. You." She sticks out her bottom lip and moves her head from side to side.

I rear back. "What? You think I'm weak?"

Grandma Dori shrugs.

Savannah giggles, opening her water bottle.

"You think I couldn't have taken over this business?"

Savannah giggles some more. Grandma Dori's eyes widen.

"Just say it."

My grandma pats my leg again. "We all have our strengths."

"But being tough isn't one of mine?"

"Let me put it this way. If you had thrown the mug, you would've broken his nose, but convincing him to drop the charges? Savannah is the gal to handle that."

I lean back and cross my arms.

"Enough with your depressed puppy dog eyes," Savannah says. "There's a reason I took the company and you took the kids, remember?"

I do actually. I would've really sacrificed my future had I tried my hand at the business. Even when I interned with Dad—after he lectured me about needing a back-up plan in case baseball didn't pan out—I sucked. Confrontation that needs to be solved through negotiation isn't my thing. Neither are balance sheets and payroll. Running a team— which is how I looked at my younger siblings when I first took responsibility for them—was definitely in my wheelhouse.

"Forget Clint Edison. Why are you here?" Savannah sits down and leans forward, eager to hear what I have to say.

She won't be so eager after I say it.

"Well..." I glance at my grandma. She looks good. Healthy. She can handle this news. My attention veers to Savannah. She's not smiling, but I'm sure she'll see that Holly's the victim here.

"What? Is it Phoenix?" Savannah prods. "Because I was thinking about it, and you should let her go with you to California."

"What? No, it's not Phoenix." She's definitely not going

with me to California, but that's a conversation for another time.

"Then what, sweetie?" Grandma Dori shifts in her seat to face me better.

"Well, you know how we ran into Holly in Greywall last night?"

Savannah points at Grandma Dori. "I was just telling her about that and how upset she seemed. What was wrong?"

"Holly is in Alaska for more than just the principal job. She took the job to get in contact with her estranged father, but..."

Savannah's eyes widen. Grandma Dori pats my thigh to encourage me to continue.

"Turns out she was having dinner with her father at that steakhouse in Greywall." I wait, but both of them sit there with curious eyes, not putting two and two together. "Her father is Clint Edison."

Savannah draws back as though I slapped her.

An inaudible sound grumbles out of Grandma Dori's mouth. "She was a sweet girl. I'm sorry, Austin."

Now it's me drawing back as though I've been slapped. "What?"

"I honestly thought she might be the one who would keep you here." Savannah gulps down her water, sharing a look with Grandma Dori.

"I'm not going to stop seeing her because of this," I inform them.

Their mouths drop open.

"She's Clint Edison's daughter?" Savannah says.

I nod. "The one *he* abandoned."

"Why would you keep seeing her? I thought it wasn't even serious, and now that you find this out... help me understand, Austin." Savannah sits up straight in her chair. "She's the enemy."

"*She's* not the enemy. Clint Edison is the enemy."

"How do you know this isn't some scheme for her to get intel on the company?" Savannah says.

I clench my fists.

"She was so very sweet," Grandma Dori says.

"She's not a spy. We're not the government. She doesn't even know him. She didn't know about the feud between our families until last night."

"So she says," Savannah says in a biting tone.

"You've got to be kidding me. You actually think she got close to me because I'm Austin Bailey?"

"You're so naive. Like we said, there's a reason I took responsibility for the business."

My heart pumps against my ribcage so hard it could make a dent as I try to keep my anger in check. "Are you so close-hearted that you actually believe what you're spewing?"

She glances at Grandma Dori and back at me. "That's harsh."

"So you're saying that Holly's using me? Does the news suck? Of course, but it's not her fault. She's not a spy, and this business has jaded you. Do you even hear yourself?"

"Now, now, kids. Calm down. We don't want everyone to hear you." Grandma Dori puts her hands up, but I'm just getting started.

I knew Savannah would be pissed, but not so much that she'd make up shit.

"You're putting your family at risk if you keep sleeping with her," Savannah says surprisingly calmly. "And by the way, Austin, everyone in Lake Starlight knows the two of you are screwing. You can keep on sneaking around, but it's common knowledge."

I shrug. I've lived here my entire life, so I figured people knew, but I tried to lay low for Holly's benefit. "It's not serious between us, but I'll be damned if I'm gonna let you cast her as the enemy here."

Savannah stands. "She is. Her last name is Edison."

I stand too. "Her last name is Radcliffe. Seriously, get a grip on reality!"

"Kids!" Grandma Dori yells.

Our heads shift in her direction.

"Stop. Who the hell cares? According to Austin, she's nobody important to him and they'll go their separate ways soon. You're fighting over nothing."

I pause at her words. *She's nobody important to him?*

"Fine. Whatever. But keep anything I tell you about the company to yourself. No pillow talk, lover boy." Savannah sits down in her desk chair and slides it into her desk.

My mind is still hiccupping over two words—*nobody important*. Holly *isn't* a nobody.

"You're delusional." I kiss my grandma's cheek and slam the door when I leave.

I pull out my phone, my thumb resting over Holly's name, ready to press the call button.

"Have a great night." Sabrina smiles even though I'm sure she heard our raised voices.

"You too, Sabrina."

I shove my phone back into my pocket and paste on a fake smile as I leave the building.

THIRTY

Holly

After another heart-to-heart with my mom last night, feeling unwanted by my dad has dissolved into the background. Maybe I'll develop a relationship with him and maybe I won't, but whatever happens, it doesn't mean I'm unlovable.

It's fourth period, Austin's free period to catch up on work, so I walk down the hall toward the bathroom as an excuse to pass by his classroom.

He didn't text or call me last night, said he had some marking to catch up on.

I glance into his classroom as I pass by, but he's not at his desk and his biology classroom is empty. Disappointment sets in, and my footsteps grow faster toward the bathroom.

Washing my hands since I don't really need to go the bathroom, I stare at myself in the mirror. *Who am I becoming?* A woman who purposely tries to put herself in front of a man to make him notice her? That's not me.

If Austin Bailey doesn't want to see or talk to me, I need to carry on with my life. How on earth do I think I'll be able to leave him in two months if I can't stand not seeing him for a single day?

On my way back to my office, I refuse to look into his classroom.

"Principal Radcliffe."

If only my body would be in agreement with my mind. Butterfly wings leave a fluttery feeling in my stomach at the sound of his voice.

I turn to face his open classroom door. He looks breathtaking in slacks and a button-down with the sleeves rolled up to his elbows, showing off his strong forearms. His hair is perfectly styled, and the extra scruff on his face completes the entire package.

How will I survive not seeing him every day?

"Do you have a moment?" he asks.

"Of course, Coach Bailey." I step into his classroom, seeing it's empty.

"Do you mind shutting the door? It's about a student and..." He lets the sentence hang there, and I wish I knew if he was saying it for others' benefit or whether it's the truth.

"Sure." I turn and shut the door.

"You can stay just like that."

I still.

"I do love to admire your ass." His shoes click along the linoleum behind me, each step bringing him closer, and a shiver runs up my spine.

I glance behind me at the windows. Thankfully, the blinds are all drawn.

"I had a movie day today," he whispers, his head nudging my ear and his hand sliding down my side until he grabs my ass.

I lift up on the balls of my feet as heat pools between my thighs.

"God, I missed you," he says in a rough, low voice.

The words a girlfriend would say are on the tip of my tongue. *Why didn't you call? You didn't have to miss me.*

"Yeah?" I say instead and swivel around to face him.

He steps into me. "How is your mom? I was giving you two, some time together." His mouth moves into the crook of my neck, kissing his favorite spot under my ear.

Was he really giving me time with my mom?

"She's good, but the bad news is that she's staying until I leave."

He steps back. "That puts a crimp in our plan."

I nod, fiddling with the buttons of his shirt. "We'll have to find somewhere else for our extracurricular activities."

"We may just have to take opportunities when they present themselves. Like right now." His hand slides up my thigh, and I lift it to rest on his leg. "You might just have to wear a skirt every day."

Goose bumps chase his fingers, and I squirm under his touch.

"We're in school." I put up a fight, but I'm so starved for him, I know I'll lose this battle.

"It's fourth period. No one is looking for me." He nibbles on the flesh of my earlobe. "I'm so hard right now." He slides my panties over, his finger sliding along the slickness of my folds. "Always so ready for me."

His seductive tone shatters the last of my resolve, and I lean back against the door in a silent offering for him to do with me as he wishes.

"I love when you agree with me." I feel his lips smiling against my collarbone.

He inserts a finger, arching it to hit the bullseye he

never misses. My hands jolt up and grab his shirt. He adds another finger as his thumb rubs slow circles around my clit. How did this man learn a woman's body so well?

I push that thought from my mind. I don't care. I don't need to care. Austin and I don't do that. There's no past and no future for us, there's just right now. It's supposed to be fun.

"Stay out of your head and with me, Hol," he says softly, his fingers sliding in and out of my slick heat, his thumb applying more pressure but not too much. He draws back, his aroused eyes locking with mine as I climb closer to coming undone.

"Jesus, Austin," I pant.

He steps closer, his hard dick straining against his pants. I desperately want to touch him, to fall to my knees and pleasure him the way he is me, but I'm selfishly taking what he's offering. I swallow, and he separates my legs farther. I raise one thigh higher up on his hip, allowing him the access to completely unglue me.

"I love watching you come." His eyes are fixed on me, and my wetness can be heard in the empty classroom as his fingers move faster, his thumb pressing harder.

"I can't hold on," I whisper.

Right as I'm about to break away to heights I've never imagined, he adds a third finger and covers my mouth with his other hand. I buck into him while blackness blocks my vision and tiny stars burst apart in my own personal universe.

When I regain my sense of self and open my eyes, Austin is staring at me with half-lidded eyes and an amused smirk.

"God, I love that." He withdraws his fingers and sets my panties back in place.

I bring my leg down and reposition my skirt. He looks like a happy man, but did he really think I'd leave him with blue balls for the rest of the day?

I drop to my knees, my fingers unhooking his belt and sliding down his zipper.

"You don't have to," he says.

But I want to. More than anything right now, I want to bring him the pleasure he just gifted me. I sneak a look up at him, watching him suck the fingers that were inside me. My insides clench with the familiar stir in my belly that only Austin can give me.

"Just so you know, I plan on really tasting you tonight."

With his promise, I smile, my hand sliding through his slacks to his boxer briefs. His dick is hard, thick, and heavy. I stare at him much like he did me as I wrap my hand around it, bringing it to my mouth.

He splays both hands on the door behind me, leaning over me as I lick his tip, his pre-cum salty on my tongue.

"Fuck," he growls. "I want to do so much to you right now."

I pump him with my hand, my mouth slowly swallowing him inch by inch.

He stays still, never directing my head, never bucking his hips to get farther down my throat. There's something alluring about that. I always liked it when a guy tugged on my hair or tried to push forward to get farther into my mouth, but Austin's patience and trust that I'll bring him where he took me makes me want to rock his world even more.

I guide him to the back of my throat, which appears to be his undoing. His nails scratch the wood of the door. After squeezing and pumping his hard length when I draw back, I hollow out my cheeks and suck him back in, wiggling my tongue around when my lips reach the base of him and he's breached the back of my throat

After a few minutes, he says in a gravelly voice, "I'm gonna come."

I don't let up in my efforts. My left hand runs up under him, playing with his balls, and he inches back, jerking in my mouth. I look up and our eyes lock as he pumps into me. I swallow and lick him clean before putting his dick back in his boxer briefs and zipping him up.

He pushes off the door, offering me his hand. "Fuck, you know how to do that too well." His hand lies on the side of my neck before moving to the back, bringing my face to his.

Our lips meet as the bell rings. Loud voices fill the hallway, and Austin draws the kiss to a close before we're caught.

"This timing sucks," he mumbles with a satisfied smile. "Tonight?"

"Sure."

"Dress in black. I'm sneaking you into my house."

The door handle jiggles, then someone knocks on the door.

"Hello, Buzz Wheel," I joke, stepping a good distance from him.

He laughs. "Who gives a shit? We're out of here in a couple months anyway, right?" He kisses me one last time before opening the door.

Kids barrel into the classroom, some clocking my presence and others oblivious as they chat with their friends.

"What's going on, Coach Bailey?" JP asks.

Elijah is right behind him with his arm swung over a small brunette. Obviously all is right in their world again.

JP eyes me. "Oh, I gotcha." He and Elijah fist-bump each other.

Elijah shakes his head. "On school grounds? I thought you'd set a better example than that?"

"If you must know, Principal Radcliffe and I were discussing your final."

Their amused faces dip into frowns.

"Thank you again for your help, Principal Radcliffe. You had some great ideas I think I'll put into action."

"Of course, any time, Coach Bailey."

I leave the classroom, weaving through a few students, already hearing their whispers. Once the classrooms are filled with students and the halls are empty, I lean against the lockers, catching my breath.

Who the hell am I these days?

Definitely not the Holly Radcliffe I'm familiar with.

But maybe the Holly Radcliffe I've always wanted to be.

THIRTY-ONE

Austin

Back home, I try to pick up around the house as best I can before Holly arrives. Sedona and Phoenix are staying at their friend's house. I don't really have to worry about Rome—he already knows, plus, it's Friday. He'll probably crash at Denver or Liam's. Brooklyn is with Jeff tonight, Kingston is still out of town, and since Juno is currently his roommate, she'll be sure to stay home and enjoy having the place to herself. Which should leave Holly and me alone.

"Why won't you take me with you on your interview?" Phoenix asks.

"Because USC is paying for me to go there. I'm not buying you a plane ticket."

Phoenix huffs from where she sits on the couch. "I don't get it. You're so hell-bent on leaving Lake Starlight because you feel like we stopped you from living your dream, but you won't let me live mine."

"First of all, you didn't stop me." I grab the food wrappers and put them in the popcorn bowl Rome failed to clean up last night and head to the kitchen, hoping Phoenix will stay in the family room.

No such luck. She follows. "Then why do you want to go to California so bad?"

I toss the kernels and papers in the trash, rinse out the bowl, and put it in the dishwasher. "Because I want to coach baseball at the college level and there's nothing up here but high school."

"Because you had to leave all that behind and come home to raise us. I get why you'd resent us, but let me come with you," she whines.

"Come with me. I'm going to Scotland with Jamison." Sedona walks in. Ever since she talked with Holly at school, she thinks it's set in stone that's she's going.

"You're not going." I point at Sedona. "You'll go to college, and then you can do whatever you want to do."

She rolls her eyes, grabs an orange out of the fridge, and leaves the room.

I turn my attention back to Phoenix. "I don't resent you."

"I would." She crosses her arms.

"Well, we're not the same people." I spray down the counter.

"Why are you cleaning? Is *she* coming over here?"

I'm thankful for the change of topic, but not for the way it went.

"Who?" I ask, playing dumb.

"The enemy. I heard all about the fact that she's Clint Edison's daughter."

I roll my eyes. This family is their own gossip wheel. "It has nothing to do with you, and no, she's not coming over. I'm not even seeing her."

"Please. I'm not an idiot. Do you know how horrible it is to hear that the two of you are having sex in your classroom? Someone said they found a condom." Her face distorts.

Mine does too. I wouldn't do that.

Then again, I really wasn't thinking when I allowed Holly to blow me. I mean, I wanted her so badly after only one night away from her. What the hell is wrong with me?

"How is that leading by example? I guess it was safe sex, but if I was screwing Pete Wertz in the chemistry lab, I'm sure I'd get expelled."

"Phoenix, I'm not in the mood for this." I move from the kitchen back to the family room.

"You're ruining my life."

I stop and turn to face her.

She's thrown herself on the couch next to Sedona, who keeps looking back and forth between us. I remember when they were eight and didn't fully understand that our parents weren't coming back. They'd cuddle on the couch and wait for me to invent some game for them to play because I was their fun older brother.

Now they're on the verge of adulthood. My heart aches for the regular sibling relationship we'll never have. The one that died with my parents against that tree.

I look at my two youngest sisters, and for the first time, I realize how far they've come. They're not little kids who need me to dictate their every move anymore. They're old enough to have an idea of what they want out of life. God knows I did when I was their age.

And here I am trying to live my life by leaving Lake Starlight, and I'm dictating what she does with hers. Both of them.

I sit down in the chair next to the couch.

Their eyes widen, sensing the change in my demeanor.

"You're right," I say.

"I am?" Phoenix asks.

I run a hand through my hair. "Yeah. I can't tell you not to live your dream while I leave to chase mine. I'd like you both to go to college. It's what Mom and Dad would've wanted. If you don't want to go, that's fine, but you don't get your college money until you're twenty-one. Same rules as Kingston. And you still need a plan for your future—college or not."

God, that felt good. The agony from the pressure of getting them to attend college lifts. Is this what I'll feel like in California? Like a thirty-year-old guy instead of a fifty-year-old man?

"Really?" they say simultaneously.

"Yeah. I have to let you make your own mistakes and live with the consequences of your decisions. Or maybe you'll beat the odds, but either way, me sheltering you isn't going to make you a better person." I slap my hands on my thighs, preparing to get up. "So, you girls do as you wish."

"Are you mad?" Sedona asks.

I turn around. I've fought so hard, I see why she's asking the question, but I'm not.

"No. I just hope you're making the right decision." I walk out of the room.

HOLLY RINGS THE DOORBELL AT SEVEN O'CLOCK. THE girls left at six, and they shouldn't be returning home. Rome and Savannah are looking at another location for a restaurant, then they're heading to Lucky's to meet Denver. Brooklyn came down a half hour ago with an overnight bag, saying she's staying at Jeff's for the entire weekend.

I straighten picture frames, hiding the one of my naked butt running through the field behind our house. My mom thought it was the cutest picture and showed it to everyone, so I don't have the heart to remove it permanently. I'll put it back tomorrow.

I half jog to the door and spring it open.

"Hey," she says.

"Hey." I motion for her to come in before I shut the door.

"So, I can just ring the doorbell and park in the driveway now?" She laughs.

"Don't worry. My family isn't around."

She takes in the interior of the house—picture frames, furniture, draperies. It's no decorating masterpiece. None of us has touched anything since my parents' deaths.

"Come in. Do you want a drink?" I ask, heading to the kitchen.

"Sure, whatever you have."

It's odd having her here. I didn't really think about it until now, but she's the first woman I've ever invited into my family's space. "I have some white wine?"

"Perfect."

"Head on into the family room and I'll be right there."

I pour two glasses of wine then find her on the couch, flipping through one of the magazines sitting on the table. I pass her the wine glass and sit next to her.

"Thanks." Her lipstick leaves a mark as she sips the wine. She leans back, looking at me as though I'm a stalker. "What?"

"Sorry. It's just..." I shake my head. "I guess I'm not used to having you alone."

She tilts her head. "We're usually alone at my house."

I nod. "Yeah, I guess." I grab the remote. "Did you want

to watch a movie? Did you eat? I could order something or whip something up?"

She laughs, placing her hand on my knee. "I'm fine and full. This is good." She brings the glass to her lips.

I blink. What is wrong with me?

"Are you sure you're okay?" she asks.

I look away. "Yeah, just a long day."

"I know. My mom being here is..." She tilts her head back and forth. "She wants to be at the next dinner with my dad, which won't turn out well, I'm sure. I think I've convinced her to wait around for me while I meet with him."

My hand finds hers as though we're teenagers and I can't bear not touching her for even a second. "When are you going to dinner with him?"

"Next week. He said he had to go out of town, so next Friday."

"Oh, I'll be in Cali for the interview."

She turns in her seat. "I completely forgot. I'm sorry. With my dad and my mom and the fact my dad is..."

"It's fine." I shake my head. "Who knows what will happen?"

"You're a total shoo-in." She nudges my shoulder. "Why aren't you more excited?"

I sip my wine. "I don't want to get my hopes up, you know?"

"I understand."

"You wanna hear something I think you'll find surprising?" I place my wine glass on the table. "I told the girls they can do what they want after high school. I'm not going to try to stand in their way."

Her eyes widen.

"I know, but damn, it feels good to have that settled."

"Do you mean it?"

I shrug. "You know, I've been so hell-bent on getting my siblings to do what my parents would've wanted, I lost sight of the fact that they aren't here. We don't really know how they would've handled it. I've done my best to guide them, but I realize now that their mistakes are theirs to make."

She kisses me. "You surprise me, Austin Bailey."

I place my hand on the back of her head, keeping her there for another kiss, and I slide my tongue into her eager mouth.

"Why?" I mumble over her lips.

"Just... I don't know. You always seem to do what's right. I mean, how could anyone doubt you should go to California? It doesn't seem like you've ever made a bad decision in your life." She rests her head on my shoulder.

I open my arms so she can snuggle into my chest. "Sure, I have."

"Really?" She pokes my stomach. "When?"

I look down at her. I've made plenty of bad decisions over the years, and I can only hope this next big life change isn't another one of them. "Do you think it's stupid? Me chasing this dream to California?"

She rests her chin on my chest and looks up at me. I tuck a strand of her auburn hair behind her ear. "You're asking a girl who left Florida to find the father who wanted nothing to do with her. I think there's a reason why people say you chase your dreams. Dreams don't knock on your door one day and announce that they're ready for you."

"They don't?" I ask with mirth, staring into her beautiful green eyes.

Her hand reaches up to my cheek. "You deserve to live the life you want."

I kiss her forehead, and she lays her head back down on my chest.

She gets me. She understands why I need to do this.

I slide down on the couch so she's lying on top of me, and we turn our attention to some show on the baking channel. My mind couldn't be further from who makes the better cookie.

THIRTY-TWO

Holly

I put in my earrings while walking down the stairs to join my mom, who insists on driving me to the restaurant where I'm meeting my father as if I'm fifteen and going on my first date.

"Guess what?" she says, standing in the kitchen with three bags of groceries on the kitchen table.

"What?" I open the fridge, searching through shelves lined with food for a bottle of wine.

"I got a job!"

I whip my head in her direction. "What?"

"I can't just sit here all day. I mean, you're busy at the school. I might as well earn a little money." She unpacks the groceries.

"Where did you get a job?"

"At the diner. I went in and explained my situation, told them about my experience. This man who doesn't even know me vouched for me. He told Rachel that she could use me during the weekend shifts, and she agreed. I start tomorrow morning."

"That's great!"

Go figure my mom has already settled in here. We moved around a lot when I was younger. All in Florida, but I changed schools numerous times, trying to escape neighborhoods that went downhill.

"I think so. Plus, it'll give you some extra alone time with Austin." She knocks elbows with me.

"Well, we only have a little over a month of that before we leave anyway."

My phone rings on the table and my stomach jumps, thinking it might be Austin. He was supposed to call me after the interview today, but I haven't heard from him yet.

"Huh. I don't know who this is." I slide my thumb over the screen. "Hello."

"Hi, Holly, this is Marc Robinson."

Marc is from the school board, and I'm surprised to hear from him on a Friday night. I grip the phone tighter.

"Good evening, Marc. Is something wrong?"

He hems and haws for a second as my anxiety grows. "Nothing wrong, per se, but we've received some surprising news."

"Oh." I wait for him to explain, glancing at my clock to see how much time I have before I have to leave.

"Principal Miller has decided not to return to work, which leaves us with an opening we need to fill."

It takes a second to absorb his words. "Oh."

He laughs. "That's my sly way of asking you if you'd like the job permanently, Holly. We've gotten so many compliments from the parents about your senior interviews, and if we could implement those earlier in the year, I think it'd give our seniors more opportunity to achieve success."

My hand moves to my chest. "Well, I have to say, I'm surprised. I wasn't thinking this was a possibility."

"Neither were we. Principal Miller had been adamant that she would be returning to work, but she's decided motherhood is her calling."

I sit there, thinking of everything this could mean. I glance at my mom dancing and singing to herself as she puts away the groceries. She hasn't been this carefree ever.

"We obviously don't expect an answer today," Marc says. "Take the weekend and think about it."

"Okay. Thank you."

"And Holly, we've heard the rumors regarding you and Austin Bailey. We don't like to endorse relationships between teachers and principals, but if you accept the job, we trust that the two of you will act in a professional manner."

Yep. I'm a *real* professional, blowing him in his classroom.

"Thank you so much for the offer. I'll be in touch next week."

"We're happy to offer it to you. You've been a wonderful asset to the Lake Starlight School District. We're eager for your response."

As I hang up, my mom must notice that something's wrong. She stops to sit down with me, and I let the phone slide onto the table.

"What's going on?" my mom asks.

"They offered me the principal's job on a full-time permanent basis. The woman I replaced doesn't want to come back."

My mom's hand covers mine. "Well, it's always nice to be wanted." She rises from her chair and goes back to putting away the groceries. "Should we leave soon so we're not late?"

She starts singing again, and though I'm surprised by her laissez-faire reaction, I'm more preoccupied with wondering what Austin will think of this. Will he like the idea of me staying?

I pick up my phone to press Austin's name. Then I remember he's in California and it doesn't matter if I stay here or not. He won't be here anyway.

"Yeah," I choke out. "I'll grab my jacket."

Good news shouldn't make me this depressed.

My dad picks a much different restaurant this time around. There's no fancy setup on the table, and this time he's dressed in jeans and a T-shirt a man his age probably shouldn't wear, but who am I to say?

"So, your mom is in town, huh?" he asks, ordering for us since he said he wants me to try something Alaskan. Whatever that means.

"Yeah, she's shopping while we have dinner."

He laughs. "She always was a control freak."

My defense is on the tip of my tongue, but I bite it back. She can be that way, and he didn't say it in a mean way. I have to accept their history isn't mine and his.

"I didn't mean that..."

I raise my hand. "It's fine."

He relaxes into his chair. "So, I got a visit this week from Savannah Bailey."

I tilt my head.

"I heard you're familiar with Austin Bailey?"

I nod but say nothing.

"I'm not sure if you heard, but after our last dinner, Savannah Bailey, who runs their lumber company, threw a mug at my face."

I snicker. "I did."

"I pressed charges, but in good faith of our budding relationship and after hearing that you and Austin Bailey are... well, friends, I've dropped them."

I can't help the feeling of warmth that settles into my chest that he did something because he thought it would make me happy. "That's nice of you. They're a great family."

He smiles, but it doesn't reach his eyes. "They own this area. It's been hard for me to get a leg up around here."

"Didn't you research them before coming here to open your business?" I sip my drink.

"At the time, they were still recovering from losing their parents."

I swallow the liquid before it spews out of my mouth. "What are you saying?"

The waitress sets a plate full of crab on our table, complete with claw breakers, melted butter, and cocktail sauce. We each get a baked potato on the side.

I'm the only one who says thanks to her before she smiles and heads to the next table.

My dad rubs his hands together, staring at the crab as though he hasn't eaten in a week.

"Clint?" I ask.

He looks at me, taking a second to remember my question. "If it wasn't me, it would've been someone else." He shrugs.

"You tried to take advantage when they were hurting?" I'm starting to wonder if there's anything redeemable about my father.

"It'd been a few years. They never should've put that business in the hands of a nineteen-year-old in the first place. The old bat was crazy to do so." He cracks open a crab.

I can only stare at him in horror. "They lost their parents."

He looks up and sees the expression on my face. "Relax. I think your friendship with Austin is clouding your view of what happened."

My voice hardens. "I don't think it is."

He pulls a piece of crab out of the shell, dunks it in melted butter, and as it drips along the table, he brings it to his mouth. He finishes chewing before responding. "Women are so sensitive. It was a power move."

"You were going to try to take them over?"

"I went to Dori—she reminds me of that blue fish from *Finding Nemo*. She wanders around like she hasn't a clue."

My gut clenches.

"Aren't you going to eat?" he asks, staring at the plate in front of me.

"She's kind and sweet and—"

"Uh oh, I see they've sucked you in. See? That's what that family does. They've put a net around that entire town. Let me fill you in—they aren't all angels. I've heard things."

I inhale deeply, anger clouding my rational thinking. "They're kind people, and gossip isn't reliable."

"I heard their dad, good ol' Tim Bailey, was screwing his secretary."

"From who?" Why am I engaging him? I understand how gossip works, how it gets exaggerated from one person to the other until it's an outright lie.

"Does it matter? He's six feet under now. Rumor is he

was a drunk, and poor Beth Bailey suffered because he was an alcoholic."

"You have no idea what you're talking about."

"Relax, it doesn't mean anything. The kids are taking everything over. Forgetful Dori was clear about that."

Before I can think, all the pain and rage of his disinterest in my life boils to the surface over his crass assessment of the Baileys and I pick up my glass and splash the contents all over his face. "Go to hell. Maybe I should enlighten everyone about you? How you abandoned your newborn daughter and could never spare one minute to call, one weekend to visit? How birthday after birthday, she sat there, and her only wish was for her dad to come visit?"

All eyes in the restaurant turn to us.

"Sit down," he bites out. "You've been in this town for two minutes. You don't know what you're talking about."

"I know that the Baileys are good people and you're not. You're a loser who tries to steal what other people build." I throw my paper napkin in his face and weave through the tables as hushed whispers erupt around us.

When I push open the doors, my mom is sitting on a bench across the road, waiting for me. She stands and opens her arms, and I cross the road and walk right into them.

THIRTY-THREE

Austin

"Finally!" Jordan, my buddy from college, hugs me, smacking my back. "It's been too long."

I sit down at the table in the bar where we planned to meet. "I know. It feels like a lifetime. I can't believe I forgot how bad the traffic is." I laugh. It took me forever to get from the airport to the hotel last night. "You must spend half your time in a car."

He laughs. "Well, the sun and beach make up for it."

A waitress comes over, and we each order a beer.

"How's life?" I ask.

He shrugs. "It's good. I heard Coach likes you. Of course, it helps that you have a great recommendation."

I nod. "Thanks again for setting the stage for me."

"Of course, man."

The interview was earlier today, and it went as well as it could. It was clear that if I got the job, I'd start low on the totem pole, that he has to put guys with more experience coaching at a Division One level before me. Which I understand.

"How's the family?" Jordan leans back and takes a long pull of his beer, his eyes on the waitress's ass.

"They're good. Phoenix and Sedona are graduating this year."

"They're the youngest, right?" His eyes are everywhere but on me.

"Yeah. Rome returned a few weeks ago."

"Is that the pilot?"

"No. The chef."

He nods, but I can tell he doesn't really know who I'm talking about. I can't fault him for that. We lost touch when he was playing professional ball and I was playing daddy. It's only been the last couple years that I reached out, knowing Phoenix and Sedona would be graduating and I'd be able to leave Lake Starlight.

"Oh shit." He waves at someone behind me. "I hope you don't mind, I invited my girl to join us. If she asks, I picked you up at the airport last night."

I glance behind me as two woman approach.

"And the other?" I ask with a raised brow.

He smiles at me. "That's my thank you for lying for me." He winks, and my stomach sours.

Jordan was always a player back in college, but after he got a one-night stand pregnant years ago, I thought for sure he'd have straightened out his act.

"Hey, baby." He wraps his arm around his girlfriend, kissing her neck and grabbing her ass.

She giggles and coos. "Stop it, Jordy."

"What can I say, I can't keep my hands off you."

I swallow the lump in my throat. I hate being put in these situations.

"This is my girl"—he slaps her ass—"Renee." He points at the other girl, who stands by my side and isn't shy in letting me know with her eyes that she wants me. "This is Sara."

"Sera," Renee corrects.

Jordan laughs. "Sera, sorry."

He sits back down, and the two women sit at the table with us.

"So, what do you do? Did you play too?" Sera asks, leaning forward so I can see right down her blouse.

Holly comes to mind, when she bent over her desk and I had a direct view of her cleavage. The difference being that Holly exudes class and this woman screams predator.

"No. I'm just a high school teacher."

Her lips dip and she sits back in her chair.

"But he's about to coach with me at USC," Jordan quickly fills in.

She smiles and leans forward again, biting the side of her lip.

Yeah, I don't need this shit.

"Excuse me," I say and head toward the bathroom.

In the hallway, I pull out my phone and pull up Holly's number. Instead of calling, I shoot her a text.

Me: *Hey, interview over. Just out for drinks with a buddy. Call you tonight?*

Three dots appear and I wait for her response.

Holly: *Sure. Just with my mom at Lard Have Mercy. How did it go?*

Me: *Good. Jordan thinks I might have gotten it.*

She sends me a bitmoji of her cheering with pom poms.

Me: *I wouldn't mind seeing you in a cheerleader costume.*
Holly: *I think this is a conversation we need to have when my mom isn't eating blueberry pie next to me.*

She puts the bitmoji with her laughing and her tongue sticking out.

Me: *Tonight then. Be prepared with a sexy voice.*
Holly: *LOL...I'll practice.*

She puts a wink emoji.

I've never missed Lake Starlight as much as I do right now.

"Hey, I thought you disappeared?" Sera approaches, and I shove the phone into my pocket.

"Just checking on things at home."

She steps in front of me, her hand on the wall next to my head, and slides a finger down the center of her cleavage. Is she for real?

"You have a family?" she asks, not pulling away.

"Kind of, but no wife or kids of my own."

She smiles. "You're so honest. I don't care if you do." Her eyes dip down my body, and she steps forward so her body is flush with mine. "Go ahead and touch if you want."

"I'm sorry." I shake my head. "I have somewhere to be, but it was nice meeting you."

I gently push her away by the shoulders, and her forehead scrunches. She's probably not used to being turned down. I walk down the hallway to the main bar. Jordan's tongue is down Renee's throat when I reach the table.

"Hey, Jordan, I gotta go. Something came up."

He turns as Renee sucks on his neck. "Something at home?"

I nod. "Kind of. Thanks a lot, and I'll talk to you tomorrow at the game."

"Sure thing."

I'm a step away when I have to wait for a line of people heading to their table to pass by.

"He have a family or something?" Renee asks.

"His parents died our senior year of college and he went back to raise his sisters and brothers."

"That's horrible. How many?" she asks.

"I don't know, like a dozen. People in Alaska sure don't know when to quit."

Renee laughs, and I leave the bar grinding my teeth.

INSTEAD OF HEADING BACK TO THE HOTEL, I TAKE A CAB to the beach.

The moon shines down on the ocean, and I snap a picture. The wish that Holly was here to see it with me settles into my bones no matter how I try to resist it.

The interview weighs on my mind. California isn't what I remember. Back then, it was all about the party and fun and I played ball year round. It feels different here now. I'm older, but still, there's this knot in my stomach that I can't get rid of.

My phone rings in my pocket and I take it out, expecting to see Holly's name, but it's a California number. I slide my thumb over the screen. "Hello."

"Austin." Coach Freeman's voice sounds happy. "I just finished talking to my guys."

I glance at the time. It's nine o'clock at night. Do they have lives outside the office?

"I know I mentioned that we planned to talk to other candidates as well, but what can I say? You impressed us. It's been a long time since I've heard a guy talk about the character of a ball player. Normally it's all about velocity off the bat and over the mound. Rarely do we hear a coach say he thinks that a player isn't all about his numbers."

"Well, it's something I try to teach my boys at Lake Starlight."

"I know, and that's why we just offered Elijah Crupe a full ride."

"What? That's amazing!" I know a lot of colleges are looking at Elijah, but he hasn't had anyone offer him a full ride yet.

"He's one of yours, so we'd like to ask you to come on board with us. But you should know that there's a slightly different plan than we originally talked about."

"Okay?"

"We told you that you'd be learning the ropes the first year, but we'd like you to take Jordan's place. I know you two are friends and he's the one who got you the interview, but between us, he was a better player than he is a coach."

I sit down in the sand, resting my elbows on my knees. "I don't know what to say."

And I don't. I've waited so long for this opportunity and now that it's here, I feel shell-shocked and unable to process what this means.

"Well, say you'll take the job."

"Can I think about it? I can't help but feel like I'm stabbing my friend in the back." I'm not sure that's something I can do.

"This isn't Lake Starlight, Austin. But you think it over. I think it's a tremendous opportunity for you. More than you were asking for. But we understand how a guy who talks about sportsmanship and handling yourself off the field won't take lightly that he'd be taking over his friend's job. Let me tell you this though—Jordan is out come next year whether you come on board or not. And of course, we'd appreciate your discretion where that's concerned."

"Of course. Thanks, Coach. I'll get back to you soon."

"You're welcome. Have a great night, and we'll see you at the game tomorrow."

"See you then."

I hang up and let my head hang between my arms, my phone dangling from my hands. I stare at the ocean again. The same one that extends all the way up to Alaska, where everything I've ever known is.

For the first time in forever, I pull up Buzz Wheel, wanting to see if Elijah made the page and what his reaction was. Although they never feature underage kids, Elijah just turned eighteen, so he's fair game now.

There's the current weather at the top, and a picture of Main Street across the header. There's no word on Elijah, but there is a piece that says the charges against Savannah have been dropped. Thank God. Looks like Grandma Dori was right, and Savannah was the one to deal with Clint Edison on that.

I scroll down and see Holly's name.

"What now?" I mumble.

Then I read the headline.

"Rumor has it Principal Holly Radcliffe might become a permanent fixture in Lake Starlight."

I read the article that says Miranda Miller has decided

to stay at home with her son and her job has been offered to Holly.

Huh. Why didn't she say anything?

I hammer out a text message.

Me: *How was dinner with your dad?*

The three dots appear quickly, like they usually do when I message her.

Holly: *Eventful. (Sad face emoji)*
Me: *I'm sorry. Wish I was there.*
Holly: *It's okay. (Smiley face) My mom is here. Hence the pie.*
Me: *I should've asked sooner. I'm sorry.*
Holly: *Stop it. I'm good. Thank you.*
Me: *Any other news?*

The three dots don't appear and my gut twists. Then they pop up.

Holly: *Nope.*
Me: *Still on for later tonight?*
Holly: *Of course, let me know when you get back to your hotel.*
Me: *I'm on my way now.*
Holly: *Always so eager. ;)*

I stand and shove the phone into my pocket, staring at the moon as though it might have all the answers I'm looking for.

Why wouldn't she tell me about the offer?

Should I take the job?

Would I want to if Holly were to stay in Lake Starlight?

I come up empty, so I walk away from the water to head to the hotel. A little phone sex can't hurt, and at least it'll take my mind off my problems. For a bit anyway.

THIRTY-FOUR

Holly

My phone rings right after I snuggle into bed, wearing a piece of lingerie that's been in my drawer for years. I'm not even sure why I packed it, but right now, I'm happy I did.

"Hey, hot stuff," I say in my sexiest voice.

"You dirty little slut."

I sigh, hearing Dana's voice. "I gotta go. Talk to you later."

"Wait! Don't hang up! I'm your best friend and you didn't even tell me! I've been supporting you from thousands of miles away and you hide the fact that you're never coming back?"

"Whoa. What are you talking about?"

I hear shuffling in the background. "Buzz Wheel says you're staying there?" There's a depressed twang in her tone.

"God, I hate that thing. They just offered me the position today."

"The fact you didn't immediately call me says you're thinking about it."

I bolt up in bed. "I'm not. I'm just letting it marinate."

"Bullshit. Tell them you have a very lonely best friend in Florida you need to get back to."

"Dana," I sigh.

"I knew it. You are going to stay." She sighs.

"I honestly don't know, okay? I have to give them my decision next week. Austin isn't here, and I can't figure out if that's good or bad."

"Where is he?" she asks.

"Interviewing at USC."

"Ohhh... so there's a chance you'll come to your senses and return to where you belong." Her sullen tone turns sarcastic.

"Why do you say that?"

"I bet Lake Starlight isn't nearly as desirable without Austin in it."

She's right about that.

My phone beeps, and I pull the phone away from my ear to see Austin's name on the other line. "I gotta go. He's calling to... talk."

"Whatever, I'm not Karen. Love you." She hangs up without needing any more of an explanation.

I click over. "Hey."

"Hi."

"Are you enjoying the action of the big city?"

"I'm enjoying your voice more."

Butterfly wings flutter in my belly. Austin has a way with words.

"I have some news," he says.

"Yeah?"

"Coach Freeman called."

The butterflies lose their wings and sink to the depths of my stomach.

I put on my best happy tone. "Really?"

"They offered Elijah a full ride."

I release a breath. "That's awesome."

"And they offered me the job."

My stomach churns. "Wow. That's great." I force myself to sound happy even though I feel anything but.

I want him to be happy and live his life. I do. But for a little while tonight, I envisioned us working together at the high school. Me bundled up at his baseball games, cheering on the team. Us going home together and sliding into bed. Living a life in the town he was raised in and where we'd raise our own children.

And I feel like a fool for it.

Dana was right. I was stupid to think I wouldn't be invested.

"Yeah," is his response.

"So, when do you leave?"

"I haven't accepted yet, but if I do, I'll join them on the road after graduation."

"Well, I'm super happy that you're getting what you wanted." My voice cracks, but I swallow down the pain and fill my tone with excitement. I truly am excited for him. It's just that I'm equal parts devastated for myself.

"Thanks. I, um... read something."

I sag into my mattress. "I thought you didn't read Buzz Wheel?"

"I wanted to see what I missed today, and it seems I missed something pretty big."

"Marc called today."

"So, what are you going to do?"

"I haven't decided. It's... tempting, but I don't know.

Maybe if Buzz Wheel stops posting articles about me, I'd be more likely to stay." I laugh.

He doesn't. "Ironic, isn't it? You'd be there and I'd be in California."

"Yeah." I roll over on my pillow, my mind now far away from phone sex.

It doesn't escape me that he doesn't tell me not to take the job and follow him to California. I gather that previous offer was a slip of the tongue. I have enough pride that I won't invite myself along where I'm not wanted, and no way would I ask him to give up the dream he's wanted since before I arrived in his life.

"Austin?" I interrupt our silence.

"Yeah?"

"Take the job. Chase your dream."

His silence says exactly what I thought—he'd actually consider staying here for me. I would never want that. I always thought the saying was stupid, but it turns out if you really do love something enough, sometimes you have to let it go. And I don't want Austin to come back to me. I want him to soar to the heights he was destined for.

"I'm kind of tired," he says. "Do you mind if we continue this tomorrow night?"

"Of course. I'm tired too. Sleep well."

"You too."

The line dies, and I grip my phone, tears burning behind my eyelids. I have no reason to be upset. The agreement was supposed to stop this from happening.

Stupid Dana.

She's always right.

THIRTY-FIVE

Austin

You know that saying, time flies when you're having fun?

It's true. Who knew?

I've spent most of the past six weeks with Holly. I tried to show her all of Alaska. Even took her on a fishing boat but turns out she gets seasick. That was eventful. We hiked a bunch of trails and toured the glacier.

Now it's graduation day for Lake Starlight High School, and in two days, I'm off for California.

"I hate this dress."

The disdain in Phoenix's voice draws my attention from my thoughts, and I look over to see Phoenix straightening her pink dress.

"I look shitty in pink."

I straighten my tie in the mirror by the front door. "You look beautiful, and the gown covers your dress anyway."

She stops and stares at me. "Why are you being so

nice?" She smacks her forehead. "That's right, because you're abandoning us."

I blow out a breath. Teenagers and drama go hand in hand, even when they're getting what they want.

"Grandma Dori and Uncle Brian are meeting us at the school." Brooklyn barrels out of the powder room, holding some medieval-looking contraption to her eyelash.

"Okay, we have to get going soon," I say.

The door opens, and Savannah steps inside the house.

I look at her through the mirror. "Hey."

"Hi."

Over the last six weeks, Savannah and I have talked very little, only checking in over finances concerning the twins and who will be moving into the house after I leave. Phoenix will join me in California after the season is over, and Sedona finally came to her senses and will attend NYU in the fall to study journalism. I suspect the reason for her decision is because something happened between her and Jamison, but she's keeping tightlipped about it.

"Can I talk to you?" Savannah says.

"We're running late. Later, okay?"

She nods and heads into the kitchen behind Phoenix. "I can't believe you guys are graduating."

Savannah gushes on as though she's the one who raised them. I'm the one who made sure they were bathed and fed. Who put on their Band-Aids and separated them when they tried to yank out one another's hair?

I know I'm being hard on Sav, but I'm returning the favor for her attitude about Holly.

"We gotta go, guys," I call to anyone who's listening.

Rome slides down the bannister. "Let's go." He leans into me. "Wanna smoke a joint before we head out?"

"Uh, no. And you won't be either."

He shrugs. Great, now I have to keep a closer eye on him. This guardianship thing never ends.

"I'll drive," Savannah and I say at the same time.

"We'll both drive," I say, which is good, because I don't want to be stuck in a car with her anyway.

We leave the house, Phoenix and Rome tagging along with me while Brooklyn and Sedona go with Savannah. Kingston is out of town, doing what he does, but Juno will meet us there.

I drive through Lake Starlight to the high school for my last time as a teacher, and it feels a little surreal. I can't believe I'm actually going to help coach an USC baseball team.

The town had a parade for the graduating class last weekend, a sendoff to show how proud they are of them. It was nice to see JP on Elijah's USC float, raising his hands for people to cheer for his friend.

"Just wait until you're on that plane. Then you'll feel the relief of leaving all this behind." Rome slaps my shoulder.

I nod. He had no problem leaving, so I should take what he says to heart. I just didn't think leaving to live out my dream would be as hard as it's becoming.

We pull into the parking lot of the high school as Jack and Francie are climbing out of their truck.

"It's freedom day!" Jack opens his arms and stares at the sky. "After this, your obligation is over." He smacks my back.

"Jack." Francie nudges him.

"What? This is what he's been waiting for. Just don't totally forget about us up here, okay?" His big hand grips the back of my neck.

"Never," I croak.

Francie slides her arm through mine. "Who will eat most of Fay's butterscotch candies?"

I laugh. "My replacement, I suppose."

"Rumor is they haven't found anyone yet." She cringes. "But you know rumors."

I nod. "They have all summer to find someone."

"True."

We enter the school, the hallways bustling with proud parents and family members. I've been to eleven Lake Starlight graduations, including mine and Savannah's, so I know the drill well.

"I'll meet you guys in there." I head down the hall to the office.

The lights are off in the main office, but the one in Holly's office is on, and she's pacing around, looking at her notecards. She blows out a breath and stares at the ceiling. She's gorgeous in a spring dress with a floral pattern and her hair pinned to one side. Her attention returns to her note-cards, but she spots me and does a double-take.

She gives me a heart-stopping smile.

Not once during these past six weeks, has she given me a reason to think she wants me to stay here now that she's accepted the principal's job. If anything, she's encouraged me to go—looked at apartments with me online, shopped with me online for furniture, helped me pack up some of my things. We have plans for her to maybe come down for a visit but didn't set anything in stone.

I can't deny I'll miss her. Even more than I'm willing to admit.

I walk through the main office and through her office door. "Nervous?" I want to touch her, but I stuff my hands into my pockets.

"Very. Feel like making up some interesting things about me?" She laughs, staring at her cards.

I take her robe off the coat hanger and hold it out for her. "First let's get you dressed."

She slides her arms through the openings and zips it up.

"Get used to it. This is your first of many."

She smiles. "I know. I must be crazy. You're fleeing and I'm staying."

"You love this town. It suits you."

She blows out a breath. "After they stopped reporting about me in Buzz Wheel."

"Oh, you're not in the clear yet." I tap her nose with my finger.

"True. I'm sure they'll post some heartbreaking goodbye scene between me and you." She blanches and her words stall me for a second. She turns around and straightens everything on her desk. "I mean, you know how they love drama."

"Holly?"

She looks to the side so I can see her profile, and she shakes her head, swallowing. "No, Austin. Let's just go get this over with."

She beelines it to the door before I have the guts to stop her and ask her what's really going on behind that fake smile. By the time I reach the hall, she's gone, so I walk to the gym by myself, my shoes clicking on the linoleum floor. Our auditorium isn't big enough for all the parents and family members, so we have a stage brought into the gym. I walk into the room and see Grandma Dori in the front row of the audience section on the right side in the stands, exactly where she's been for every Bailey grandchild's graduation ceremony since my own. Phoenix and Sedona are seated with the graduates on the gym floor, facing the stage.

I climb the stairs of the stage and sit in my seat next to Francie. The faculty are all here to watch the kids we've witnessed grow up set out into the world.

"Giving the principal a pep talk?" Francie asks.

"Yeah." I fiddle with the hem of my pants, pretending to fix something.

Holly approaches the microphone and taps her note-cards on the podium to straighten them. "Hello, parents, family members, and friends of our graduating class. It's been my pleasure to reside as your principal for the remainder of this year. I think I can speak for your teachers when I say that we're sad to see you go, but happy at the same time. Your hard work and dedication has paid off, and today you graduate from high school to begin charting your own course. Some of you are staying local and others are moving away but know that wherever you end up in the world, we're all here rooting for you. We're going to start off with a few words from your valedictorian, and we then have a special tribute to one of our staff members who is leaving us this year."

Francie nudges me.

I figured they'd do something. They do it for everyone who leaves. Too bad they didn't forget in my case. It's only going to make this harder than it already is.

"On that note, I give you your valedictorian, Becca Lancaster." Holly steps away, clapping as Becca walks up to the podium to hoots and hollers from the crowd.

Becca delivers her speech about the future and living your dreams and how she hopes everyone fulfills them even if they seem impossible and scary. I can't see Becca's face, but I see Elijah's fixated on her, heartbreak in his eyes. Becca got into Duke, so she's heading there in the fall. They'll be on opposite sides of the country, and I haven't asked Elijah if they're going to try the long-distance thing. I kind of hope for both their sakes they aren't. I think it's better to cut ties all at once, rather than prolong the pain with a slow, gentle tear through the fabric.

After Becca leaves the stage, wiping tears from her eyes, Holly takes the microphone again. "Thank you, Becca. Now we have a special tribute to our own Coach Bailey, who's leaving us to head to USC to reside as the assistant baseball coach, where he'll continue coaching Elijah." She claps, her eyes glancing at me. "JP Andrews will be giving the tribute on behalf of the team."

"Seriously? At least I won't get emotional," I murmur.

"True." Francie pats my knee.

Holly takes her seat, and JP gets up on the stage with a baseball in his hand. He takes the microphone and looks back at me. "What can I say about Coach Bailey? I've called him just about every name in the book since freshman year."

The crowd laughs.

"He's a ball buster." His eyes shoot to his mom. "Sorry. But it's true. He also made me what I am today."

"That's not a good thing!" someone from the student body yells.

"Yeah, yeah, I can be an ass—jerk at times."

Everyone laughs.

"Before you go off to college and work with perfect guys like Elijah." He winks at him, and Elijah shakes his head with a laugh. "I think it's important for you to know these last nine years with us weren't wasted. Because you've gotten me and hundreds of other guys who couldn't handle their emotions"—he moves his head side to side—"or hormones maybe, ready for adulthood. You taught us that we can handle whatever comes our way and gave us the skills on and off the field to deal with the ups and down of life."

He clears his throat, and a knot forms in the middle of mine. "We all know that day nine years ago was the worst day of your life. Not only did you lose your parents, but you had to come here and teach a bunch of ungrateful kids. And though I wish your parents were in the stands right now, I'm happy you came here to teach, because I wouldn't be walking out of this school believing in the man I am and the man I know I can be."

JP sucks back a tear.

Francie is sniffling next to me.

Brooklyn's a mess in the stands.

Savannah's lip is quivering.

Even Grandma Dori is asking for a tissue.

I rise from the chair and head to the podium, using every ounce of willpower in my body to keep from breaking down and crying.

"So." JP clears his throat again. "This ball is for you, signed by each player from this year. We might not become professional ball players, so it won't be worth millions of dollars someday, but who knows... we might be able to become *you* one day, and that would be an even greater achievement." He hands it to me, and I roll it around in my palm.

I hug him, but he shakes his head and shies away.

"Thank you, JP," I say, gripping his shoulder. "And all of you. My players, my students, my coworkers, my bosses." My eyes land on Holly, who's dabbing her eyes with a tissue. "My family and the entire town of Lake Starlight, because you all made me the man I am. I'll never cherish a baseball more than this one." I hold it up. "It's not goodbye, it's see you later."

I step away, knowing I didn't say nearly enough, but unable to say more.

Holly squeezes my forearm as I pass, a small smile on her face. She steps back up to the podium. "Now, let's get you guys graduated!"

Everyone cheers, and Francie leaves my side to announce A through F.

I stand when Phoenix and Sedona's names are announced, and I hug each of them before they descend the stairs back to their seats.

Elijah gives me a thumbs-up.

JP smirks.

Becca smiles from ear to ear.

All my students are looking ahead to their future, so why am I staring back at my past?

THIRTY-SIX

Holly

"Everyone, move your tassel over to the other side of your cap." I wait for all the students to do so. "Congratulations, you have now graduated high school!"

We asked everyone not to throw their hats, but JP is the first to do so. No surprise there.

As the teachers descend the steps to offer their congratulations to the students, I wind around the back of the stage and head to my office.

My coat is on and I have my purse in my hand before Austin catches up to me. *Shit.* I wanted to be gone before he found me.

He knocks on my door even though it's open. "Hey."

"Hi."

"You have somewhere to be?" he asks and steps in.

"Um... I have to pick up some bread."

He quirks an eyebrow. "Bread?"

"You know my mom, she's always saying we need more groceries."

"Even after she moved out?"

Fuck. Where is my brain? My mom decided to relocate here after I told her I was staying, and she's since found her own place. "I forgot, what with it being only a few days now without her."

"How does she like her new place?"

I nod. "She likes it. I think it's a little too close to your uncle Brian's, but she insists they're just friends."

He laughs and steps further into the room. "Next thing you know, they'll be on *Lake Starlight Buzz Wheel*."

I smile. "Yeah. You'll have to keep up with it from now on to know what's going on."

He nods and stuffs his hands in his pockets. "We're taking the twins out for dinner. Did you want to join my family?"

"Oh, I don't think so. With Savannah and everything."

He takes my hand. "I only have two days, and I'd like to spend every minute I can with you."

There goes that tingling in my nose. What am I supposed to say to that?

"Okay," I whisper. The truth is, I want to spend it with him too. "What about your family and the fact..."

His lips land on mine. My knees weaken and I grip his shirt, never having enough of his kisses. I push him away.

"Whoa, we're still at school." I wipe my mouth.

He smirks. "I'm no longer a teacher here."

"Oh, that's right." I smile, and he corners me against my desk, his hands on either side of my hips.

"Yeah, so I could lay you down right here on your desk..."

I place my hand on his chest. "Except for the fact that I'm still employed here."

He shrugs. "True. So." He grabs my hand and pulls me

forward until I fall into his arms. "No one can argue if I save you from falling on your face."

I laugh, and he nuzzles his face into the crook of my neck. I'm really going to miss that.

"I suppose that's true," I say.

Knock. I dislodge myself from Austin's arms.

Fay stands in the doorway. "Sorry to interrupt."

"It's okay, Austin was just trying to..." I wave her off. "Forget it. I'm exhausted from trying to cover it up."

Fay laughs and enters the room. "I just wanted to say goodbye, Austin."

"Oh, Fay, like I said, it's not goodbye. I'll be back for Thanksgiving." He opens his arms, and Fay walks right into them.

"I know, but it's not the same. Who will eat my butterscotch candies if the Baileys aren't here?"

I sit on the edge of my desk, feeling as though I'm witnessing a private moment I probably shouldn't.

"Holly will steal one a day." Austin looks over his shoulder at me.

"Yep. Maybe two some days."

Fay smiles and playfully hits Austin's shoulder. She steps back and grips his hands. "Your parents would be proud."

"Would they? I've had my doubts these last weeks," he says.

She shakes her head. "All they ever wanted was for all of you to be happy. They never cared whether you lived in Lake Starlight or Timbuktu. As long as you're happy."

"Yeah?"

She nods. "The day you were born, I went to the hospital and your mom handed you to me. Your parents were the first of our friends to have kids, and I jokingly asked how bad childbirth was."

Austin and I wait with bated breath.

"She said it hurt like a bitch, like squeezing a bowling ball through a straw."

Austin looks at me behind him, laughing.

She squeezes his hands. "Then she told me that she never really knew where she fit. With her traveling so much for work, she worried about giving that up for a family and whether she'd be able to juggle the two. But she said one look at you, and she knew."

"Knew what?" Austin asks.

"She knew where she fit. That her most important role was motherhood."

"I always thought she resented having me early. That she wasn't able to travel as much as she wanted."

Watching the two of them interact is mesmerizing, and although I should be excusing myself, I don't.

Fay sneaks a peek at me. "You'll find out one day that life has a way of changing what's most important to you. That's the great thing about life—nothing is ever really set in stone." Fay kisses his cheek and falls back down to her heels. She points at me. "I'll see you for summer school."

As Fay leaves the room, Austin turns around his grin wide and his eyes thoughtful.

"We should probably get going," I say, pulling the strap of my purse onto my shoulder. "Where are we headed?"

"We're going to Lakeside Grill. It's family style."

He grips my hand, and as he guides us out of the building, a thought plagues me like the flu. This is the last time we'll walk out of here as... well, I can't give us a specific classification. But in two days, things between us are going to change forever.

"Do you mind if we come back for your car?" he asks when we hit the parking lot.

My gaze shifts to the families talking and lingering around the grounds, taking pictures.

"Remember, I don't work here anymore," he whispers, opening the door and waiting for me to climb in.

As we drive away, Austin waves with the smile of a man who's bound for greatness. I admire that smile, because that feeling has to sustain me the next two days. Austin deserves this chance, and I'm not going to be the one asking him to set it aside.

THE RESTAURANT IS ON THE SHORE OF LAKE Starlight, and I have no idea why I've never heard about it.

"What kind of food do they have?" I ask as we approach.

Austin parks in the lot. "American. A little of everything."

I climb out of the Jeep before he reaches me.

"One day you'll let me open that door for you."

I smile at him. "Sure, tomorrow you can open my door."

"I'm gonna hold you to that."

In the last few weeks, Austin has treated me like a girlfriend even though we were sneaking around and I'm not officially anything to him. Boyfriends open girlfriends' doors, and I have no idea why I pick that stupid sign of chivalry to rebel against, but it seems like a line I don't want to cross.

On the way into the restaurant, his hand rests on the small of my back. We step into a dark room with windows looking out over the lake and hear the loud clatter of noise from a private room off to the side.

"That would be them." His hand slides down my arm, and he clasps my hand.

Everything about this feels like he's mine. Like he's not leaving in two days. Like we're on our way to being something real. I keep telling myself to push away that hope, remembering the agreement, otherwise I'm going to be left brokenhearted, but that's getting harder and harder to do.

We step into the room and all eyes shift to us, the chaos of a large family silenced.

"Hey, you guys know Holly." Austin drags me through the room and deposits me across from Savannah as he takes the seat next to me.

I look at her, and she turns her attention to Grandma Dori. "Grandma, can you pass the bread?"

"I thought you didn't eat bread?" Grandma Dori asks her, winking my way.

"Today's a special day." She snatches the basket out of Grandma Dori's hands before she can fully hand it to her.

"Do you have your period?" Grandma Dori asks, which gets the guys all cringing and groaning.

Uncle Brian surprises me by coming to sit next to me. "So, is Karen coming?"

I draw back. "No."

"Oh, too bad. You know, she's really got quite the green thumb. I mean, her garden is looking marvelous and she just moved in."

I nod.

"We talked about maybe selling some of her vegetables at the farmer's market. You're going to love it here in the summer. There's a farmer's market every Saturday and Sunday morning in the parking lot of the library. If spring was enough to get you to stay here, wait until summer."

I smile. He seems like a nice man. "I'm a little scared for winter."

He laughs. "You should be. Aust—one of us will make sure you have enough wood for the fireplace and help you clear the driveway if we get dumped on with snow."

"I can come over and check on you, Holly," Denver says. At least I think it's Denver. I still have a hard time telling the difference between him and Rome.

"Like hell you will." Austin throws a roll at him, which he catches and chomps a big bite out of it.

"Hey, you'll be in sunny California while we're stuck in darkness for days," Rome says. Again, I think it's Rome and not Denver.

Austin's hand lands on my thigh under the table. I slide my hand under, linking our fingers. How can something so right come with the worst possible timing?

"How's that relationship with your dad?" Savannah asks, silencing the table.

"Savannah," Austin warns, but I squeeze his hand.

"Actually, it turns out that it's not going to go anywhere."

Now it's Austin squeezing my hand.

I never told him about my outburst at the restaurant or the nasty gossip my dad told me. I left it at the fact that he'd never wanted a relationship with me before and doesn't really want one now. Which seems to be the truth, since I haven't heard from him since that day.

"Oh," Savannah says, looking chagrined.

"I'm very sorry, sweetie," Grandma Dori says in a genuine tone.

"Thank you. I can't be too mad. He's what led me here."

Austin removes his hand from mine, standing from the table. "Excuse me."

He can't leave. What is he thinking? Leaving me mid-conversation with his family? With longing, I watch him go, because I feel Savannah's eyes on my face, and I have no idea if she's done prodding me or not. I turn, and there are her brown hues that match Austin's.

"Why did you decide to stay in Lake Starlight then?" she asks, breaking apart her second roll.

"I... um... I just like it here." I shrug.

"What's not to like? You're not the first person who got sucked in," Grandma Dori interjects, shooting a warning glare at Savannah.

Austin comes back into the room, Savannah's gaze following him all the way to his seat.

"Don't forget, Grandma," Savannah says. "Some people want to get out too. It's usually an either/or, never in between."

Austin places his napkin in his lap. "What is?"

"Loving Lake Starlight. Some people love it and others don't. We were trying to figure out why Holly wants to stay here."

"Let it go," Austin grumbles.

"Do you need some of my oils, Savannah? I have a lavender/bergamot mix in my bag. It might help chill you out," Brooklyn says.

Savannah ignores her and leans forward in my direction, dropping the rest of her roll on the table. "I'm sorry, what?"

Grandma Dori pats Savannah's hand. "Now isn't the time."

"Isn't it? It's perfect. The twins have graduated, and

Austin gets to flee from his responsibilities in a couple days. Might as well hash it all out now."

"Why are they called the twins? We're twins too." Denver leans back, resting on the two back legs of his chair.

Everyone's gaze shoots to him before they move back to Austin and Savannah having a showdown as though they're eight and playing who blinks first.

"Get off the damn soapbox. You said you understood why I was leaving," Austin says.

Savannah stands and throws her napkin on the chair. "You're so fucking blind." She storms from the room.

"Austin," Grandma Dori's tone insinuates a lot.

"This is bullshit." Austin throws his own napkin on his chair and leaves the room.

"So, like I was saying about your mom..." Uncle Brian moves the conversation along as if nothing happened.

"It's just a little sibling spat," Grandma Dori says when she sees my puzzled expression.

I smile at all of them, thinking I should've declined Austin's invitation to dinner.

THIRTY-SEVEN

Austin

I find Savannah on the patio overlooking Lake Starlight, her back to me as she sways on the porch swing installed there.

"Mind telling me what the hell is wrong with you?" I ask.

She looks at me, her eyes rimmed with red and her fingers brushing away tears. "You know I can't handle my feelings."

I chuckle, easing the tension and breaking the distance between us. "At Mom and Dad's funeral, you yelled at the funeral director for going too slow on the way to the cemetery."

I sit down beside her on the swing, and she knocks shoulders with mine.

"I'm sorry. I know I put on a good face about you leaving and you have every right to, but I just... I can't help but feel like everything's being dumped in my lap and I don't know if I can handle it all without you. The business is finally starting to do really well since I took over. Rome is back and wanting to open a restaurant. Brooklyn's wedding is next year. We were a team, and I think I probably feel like Holly should be a mess too. Obviously she can handle her feelings." She laughs. "Remind me to apologize to her. I'm sorry about all the crap I'm giving you and her."

I nod. This is Savannah—she runs hot. Especially when she's feeling emotions she doesn't want to. "So, you don't think she's a spy now?"

She giggles. "No, I don't. At the time, I thought that she'd be another reason for you to leave here, that the two of you would go to California together, and if you had her, you might be more okay with leaving Lake Starlight."

"That's why you thought she was the enemy?"

Savannah shrugs, her eyes never meeting mine. "That, and a little bit of who her dad is. She's not from here. I never thought she'd want to stay. Especially after all the shit she took about you and her outside Lucky's." She looks at me. "She's tough."

I nod. "Yeah."

"I actually like her." She huffs as though she can't believe it herself. "You guys fit well together."

I think back to what Fay said my mother felt after having me. "You know I'm only a phone call or plane ride away. If the family becomes too much, call me. I'm not going to California and forgetting my family."

"That's too rational for me to comprehend." A smile tips her lips. "You know, you've sacrificed so much. You deserve to get what you want."

"Thanks."

I'm so sick of everyone saying that. I didn't sacrifice, I changed course for a while. My life in Lake Starlight hasn't been a prison sentence. I reconnected with Jack and got to be his best man when he married Francie. I saw my siblings grow up, and I grew closer to them than I would've had I stayed in California. I was able to spend more time with Grandma Dori as she aged.

"We don't know what my future would have been if they hadn't passed away," I say.

"That's the thing, right? We're always chasing what we think it was supposed to have been like. I wonder if I'd stayed on course, would I really want to run Bailey Timber Corp? What if none of us had wanted to take over the company from Dad? Would a sleazeball like Clint Edison have bought it? There're so many unanswered questions we'll never know the answers to. They died and you came back, and I took over the company. I think it's time we forget the what-ifs and live for the what-can-bes." Her hand lands on my knee, and she squeezes before she walks to the railing.

"You have a point, I guess." I meet her at the railing.

Both of us stare at the lake, Main Street on the other side. I spot a few graduates and their families smiling and laughing as they make their way along the sidewalk. Bright futures, venturing out to live their lives.

"Just do me a favor." Savannah's voice is low and melancholy.

I turn and face her. "What?"

"Don't live for the past. Live for the future you really want to have."

I nod.

"Now I'm going to apologize to your girl—to Holly." She squeezes my shoulder before she walks away.

Crossing my arms, I feel her words about the future I want wrap around me and squeeze the breath out of my lungs. I stare at the lake, and again that nagging feeling tugs at my gut.

I shake off the feeling and head back inside. Things can go south with my family pretty quickly.

"I can't believe your sister apologized," Holly says from the passenger seat of my Jeep.

The rest of dinner was good, and the conversation stayed lighthearted after Savannah and I returned to the table.

"Yeah. One thing about Savannah, she usually admits when she did wrong."

"It was nice of her." Holly's smiling as she watches Lake Starlight go by in the window.

"You really like it here, huh?"

She smiles and nods. "I do. I can't describe it. I mean, I get why you want to leave. It's not the town or the people, it's the opportunity that lies elsewhere. For me though, I feel like I've tried to find somewhere I fit all my life, and it just feels right here. That's the best way I can explain it."

I clear my throat. There's that word *fit* again.

"It's a good explanation, and I get what you mean. I'm sure I'll miss it. Both good and bad." I pull up to her car in the high school parking lot. It's dark now, no life inside the building. "Can I come over tonight?"

Her hand is already on the handle. "Um..." Her head turns down, and she takes my hand. "I think we need to rip off the Band-Aid."

I shake my head. "No. I have such little time left here."

"That you should be spending with your family."

"They don't care."

She looks at me with that "you're wrong, they do" look. I sink back in my seat.

"What about tomorrow?" I ask.

She brings her face to mine, placing the softest kiss on my lips. She draws back, and a tear slips from her eye. "We have to say goodbye."

A stabbing sensation pierces my heart because I know her answer before she even says it. "I can't change your mind, can I?"

She smiles and shakes her head. Her lips press to mine once more, and this kiss feels like a goodbye. She rests her forehead to mine. "You got this."

One last kiss, then the interior light illuminates us and she's climbing out. As I try to pull air into my lungs, I feel as if I was just punched in the gut.

"Wait." I grab her hand. "We could do the long-distance thing. Why are we saying goodbye? We don't have to."

A small smile forms on her lips. "We're both too old to pretend that would work. This is your time. Take the opportunity." She shuts the door, and the sound feels final somehow.

She unlocks her car and slides in. I wave out the window, and soon it's only my Jeep in the parking lot as I stare at the dark high school that's as empty as I feel right now.

THIRTY-EIGHT

Holly

I throw my keys on the couch, run up the stairs, and trade my dress for pajama pants and an oversized T-shirt. Back downstairs, I grab a bottle of white wine from the fridge and plop down on the couch, ready to commence the ritual of ridding Austin Bailey from my memory and my heart.

A tub of ice cream is in the freezer. Cookies are in the cupboard. An array of pizzas are stuffed in the freezer, so I don't have to see anyone for days.

"Wine first," I mumble, pulling out the cork, then I guzzle a huge gulp straight from the bottle. I reach for my phone and dial Dana.

"How are we?" she asks, and I can hear that she's eating something—again.

"It's done."

"Good. I thought you'd cave and spend his final night with him."

"I really wanted to." One tear slips free. "Remind me of

this moment should I ever come up with another brilliant idea of sleeping with someone I'm not in a relationship with, okay?"

"Gladly. I hate hearing the devastation in your voice. What'd you pick first?"

"Wine."

"Good choice. I'll join you." I hear her open a bottle, and she swallows something. "I even forewent the glass."

I let a sad chuckle loose. "How did you know?"

"It's not the first heartbreak I've helped you through."

"This one hurts the most though," I tell her.

"Well, I think he might've actually been a good guy worth getting your heart broken for."

I sniffle, trying to stifle the tears building. "I shouldn't have begged him to stay, right?"

I think back over the weeks I smiled and assured him that he was doing the right thing by leaving, that he was making the right choice.

"Definitely not. Even if you guys would've worked out, he would have resented you at some point."

I know everything she's saying is right. I really do want Austin to be happy. To find whatever it is he feels he lost the day his parents died. That's the only reason I kept my true feelings to myself—because he's the kind of man who would've honored my wishes and stayed.

"Maybe I should've gone with him." I lift the bottle to my lips again.

"Stop torturing yourself. I know it sucks."

"Yeah." I gulp down another glass' worth, the sweet liquid coating my mouth.

"So, hunker down and don't pull up Buzz Wheel. And no watching romance movies."

I click on my Netflix, looking up romantic movies that make you cry. "Okay."

"I mean it. Do not put on any Nicholas Sparks movies!"

"Okay." I debate between *The Notebook* or *Dear John*. Ryan Gosling or Channing Tatum? Decisions. Decisions.

"You're doing it, aren't you?"

"Yes."

She blows out an annoyed breath. "Fine. Pick *Dear John* though. I can never get enough of Channing. Especially now that he's single."

I click on *Dear John* and put the bottle in my lap.

The movie begins.

"Hey, Hol?" Dana says.

"Yeah?"

"I'm really sorry."

The tears I was trying so hard to keep inside fall free. "Thanks."

I grab one of the two boxes of Kleenex I bought. After two boxes, Austin Bailey should be long gone from my memory and my heart.

I'm always the best at lying to myself.

THIRTY-NINE

Austin

"That's all of it." Savannah bundles together all of the paperwork for the girls and puts it in her file folders. "I'll have Sabrina make sure it's all ready to go. Do you think after the season is done in a couple weeks, we could meet up in New York to find Sedona a place to live?"

"Sure."

Rome comes into the kitchen with bags full of Chinese food. "Li sent you some goodbye food."

"Did he think we were feeding the entire town?" Savannah helps Rome pull out the containers.

Rome dumps a pile of fortune cookies on the counter and I laugh, wondering what funny pieces of paper Li put in them this time around.

"Why were you there?" I ask.

"I was picking his brain on some fusion recipes." Rome grabs a pair of chopsticks, while Savannah and I each take a fork.

"So how was that restaurant you guys went to look at?" I

ask, grabbing us some plates.

Phoenix comes in and inhales deeply over the container of orange chicken. "Wok For U!"

"That must be the vegetarian in you speaking," I say, and she rolls her eyes.

"Yummy. I'll miss this in New York." Sedona grabs a fork and pierces a piece of chicken.

We all pile food on our plates and sit down at the harvest table. Savannah's eyes fall over each of our siblings, and I know what she's thinking. This is one of our last times eating together before things change. Not that we're not used to change. Everyone has had their turn to leave. Somehow things went on, and they will again.

"You going to Holly's tonight?" Savannah asks.

"No. We said goodbye last night." I concentrate harder than necessary on my fried rice.

"You know, I actually liked her. I mean, she was a little uptight, but so is Savannah." Phoenix smiles.

Savannah throws her napkin at her. Phoenix dodges it.

"Hey!" Denver barrels in. "Li is the man." He piles food on a plate then sits down next to Phoenix, giving her a noogie.

She wiggles out of his hold and punches him in the stomach.

"Juno's just behind me."

The words aren't out of his mouth before she walks in and kisses my cheek before grabbing her own plate and sitting down. Emotion overcomes me, but I push it back, forcing myself to enjoy this dinner with my family.

"Kingston wishes he was here," Juno says. It's fire season, and we all understand why he can't be here.

Brooklyn stomps down the stairs. "Hey, someone was supposed to get me."

"You said you were on a diet, so you'd fit in your wedding dress," Rome throws her words back at her.

"Tonight, is special." She smiles at me.

Soon we're all around the table. Everyone minus Kingston, but we spoke earlier, so I'll take it. My siblings converse in ten conversations between each another. Rome is telling Juno about the building he has his eye on. Savannah's telling Sedona she'll pick out where she's living, and Manhattan isn't it. Denver's razzing Brooklyn about Jeff and the fact that he's not a real man. I lean back, my eyes finding Phoenix, who is also taking in the scene. She'll be leaving soon too.

That tugging feeling grips my gut again. But I push it aside, helping Savannah reason with Sedona.

Savannah shoots me a thank you look when we finish.

And as we've done for the last nine years, the Bailey siblings endure change.

***

ROME TOSSES ME A FORTUNE COOKIE LATER THAT night when I'm sprawled out on the couch, watching the Cubs play the Brewers. "You didn't open your fortune."

I crack the cookie open and pull out the white paper.

IT'S NEVER TOO LATE TO DREAM A NEW DREAM.

I LOOK UP, BUT ROME'S GONE.

I place the paper on the table and eat my fortune cookie.

Damn Li.

FORTY

Austin

I picked Denver to take me to the airport. He's a safe bet to not make this emotional.

"Be safe and don't forget to call." He straightens the collar of my shirt, running his hands down my shoulders like a mom before her son jets off to college. He even imitates a mom voice. "Remember those girls only want one thing."

I laugh and shake my head. "See you in a few months."

He pauses like he wants to say something but doesn't. "See you."

I turn around and head through the sliding doors of the airport.

"Austin!" he calls, and I circle back.

"Be happy."

"You too." I nod, turning back into the bustling airport.

His words don't register until I'm at the ticket counter.

Do people think I wasn't happy in Lake Starlight? I was happy.

I check my bags and get my boarding pass to head through security. I don't know why it feels so final. This is the twenty-first century—I could come back in a day if I wanted.

I make my way through the airport, heading straight to my gate, and take a seat in front of the wall-to-wall windows so I can watch the planes take off. I'm only there for five minutes before I hear a voice I'd recognize anywhere.

"Excuse me. Yeah, I need to sit there."

I look up to see the man next to me sliding over as Grandma Dori smiles at him, though he looks annoyed.

"Thanks. Your grandma would be proud," she says.

"She's dead but thanks." The man is barely up before she sits down.

My face must be twisted in confusion. "Grandma?"

"Well, I have to say you're a stubborn one. I can't believe you're here." She pats my knee.

"You knew I was flying out today."

"Yes, but I always thought you were a bright boy. Maybe I'm mixing you up with Rome or another one of your brothers."

"How did you get through security?" I ask.

"Well..." She leans forward and whispers, "the Thompson boy let me through."

"There you are!" Savannah stands at the end of the row of seats, gasping for breath. "It's not cool to jump on the ride mobile and leave me to fend for myself, Grandma." Savannah winds through the people's legs. "Excuse me. Sorry. Excuse me."

"Why are the two of you here? And I seriously think Duke Thompson needs to be fired."

Savannah sits on the window ledge in front of me. "He

was my first kiss, remember? Spin the bottle. Weak lips though." Her face distorts into disgust.

"Let's get back to why you guys are here…"

The gate attendant comes over the speaker and calls off the names of some passengers she needs to see at the kiosk before takeoff. I'm one of them.

Savannah looks at Grandma Dori. "Okay, tell him, Grandma."

"Did you know that your grandfather didn't want to take over Bailey Timber Corp?"

I stand and secure my bag around my shoulders. "Sorry, Gram, I don't have time to go down memory lane right now." Maybe the old bird is finally losing it.

"He didn't. He wanted to be a fisherman. Work on one of those crab boats. He tried to convince his father to buy a boat so he could captain it. His dad said hell no and demanded he come work for the company."

"So, what did he do, Grandma?" Savannah asks.

I shoot her a look to say *why the fuck are you encouraging her?* Savannah ignores me.

"He left."

"Great story." I pat her shoulder and step over the legs of a man reading.

"The story isn't over." Grandma Dori gets up. "Excuse me, do you think this is your living room? Sit up straight and pull your legs in."

"Sorry," Savannah says to the man.

I blow out a breath and turn to see them behind me.

"Let me finish," Grandma says.

A few people file into a line at the kiosk.

"He came home for Christmas. Such a beautiful time of the year. All the snow had fallen, and well, I was ice skating on the pond over there by Hickory Lane. You know, where the elementary school is now?"

"Yeah," I say.

Savannah smiles at Grandma as though she's enjoying her story. Maybe they're both losing it.

"I was a really good ice skater. Maybe even good enough to do those Ice Capades."

I roll my eyes.

"He asked if he could buy me a hot chocolate, and I said yes."

"Heartwarming story, Gram." I kiss her cheek. "I'll see you in a few months." I take a few steps toward the kiosk.

"*Austin Bailey!*" she scolds.

I turn, as does almost everyone in the airport.

She points at the floor in front of her. "You will listen to me."

Savannah laughs not embarrassed for me in the least.

I walk over to her. "What?"

"Hot chocolate turned to him asking to walk me home, which turned into asking to escort me to the dance, which turned into asking me to church with him on Sunday. Eventually he asked my daddy for my hand in marriage, he went to work for Bailey Timber Corp, and we built a life together in Lake Starlight."

"I know all this. Well, I didn't know about the crab boat thing and I've always enjoyed hearing your stories—"

"Do you think your grandfather resented me?" she asks.

More people pass me to line up for the plane.

"No," I answer, speaking the truth. I saw it in my grandfather's eyes until the day he died how much he loved my grandmother.

"So...?" Savannah says.

I blow out a breath. "I know what you're trying to do

but sliding through security and insinuating I need to do something now... it's too late. I've accepted the job and she's staying here. She never even asked me to consider staying. It's not our time. She doesn't feel that way about me." I kiss my grandma on the cheek and hug Savannah goodbye. "Love you guys. I'll call you when I land." I turn and get in line.

"*Austin!*" Savannah screams.

I turn around.

"Just go read Buzz Wheel right now."

I shake my head. "Can you not see I'm busy?"

I head over to the kiosk to wait until it's my turn to deal with the airline employee. When I turn back around, thankfully my grandma and sister are gone. *I need some caffeine.*

The gate attendant told me I had enough time to hit the cafe next door, so when I reach the small coffee shop, I peruse the menu for food but decide to skip it. I can eat on the plane if I need to.

A girl probably only a little older than Phoenix and Sedona comes over to help me.

"Coffee. Black." I pull out my wallet and grab some cash. A small piece of white paper floats from it to the floor.

The barista takes the cash as I bend down to pick up the paper—until I realize it's the fortune I opened last night.

When did I put this in my wallet?

"It'll be ready down there." The girl directs me to the pick-up line, and I walk over, flipping the fortune over.

IT'S NEVER TOO LATE TO DREAM A NEW DREAM.

I HUFF, STUFFING IT BACK INSIDE MY WALLET.

With my coffee in hand, I make my way back over to my gate. A plane must've just landed, because swarms of people are walking toward me and dodging me. I feel like a salmon swimming upstream.

"Austin!"

I turn to see a woman who's probably close to my age, wearing yoga pants and a large sweatshirt, her red hair pulled into a high bun.

"Austin Bailey, right?" she asks again.

One person hits me with their messenger bag as they pass me.

"Yeah?"

"You look the same as on Buzz Wheel."

I draw back. "You're from Lake Starlight?" Why does this woman not look familiar at all?

"I'm Dana. Holly's friend."

"Oh." Just the mention of her name makes me feel things I shouldn't. Regret being the biggest one of those things. "You're coming to visit?" Holly hadn't mentioned it.

Another person passes us. If I was thinking straight, I'd move to the side, but meeting someone from Holly's world has me off-kilter.

"I'm here to pick up the pieces you left her in."

I tilt my head. "What?"

She smiles. "Totally kidding. Yeah, I'm here for a visit."

"Well... enjoy." I don't know what else to say. Give her a hug for me? Give her a kiss for me? It all feels so superficial, and what Holly and I shared wasn't superficial. At least not to me.

"Thanks. I heard you have some hot brothers. Maybe one of them has a Jeep I can steam up the windows in?" Her laughter is so loud, twenty people look at us as they pass by. "I'm totally fucking with you."

I smile. "You're about as opposite of Holly as they come."

She nods toward the side of the walkway and I follow, weaving through the grumbling people I'm inconveniencing.

"I am. That's why I knew this little plan you guys hatched was bullshit."

"What plan?"

"The agreement. The whole 'sleep together and not develop feelings' thing."

"Oh, right."

She touches my arm. "Anyway, have a nice life. I'm glad I got to meet the infamous Austin Bailey before he bolted."

"Infamous, huh?"

She smiles. "You seem nice."

"You say that like you're surprised."

"It's easier when the guy who breaks your friend's heart is an asshole."

I tighten my grip on the bag over my shoulder as my stomach churns. "What do you mean about breaking hearts?"

She covers her mouth. "Oops? Oh... hmm... I don't know." Her eyes say she does.

I step closer to Dana. "Is Holly upset?"

Holly has been nothing but encouraging. Never once, other than our moment in the truck the other night, did I see any semblance of her feelings being similar to my own. Even then, I thought it was just a goodbye thing. They suck no matter what. Is it possible she feels the same way for me that I feel for her?

"No." Her face is void of emotion now. She steps backward. "She's peachy keen. I need to go though. Karen is probably waiting for me."

"Wait." I step forward, my hand landing on her wrist. "Am I missing something?"

She smiles. "Don't all guys? Really, Austin, have a great life. Knock California upside its head." She turns then circles back around. "Do me one favor though?"

"What?"

She opens her mouth just to shut it again. "I know you owe me nothing, but for Holly." She inhales a deep breath, her eyes locking with mine. "Don't reach out to her."

"What? Why?" This woman has me totally confused.

She tilts her head. "This is something that could ruin my friendship with her, but I'll risk it because she deserves to find her happily ever after. Don't you agree?"

"I do," I say, nodding.

"Then once you board that plane, leave her behind. I know your paths might cross when you come back to visit, but don't call her or reach out to her after you leave. If this thing between you isn't permanent, let her live her life."

Her words blow me over like a hurricane. Never talk to Holly again?

Dana's phone rings and she pulls it out of her bag. "That's Karen, and she's not going to take kindly to waiting. So, you'll do it?"

I focus on the floor. The thought of never hearing Holly's voice or holding her again guts me. Never hearing her laugh or talking to her about the mundane parts of my day? Knowing I can't fire off a text when the mood strikes? But Dana's right. I can't have the best of both worlds. I hadn't really considered it a choice until this moment. Holly can't hang out in the wings, waiting for me to roll through town every few months for a quickie.

"Yeah. I will," I agree, my voice hoarse.

She grips my forearm. "Thanks. Well, safe travels, Austin."

I nod, not looking up to see her leave.

When I take a seat near my gate again, my thoughts all jumble—the fortune, Dana's comments about Holly, her request that I not reach out to Holly again, my grandma's words when she was here. This is what I want, right? To be a coach at the college level? That's what Holly wants too, right? I mean, I can't play ball anymore and coaching at a college is the next best thing. Not at a high school.

JP's speech comes to mind, and I shake my head, thinking of how much I thought I never got through to him. But I guess in my own way, I did make a difference in his life.

I smile until I think of the inevitability of Holly moving on. Who will win her over? She'll find someone else to show her all the hidden gems in Alaska. He'll be the first one to take her camping and make love to her in a tent. I never got to skinny-dip with her in the pond on our property. He'll be the one who gets to hear those small moans she makes with the softest of touches. Her wavy auburn hair will lay on someone else's pillow. The lucky bastard will be able to kiss her whenever he wants. To bring her home white wine on the hard days. Some other guy will be the one to pick her up when she needs it and show her the gorgeous and strong woman she is.

The lid pops off my coffee, I'm gripping it so hard. I pick it up off the carpet and toss it into a nearby garbage can. When I sip my coffee, it just tastes bitter.

I close my eyes, trying to push those thoughts away.

She deserves to find a guy like that.

She deserves to be someone's everything.

I was lucky to have her be *my* everything, if only for a

few short months. It's not her fault I couldn't be *her* everything.

Ten minutes pass while I question everything I ever thought I wanted. The airline employee calls the boarding for my zone on the plane, and I head over to stand in line. As I make my way down the jetway toward the plane's entrance, the sick feeling in my gut intensifies.

I'm doing the right thing.

I stop when I reach the end of the line of passengers waiting to board.

"That was cute," a woman says behind me. When I scrunch my forehead in confusion, she continues. "I overheard your grandma, I think it was, talking to you earlier. What a great story."

She's close to my age. Petite with blonde hair and tanned skin. My guess is that she's returning to California.

"Yeah, my grandma is pretty unique."

"It's sweet. So where are you seated?"

I look at my ticket. "12A."

"Oh great, I'm only a few rows away. Maybe we can convince someone to switch." Her gaze runs down my body and back up, her tongue sliding out of her mouth and licking her lips. "What's Buzz Wheel anyway?"

"Just a gossip blog from my hometown."

She laughs, and I turn around and groan at the long line of people waiting to board the airplane.

"How do you spell it?"

I turn back to face her. She has her phone out, showing me a screen that says the website isn't in service. "You need to add Lake Starlight to Buzz Wheel."

Her thumbs move over her screen. "Oh, here it is."

I take one step forward.

"This is the funniest thing. Oh man." She laughs some more. "That sucks."

I finally relent and glance down to see a picture of Holly sitting across from Clint Edison wearing a lobster bib.

"Do you mind?" I hold my hand out for her phone.

She smiles. "Not at all."

I scan the article. The breaking news of the day is that weeks before, Holly told off her estranged father when he said horrible things about the Baileys. Apparently she threw a drink in his face and defended my family name then stormed out. They apologize for not posting about it sooner, but news from neighboring towns about Lake Starlight residents takes longer to reach them.

It goes on to call Holly one of our own and praises her after Austin broke her heart and left. Then there's a picture of Holly with no makeup on, her hair in a messy bun, dressed in sweats, with a frown while she holds a takeout bag from Wok 4 U in one hand and a bottle of wine in the other. She looks miserable. She looks as miserable as I feel.

Something finally clicks in my brain and I realize what an idiot I've been.

All this time it's been her. *She's* the dream I need to chase, not my coaching career.

I hand the woman back her phone. "Excuse me." I rush back up the jetway, saying to myself, "I'm so fucking stupid."

My grandma was right—men are idiots sometimes.

"Sir!" the gate attendant says.

"I'm not taking the flight."

I run down the hallway, weaving through the throngs of people coming toward me. Once I'm past security, a golf cart pulls up beside me. It stops, as do I, and Grandma Dori steps off.

"See, I knew you weren't stupid."

A panting Savannah comes up behind her. "We really need to talk. If you want to be Thelma and Louise, you can't leave me behind."

Grandma Dori waves her off. "Not now, Austin needs to get back to Lake Starlight. I told you he'd come to his senses if we waited around."

Holly

"I get the appeal. This place has a rustic vibe." Dana looks around Lucky Tavern, sliding into her side of the booth. "You look good. I thought I'd find you under your blankets, not on the couch with a tub of cookies and cream in your lap."

"Thanks."

"Hey, Holly, what can I get you?" Nate asks when he approaches the table.

"Hey, Nate. I'll just have a glass of pinot. This is my friend Dana from Florida."

Nate turns to Dana. "Nice to meet you. What can I get you?"

"I'll have a vodka on the rocks with a lime."

He nods. "Be right back."

"So..." Dana starts.

"So, nothing. I have to move on with my life." I play with the bar coaster Nate left on the table.

"Two days and you have no more tears left?" she asks skeptically.

I shrug, the burning behind my eyelids ever-present. "They're not dried up yet."

"I'm not surprised." She shakes her head.

"Whatever."

Nate returns with our drinks and I swallow half of mine, apparently alarming Dana.

"Slow down," she says.

"I'm kind of on the forget phase. You know—forget he ever existed."

"Moving right along."

I don't tell my best friend that my heart is aching so badly that I'm thinking a long-distance relationship might've been better than this. "Should I have volunteered to go to California?"

"Uh, no. We've been over this."

"You say it like California's a bad thing."

"I'm going to give you a pass because you're obviously hurting, but don't second-guess what happened." She sips her vodka and relaxes into the booth. "Let's change the subject. I get why you like this town so much, but it feels like a little bigger version of Mayberry."

I roll my eyes.

"But for real, I felt the stress leave my body the minute Karen drove past the cute little sign into town. That said, we need to discuss something."

I still with my wine glass halfway to my lips. "What?"

"How on earth are you going to move on when the Bailey name is everywhere? I mean, their name and logo is right below the Welcome to Lake Starlight sign."

I shrug. "Honestly, I'm kind of immune to that by now.

The only thing I couldn't do is live in the same town as Austin. To see him every day and know he couldn't be mine."

I look over at the bar stools where he approached me, remembering the instant attraction I felt. The way we kind of knew we might leave together. He asked if I wanted a ride home and I accepted, even though I was within walking distance. We didn't need names or occupations. Nothing to fill our conversation. Our connection sparked to life that night, and it's still burning.

"It's funny, if I believed in love at first sight, I might've thought I felt it."

"Let it all out, girl. I'm here." Dana lets me say all the stupid shit we women do after our hearts are broken.

"There was a connection between us right away." My eyes fixate on the two empty chairs where it all started. "Have you ever felt like everything in your life, all the pieces, finally fit? Like you'd found the last piece of the puzzle?"

"You were already complete," a deep voice says next to me.

A voice I'd recognize anywhere.

I turn my head. Austin's there, crouching beside the booth.

"Holly."

His hand runs along my cheek, and I close my eyes and let the sensation of his touch sink into my skin. I swallow, staring at him as though I may have conjured him up in my mind. He's just as gorgeous as the night we met under the dim lighting of this neighborhood bar. I cover his hand with mine, unable to speak.

"I'm stupid. Please forgive me for being so stupid." All

the love I've been drowning in, suffocating on for the past couple of days, peers back at me in his dark eyes.

"Thank God," Dana says but I don't spare her a glance.

"You're not stupid. Why are you here? You should be on a plane."

He gets up and slides into the booth. "No. This is where I should be."

I turn my face away from him, wiping tears with the backs of my hands. "No." I find my voice and shake my head. "You need to go, Austin."

He laughs as if there's something funny. "I need you. That's *all* I need in this life. You next to me when I fall asleep and you there when I wake up in the morning. And all the hours in between."

"I can't be someone you resent in a year or two," I whisper.

He's already shaking his head. "How could I resent you? I mean, my dream was always something I couldn't have, and somewhere along the line, I convinced myself that's what I needed to be happy. But then you walked into this bar and sat on that stool."

"It's only been three months. I should tell you that I drool when I'm really tired, and I'm a bear to wake up in the morning. There's so much you might find out that you don't like about me."

He takes my face in his hands. "And I can't wait to find out the things that annoy me, because there'll be a million more things that I love. I want the good and the bad. The beautiful and the ugly. The only stipulation is that I experience them with you."

"But you can't be a college baseball coach here."

"Holly," he says.

"What?"

"Please just accept that I'm a smart man and I know what I'm doing here. I'm telling you I was stupid. Sometimes us guys are slow on the uptake, what can I say? I didn't see that after you entered my life, my dream changed. You'll give me so much more than a stupid coaching career. I want to watch you walk toward me in a white gown. I want to see you sign your name as Holly Bailey. If you're willing to change your name." He smirks. "I want to practice getting you pregnant over and over again and rub my hand across your growing belly." He tips his head down and brings his forehead to mine. "I want to argue about what to name our kids. Hold your hand while a part of us, a part of our love is born into existence. Every moment of my future... I want you in it." Tears run down my face, and he pulls back and brushes them away with his thumbs. "What do you say?"

"What's the question?" I laugh, trying to compose myself, because right now, I feel as if I could float away like a balloon from the sheer amount of joy bursting in my chest.

"Can I drive you home?"

I smile.

"This time you'd better take her home and not to your Jeep," Grandma Dori says, and Austin raises his hand toward her. I didn't even notice that she was standing behind him.

"This time our agreement is different. Sleepovers every night, shared meals where I get to cook breakfast in the mornings, and as many dates where I hold your hand down Main Street as I want, *and* I can kiss you whenever the mood strikes. Those are the stipulations, Holly. Do you agree?"

I smile and nod. "Yes."

"And this time we're sealing it with a kiss." He leans in, pressing his lips to mine.

Applause rings out around us as I hold his head to mine. I'm never letting him go again.

Austin

I slide into bed, kissing Holly on the cheek.

"What are you doing?" I ask, trying to take a peek at her tablet.

"She pulls it flush to her chest. You probably don't want to know."

I tickle her ribs and she squirms under me, my lips nibbling on her neck as my fingers torture her.

"*Austin!*" she screams, wiggling around on our bed.

Our bed. I love that I can say that. Holly moved in with me in the family home shortly after I professed my love for her, and we've slept beside each other every night since.

"Say you love me," I say.

"No."

"Say it?"

Her cami rises and my plan to get an early night's sleep fades away. I stop tickling her and slide my hands under the thin cotton.

"You said you were tired." Her head falls back as my

mouth latches onto her nipple through her cami, and once I free the fabric from her body, I suck directly on her nipple.

Myles jumps on the bed and onto my back.

I push him off. "Down, Myles."

She giggles.

"I swear this dog is going to cockblock me again," I grumble. Myles jumps up again, and I hop off the bed. I point at the open door. "Get out, Myles."

"He looks so sad," she says.

"Believe me, I'm going to look sadder if he doesn't leave."

Myles slowly walks out of the room, and I shut the door.

I crawl up the bed, Holly giving me her seductive "come and get me" expression that makes my dick harder than steel every time. Her arms open, and I fall on top of her. Heaven on earth.

I think she still worries I made a rash decision by declining the coaching position at USC, but one day she'll realize I knew all along where I should be. I just refused to listen.

The words I spoke in front of everyone that day in Lucky's were the truth. Every morsel of my happiness is wrapped up in her. I haven't regretted my decision once since I've been back. If anything, I feel more myself than I have in nine years.

Sedona's at NYU.

Phoenix still went to California, although she's living in a studio apartment that makes me cringe.

Savannah is rocking it at Bailey Timber Corp.

Rome just bought a restaurant on Lake Starlight.

Kingston is hardly home, which I have my theories about, but those are his issues. I solved mine and he has to solve his.

Denver is Denver, forever the Bailey bachelor.

Juno is trying to use Holly and me to convince me she really is a great matchmaker. Unless she convinced Holly to step into Lucky's that night, she'd better try again.

And Brooklyn... well, I knew that fiancé of hers was an asshole.

My lips fall from Holly's, and I pick up the tablet to see what she was hiding. No way I'll let her outdo me on our one-year anniversary presents.

"What is it?" I ask.

"I just had to see what Brooklyn was facing when she returns." She leans her head on my shoulder as the two of us read tonight's *Lake Starlight Buzz Wheel*.

HONEYMOON FOR ONE

Well, the news is out, and unfortunately, Brooklyn Bailey has been left at the altar. After two years of preparations, the Bailey clan—including the newest addition, Holly Radcliffe—were ready to give away their sister, but no one was at the end of the aisle to take her off their hands.

Rumor has it, she's considering going on her honeymoon by herself.

Oldest brother, Austin, was rumored to say that "the guy has a death wish." He and the other three Bailey brothers stalked out of the wedding in search of the Runaway Groom. I sure hope he's hunkered down somewhere safe tonight.

All in all, it's sad news, but many men in Lake Starlight are asking, how soon is too soon to ask Brooklyn Bailey out?

IF THE JEEP IS ROCKIN', DON'T COME KNOCKIN'

In other news, our favorite Coach and Principal were seen once again, steaming up the windows of a Jeep behind Lucky's. If I didn't know better, I'd say those two like to be in Buzz Wheel. (Picture included)

I TURN OFF THE TABLET AND TOSS IT ON MY nightstand.

"Will our names ever not be in that thing?" she asks.

I hover over her, my lips millimeters from hers. "Stick with me and we'll always give people something to talk about."

Just as the anger is finally leaving my body over Jeff screwing over Brooklyn, scratching commences on the other side of the door. Holly and I sit up.

"Lie down, Myles," I call.

We hear a whimper behind the door.

"Nope," I say to Holly, whose lips turn down at Myles's displeasure. "One day we're going to have five kids and a dog in this bed with us. I'm making the most of our time alone."

She cocks an eyebrow. "Five?"

"I made it clear in our new agreement that I wanted to practice over and over again."

She giggles, and I swallow her amusement with a kiss.

Sometimes you don't even realize you're missing a piece of your puzzle until you find it.

The End

COCKAMAMIE UNICORN RAMBLINGS

The Baileys came to us a little differently than normal. Usually one of us has an idea and tells the other and the series spider webs out from there. With this series, all we knew was we wanted a new series, unrelated to our existing world that would be a longer than our usual three books. One where readers could pop in and out with ease. Maybe because we wished the Bianco family had five more siblings that we could've kept writing about them. You wish that too, right? LOL

If you follow us on social media you might remember that in September we met up in Florida for the NINC (Novelist Inc.) annual conference. It was 4 days, 5 nights of us actually face-to-face, not in two different countries. Bonus, we brought our assistant, Shawna, with us. In our minds we were going to flush every story out in this series before we parted ways. We were going to accomplish everything on our lengthy to-do lists because hello, we were kid free! Best laid plans and all that.

Before arriving in Florida we knew the series would be about family in Alaska who probably owned a lumber company. At least, I think we were going with family, but still not completely sure (granted, we were probably knee deep in another series. Oh, yes, Rayne was finishing up writing and Piper was editing Crushing on the Cop so we'd make the deadline for our editor. I don't even think we had named the town yet. No... we hadn't because one night we threw names out as we sat in our hotel room. Before Lake Starlight there was Bears Landing, Twin Rivers, Kings Crossings. I love looking back at our notes after we finish writing a book because the story NEVER ends up where we started.

Anyway, after the conference (we're sure this is the same for anyone when they love their job), after the lectures and workshops we were inspired and revved up to plot this next series.

Rayne was sitting in a class presented by Jennifer Lynn Barnes by herself—because we tend to divide and conquer to gain more knowledge. As Jennifer was talking, her mind was on the new series. Jennifer said people probably love what you love. It got her thinking of the family dynamics she loves in television or in books. Somewhere in her head, the sitcom Party of Five popped into a little bubble. When they got back to the room, Rayne pitched the idea of our family being orphans to parents who died years before (because this is a rom com after all) to Piper and she loved it.

Then came the hard work. Titles and storylines and... everything that makes the book a book... everything that makes a series a series! If you think we struggled to name a town, can you imagine coming up with NINE similar titles? And NINE different siblings all with their own personalities?

Piper came up with Secrets of the World's Worst Matchmaker first. Other possible titles we threw out there were Match Me, The Matchmaker who Miss Matched, Lies of a Matchmaker, Secrets of a Matchmaker. We then tried to find a title using the trope we were writing for each book. Sounds a lot easier than it was. Now that we see them all together, we're in love! But there's a time when you're throwing things out there and they aren't sticking that you think to yourself, this will never work.

But it did and before we left Florida we might not have had every story outlined but we had the gist of every story and all the Bailey siblings had names! As we sadly parted after the conference knowing we wouldn't see each other's beautiful faces until May 2019, we each were optimistic that we had a pretty great series coming your way!

And not for nothing but we LOVE this family! LOVE!!! Starting out on this new series we had our doubts but in the end we love the dynamic between all these siblings. Loss and love has made them a tightknit group, but like any family that means they know all the buttons to push to make you crazy. LOL

We both hope you loved Lessons from a One-Night Stand. Austin and Holly were so fun to write, as were all the Baileys and the town of Lake Starlight. Buzzwheel might be the most fun! Head on over to LakeStarlightBuzz-Wheel.com and check it out! ;)

As always, we have a long line of people to thank...

- Danielle Sanchez and the entire Inkslinger family for spreading the word and so much more!
- Ellie from My Brother's Editor for first round edits.
- Cassie from Joy Editing for second round edits.
- Shawna from Behind the Writer for proofreading.
- Sarah from Okay Creations for the cover and branding for the entire series.
- Sara from Sara Eirew Photography for the hot picture of our 'Holly' and 'Austin'.
- Bloggers who carved out precious time to read, review and/or promote us.
- Piper Rayne Unicorns who get just as giddy and excited as we do. Who spread the word about us and our books and who we'd be nothing without!
- Readers who took a chance on our book when you have so many choices.

Mwah to everyone!

Oh wait, you need a tease...

Be on the lookout for Brooklyn Bailey's book, Advice from a Jilted Bride next. We hate to see her heartbroken, but we're pretty sure the guy moving in next door might just be Mr. Right. Of course, love's journey is never as easy as that though, is it?

Xo

    Piper & Rayne

ABOUT PIPER & RAYNE

Piper Rayne is a USA Today Bestselling Author duo who write "heartwarming humor with a side of sizzle" about families, whether that be blood or found. They both have e-readers full of one-clickable books, they're married to husbands who drive them to drink, and they're both chauffeurs to their kids. Most of all, they love hot heroes and quirky heroines who make them laugh, and they hope you do, too!

My Famous Frenemy

The Greene Family Vacation

My Scorned Best Friend

My Fake Fiancé

My Brother's Forbidden Friend

The Modern Love World

Charmed by the Bartender

Hooked by the Boxer

Mad about the Banker

Complete Set (all 3 books)

The Single Dad's Club

Real Deal

Dirty Talker

Sexy Beast

Complete Set (all 3 books)

Hollywood Hearts

Mister Mom

Animal Attraction

Domestic Bliss

Bedroom Games

Cold as Ice

On Thin Ice

Break the Ice

Complete Set (all 3 books +)

Charity Case

Manic Monday

Afternoon Delight

Happy Hour

Complete Set (all 3 books)

Blue Collar Brothers

Flirting with Fire

Crushing on the Cop

Engaged to the EMT

Complete Set (All 3 books)

White Collar Brothers

Sexy Filthy Boss

Dirty Flirty Enemy

Wild Steamy Hook-up

The Rooftop Crew

My Bestie's Ex

A Royal Mistake

The Rival Roomies

Our Star-Crossed Kiss

The Do-Over

A Co-Workers Crush

Hockey Hotties

Countdown to a Kiss (Free Novella)

My Lucky #13

The Trouble with #9

Faking it with #41

Sneaking around with #34

Second Shot with #76

Offside with #55